KILLING

KILLING

(The Making Of Riley Paige—Book 6)

BLAKE PIERCE

BLAKE PIERCE

B lake Pierce is the USA Today bestselling author of the RILEY PAGE mystery series, which includes seventeen books. Blake Pierce is also the author of the MACKENZIE WHITE mystery series, comprising fourteen books; of the AVERY BLACK mystery series, comprising six books; of the KERI LOCKE mystery series, comprising five books; of the MAKING OF RILEY PAIGE mystery series, comprising six books; of the KATE WISE mystery series, comprising seven books; of the CHLOE FINE psychological suspense mystery, comprising six books; of the JESSE HUNT psychological suspense thriller series, comprising seven books (and counting); of the AU PAIR psychological suspense thriller series, comprising two books (and counting); of the ZOE PRIME mystery series, comprising three books (and counting); of the new ADELE SHARP mystery series; and of the new EUROPEAN VOYAGE cozy mystery series.

ONCE GONE (a Riley Paige Mystery—Book #1), BEFORE HE KILLS (A Mackenzie White Mystery—Book 1), CAUSE TO KILL (An Avery Black Mystery—Book 1), A TRACE OF DEATH (A Keri Locke Mystery—Book 1), WATCHING (The Making of Riley Paige—Book 1), NEXT DOOR (A Chloe Fine Psychological Suspense Mystery—Book 1), THE PERFECT WIFE (A Jessie Hunt Psychological Suspense Thriller—Book One), and IF SHE KNEW (A Kate Wise Mystery—Book 1) are each available as a free download on Amazon!

An avid reader and lifelong fan of the mystery and thriller genres, Blake loves to hear from you, so please feel free to visit www.blakepierce-author.com to learn more and stay in touch.

TABLE OF CONTENTS

PROLOGUE

Julian Banfield breathed in deeply as he stood in his kitchen. He simply loved the mingling smells of fresh-brewed coffee and frying bacon for a late night snack.

Enjoy it one last time, he told himself as he turned the bacon with a spatula.

His wife, Sheila, would get home from her book tour in just a little while, possibly before he went to bed. Julian needed to make sure not to leave any evidence that he'd been indulging in bacon and other high-cholesterol luxuries during her absence. He reminded himself to spray the kitchen thoroughly with air freshener to get rid of the lingering, delicious smell.

As much as he loved Sheila, and as happy as they had always been together, he had to admit he'd enjoyed her absence during the last week. After thirty-five years of marriage, he couldn't say that he'd especially missed her, nor did he imagine that she'd especially missed him. Instead, it had been an interesting change, probably for both of them.

And it had been refreshing not to have to listen to her gentle but persistent scolding about his mild vices and indulgences. He'd been able to eat donuts and pizza, skip exercise sessions at the gym, and have an extra bourbon or two after dinner.

All that was going to end when Sheila got back.

Seize the moment, he told himself.

He removed the bacon from the pan and broke a couple of eggs into the bubbling bacon fat. Then he pushed a slice of bread down into the toaster and poured himself some orange juice. When the eggs looked ready, he flipped them over for just a few seconds and flipped them back again. Pleased with the flawlessly translucent white film over the yoke, he scooped the eggs onto a plate just in time for the toast to pop up.

He set the plate of bacon, eggs, and toast on the kitchen table, then sat down and smeared sinful gobs of butter on the toast—another luxury he was going to have to forgo when Sheila returned. As he began to eat, he found himself thinking about tomorrow's upcoming therapy sessions. His first appointment in the morning was with a young man named Dennis Jones, whose impulse control issues had led to his recent arrest for shoplifting.

Julian had done his best to convince a judge that Dennis's kleptomania was a matter of illness rather than criminality—an obsessive-compulsive disorder and not a failure of moral character. After all, the kid generally stole things that he didn't even want.

But the judge was still on the fence about Dennis's case, so in order to keep him out of jail, Julian was going to have to get him to change his behavior for good.

Tomorrow's task would be to persuade Dennis to add naltrexone to his medications, which currently included fluoxetine and bupropion. Dennis was neurotic and not especially intelligent. Although he wasn't given to delusions or paranoia, certain fringe online conspiracy sites had convinced him that the government was using psychiatric medications for mind control. Julian hoped that today he could talk him out of such a ridiculous idea.

Julian grunted with annoyance at the trouble this sort of thing was causing.

The Internet sure hasn't made my job any easier, he thought.

As far as he was concerned, social networking and other online activities were undermining the mental health of society as a whole. Sheila had adapted well to all this digital novelty, but sometimes Julian felt like a relic of simpler, saner times.

Worse, he knew that his younger colleagues considered him to be some old fogey who couldn't keep pace with the changes in the world. He looked forward to retirement, which was still at least two or three years away.

Savoring his snack, he found himself envying Sheila. She'd been able to give up her own family therapy practice after writing a bestselling book about the very issues that troubled Julian. And now she was getting to travel around the country, speaking and lecturing and signing books and just generally basking in the public's admiration.

It must be nice, Julian thought.

But he was determined not to give in to jealousy. After all, Sheila's publishing royalties were going to make both of their senior years a lot easier. And he was happy that she was enjoying her new life.

Julian finished eating and took his plate, glass, and silverware over to the sink. As he started to wash the items, he thought he heard a noise over the sound of running water. He turned off the water and listened.

Had Sheila gotten home earlier than expected?

If so, there would be no hiding the aroma of fried bacon.

Busted, he thought.

He'd just have to put on an embarrassed grin and admit to his wayward behavior. Sheila would be cranky about it but not really unpleasant. They'd both laugh good-naturedly as he made promises for the future that he surely wouldn't keep.

He stood listening for a moment and heard nothing. Figuring the noise must have come from his guilty imagination, he finished washing the dishes. As he dried his hands, another sound caught his ear.

This time he was sure it wasn't his imagination.

"Sheila?" he called out.

There was no reply.

He walked into the living room and looked around. No one was there. But he was sure he'd heard something.

He turned toward the entry hallway and saw that the door to Sheila's downstairs study was closed.

He felt a tingle of alarm.

Maybe Sheila had come inside and smelled the bacon, and instead of reacting with good-natured crossness, she was genuinely mad at him and had shut herself up in her study. That sort of behavior wasn't exactly like her, but if her trip had wound up being less than pleasant, she might be crankier than usual.

He walked over to the study door and knocked.

"Sheila, are you in there?" he asked.

Again there was no reply. For a moment, Julian just stood there in a state of confusion. Had anyone actually come into the house at all? He was certain he hadn't imagined those sounds. But no luggage had been deposited there in the hallway.

Was it possible that Sheila had hauled her bags into the office and shut the door behind her and now wouldn't even talk to him?

That would be silly, of course. And he knew it was neurotic of him to even imagine it.

Shaking his head in amusement at his own speculations, he opened the study door and walked inside. At a glance he saw that Sheila's typically immaculate workplace, so unlike the chaotic clutter of his own upstairs office, was unchanged and unoccupied.

Maybe she went upstairs, he thought.

But surely he would have clearly heard that much activity in the house. It was much more likely that his imagination was playing tricks on him.

Suddenly he heard a noise behind him, in the hallway just outside the study. It sounded like swiftly moving footsteps. Before he could even turn around, he was seized from behind in a viselike grip. A strong hand pressed a wet piece of cloth over his mouth and nose.

Julian immediately recognized the pungently sweet taste and odor from his medical training.

Chloroform!

His mind was rushing ahead of his body, which hadn't yet been seized by panic. He knew he was in serious danger, but he simply didn't feel it.

He thrashed only briefly, dimly aware of knocking over the desk lamp.

And within a few moments, he was aware of nothing at all.

CHAPTER ONE

R iley Sweeney felt sweat breaking out on her brow. Her hand shook as she wiped her face with a handkerchief. The courtroom suddenly felt hotter than it had a few moments ago. Her heart was beating faster.

The moment she'd long been waiting for had finally arrived.

Right now, her senior partner, Special Agent Jake Crivaro, was scheduled to testify in the trial of Larry Mullins. Riley looked across the courtroom and saw her short, barrel-chested partner's face twitch with eager anticipation.

The outcome of the trial had been in doubt, but she felt sure that Crivaro's testimony might prove a turning point.

Riley reminded herself that it had been exactly a year ago today that Crivaro had come into her life and set her on course for a career in the BAU. A legal victory today would be a fine way to celebrate.

But something unexpected seemed to be happening. The chief prosecutor and Mullins's defense lawyer were huddled together, whispering intensely.

What's going on? Riley wondered.

Whatever it was, she doubted that it was good.

Finally the prosecutor turned to the bench and spoke to the judge.

"Your honor, the counsel for the defense and I would like to speak to you in chambers."

Judge Tobias Redstone frowned grimly.

With a crack of his gavel, he said, "The court will take a short recess while I confer with counsel."

Everybody in the courtroom rose as the bailiff and the lawyers followed Judge Redstone out of the courtroom. Then a murmur passed among both the jurors and the spectators as they sat back down again.

Flanked by guards, Larry Mullins was still sitting at the defense table. Although his hands were shackled together, he was well dressed in a suit jacket over a shirt and tie, and he cut a respectable figure.

Riley knew that his lawyer had gone to a lot of trouble to make sure he wouldn't be sitting there in an orange jumpsuit. Consequently, Mullins didn't look like such a bad guy. He was well-scrubbed and well-spoken, and had an earnest air of innocence about him. The guise seemed to be working. Riley sensed that the jury was still uncertain of his guilt.

That was why Crivaro's testimony was to be so crucial. If anybody could convince the jury that Mullins was not the misunderstood character he claimed to be, Crivaro was that person.

But as they waited for the judge and lawyers to return, Riley wondered—was Crivaro not going to testify after all?

She felt a deep chill as Mullins turned to look directly at her, a smug smile forming on his babyish face. Then she watched as he turned toward Crivaro with the same expression. Crivaro's lips twisted sharply, and for a moment Riley was afraid her partner would lunge across the courtroom at Mullins.

Don't do it, she thought.

She could see Crivaro turn his face away and she knew he was struggling to keep his anger under control.

Riley only hoped she could control her own rage at that self-satisfied expression.

At least some people in the courtroom knew for a virtual fact that Larry Mullins was a monster to his very core. Riley and Crivaro were two of them. The others included the parents of the two victims, who sat together looking very anxious. Their common hope was that Mullins would at least be sentenced to life without parole, or perhaps even the death penalty.

Surely, she told herself, the case was tight enough for a conviction. She reviewed it in her mind.

Larry Mullins had been working as a nanny—or a "manny," as he preferred to call himself—when he'd been arrested for the death of Ian

Harter, a little boy under his care. When Riley and Crivaro had been brought in to investigate Ian's death, they soon discovered that another child, Nathan Betts, had died under identical circumstances under Mullins's care in a different city. Both boys had been suffocated to death—obviously murdered.

Mullins had pleaded innocent to two charges of murder, admitting to nothing more than letting the two boys out of his sight during the times of their deaths, and putting on a shallow show of remorse for his negligence.

Riley had never believed for a moment that their deaths under Mullins's care had been coincidental, much less that some unknown murderer was still at large. But proving Mullins's guilt beyond a shadow of a doubt had proven to be another matter entirely.

From the very start of the trial, the prosecuting attorney, Paxton Murawski, had warned Riley and Crivaro that this was going to be a tough case. Try as they might, the agents and the police had uncovered no evidence to prove that Mullins was the only person who'd had access to the children when they were killed.

"We've got to be careful, or the bastard will walk," Murawski had told Riley and Crivaro.

Neither Riley nor Crivaro had known exactly what Murawski had meant by "careful." But she knew that some attempted plea-bargaining had been going on behind the scenes between the prosecution and the defense. And now she suspected the whole courtroom was going to learn the results of that bargaining.

Is he going to go free after all? she wondered.

She shuddered at the possibility, and also at her memory of the moment when she and Crivaro had put Mullins under arrest.

Right when Riley had been putting him in cuffs and reading him his rights, he'd turned his head and smirked wickedly at her, with a gloating expression that all but admitted his guilt to her.

"Good luck," he'd said, obviously confident about hard it was going to be to convict him.

Riley ground her teeth as the words echoed through her memory.

Good luck!

She didn't believe she'd ever been as angry as she'd been at that moment. She had truly wanted to kill Mullins right there and then. She'd actually reached for her Glock. But Crivaro had touched her on the shoulder and given her a warning look, and she'd finished the arrest in a proper manner.

And now Riley wondered—if it weren't for Crivaro, would Larry Mullins be alive today? Of course she'd have been charged with murder herself, and she might have spent the rest of her life in prison. But might it have been worth it to get rid of such a repugnant excuse for a human being?

Riley half-wished she'd shot him dead that day.

And now, judging from Crivaro's angry expression, she suspected that he felt the same way.

The bailiff returned and asked Mullins to join counsel in the judge's chambers. Still flanked by guards, the man on trial got up and followed the bailiff out of the courtroom.

Riley's heart sank.

This doesn't look good, she thought.

Several long minutes ticked by before the bailiff returned and asked everyone in the courtroom to stand again. Judge Redstone reentered, followed by the lawyers and Mullins himself.

Judge Redstone announced to the courtroom, "The counsels for the defense and the prosecution have reached an agreement. If the defendant agrees to plead guilty to two charges of second-degree, unpremeditated murder, this trial will be unnecessary and the defendant will be sentenced accordingly."

Riley gasped aloud, and so did many others in the room.

Unpremeditated murder?

The very idea made no sense to her.

Frowning at Mullins, the judge said to him, "Larry Mullins, do you so plead?"

"I do, Your Honor," Mullins said.

"Very well," Judge Redstone said. "Larry Mullins, you are hereby sentenced to two sentences of thirty years, to be served simultaneously and with the possibility of parole in fifteen years."

Simultaneously? Possible parole?

Riley had to fight down her impulse to stand up, to scream, *No, that's wrong.*

She knew it wouldn't help, so she choked back the words and stayed in her seat. But she couldn't stop her mind from spinning frantically.

The man killed two children.

Why didn't they understand that?

The judge thanked the jury for its time and service and ended the trial with a bang of his gavel. The whole room was in an uproar as Mullins was led away to his cell. When Riley finally got up from her chair, she found herself in the midst of an angry and confused mass of people.

The first thing she wanted to do was talk to Agent Crivaro and ask him what he thought had happened and if there was anything they could do about it. But she only got a glimpse of her partner as he stormed toward the entrance of the courtroom, red-faced with anger.

Where's he going? she wondered.

She couldn't follow him through the crush of bodies. Instead, she managed to make her way to the prosecution table, where Paxton Murawski was packing up his briefcase.

"What the hell happened?" she blurted bitterly.

The prosecuting attorney shook his head.

"It was the best we could do," he said.

"But it doesn't even make sense," Riley said. "All along Mullins has been pleading innocent to both murders. He was just negligent, he says. But now he's pleading guilty to second-degree murder for both of them. How could he have been merely negligent and also killed them? How can he have it both ways?"

Murawski scowled sharply at Riley.

"Agent Sweeney, you're new to this sort of business," he said. "Sometimes you've got to compromise—and sometimes these outcomes *don't* make sense. And really, this worked out better than we might have expected. We weren't going to get a conviction on first-degree murder, especially not two cases of it. It just wasn't going to happen. But the defense knew that Mullins wasn't going to get off scot-free either. That's why they proposed this deal. And we took it. End of story."

"'End of story?'" Riley echoed. "This isn't the end, and you know it. In fifteen years, Mullins might be up for parole. He'll be the same evil bastard he is today. But all he'll have to do is play his sweet-faced innocence act for the parole board, and they're liable to fall for it, and he'll be back on the streets."

Murawski shut his briefcase and said, "So—don't let that happen."

Riley could hardly believe her ears.

"But that won't be for another fifteen years," she said.

Murawski shrugged and added, "Like I said, don't let it happen. Trust me, he'll stay put until then."

Murawski turned to leave, but his eyes lit up with alarm at somebody that he saw approaching him. He seemed suddenly to change his mind about heading straight for the exit. Instead, he dodged and ducked in another direction. Riley quickly saw why.

The four parents of the two victims, Donald and Melanie Betts and Ross and Darla Harter, were pushing their way toward the prosecution table. Without either Crivaro or Murawski and his team still here, Riley knew that she was going to feel the brunt of their indignation.

Melanie Betts was weeping tears of sheer fury.

"We trusted you," she said to Riley. "You and your partner and the defense team."

"How could you have failed us like this?" Darla Harter added.

Riley opened her mouth, but she didn't know what to say.

Ironically, her first impulse was to repeat pretty much what Murawski had just told her—that they couldn't have gotten guilty verdicts on two counts of first-degree murder, and that this deal was better than it sounded, and anyway Larry Mullins was going to be in prison for a long time.

But she couldn't bring herself to say any of those things.

Instead she said, "I'm sorry."

"You're *sorry*?" Donald Betts said incredulously.

"Is that all you've got to say?" Ross Harter added.

Riley felt dumbstruck.

I've got to say something, she thought.

But what was left for her to say?

Then she remembered something that Murawski had said to her a moment ago about Mullins's possible parole.

"Don't let it happen."

Riley swallowed hard. Then she spoke with a note of conviction that surprised even her.

"He won't get parole," she said. "He'll serve his whole sentence—all thirty years of it, if he lives that long."

Melanie Betts squinted at her with a puzzled expression.

"How do you know that?" she asked.

"Because I'm going to make sure of it," Riley said, her throat catching with emotion. "I'm never going to let him get parole or early release."

She paused and thought hard about the two words she was about to say.

Then she said, "I promise."

The four parents stood staring at her for a moment. Riley wondered whether they could possibly believe what she'd just said, especially after what had just happened in the courtroom. She'd never promised them anything until now—certainly not that Mullins would be punished to the full extent of the law. She'd known better than to do that.

But now that she'd said it, she knew that she meant it.

She had no idea what it was going to take for her to keep her promise, but she was going to go through with it.

Finally, Donald Betts simply nodded. As he began to usher his wife and the other couple away, he looked at Riley and mouthed two words silently.

"Thank you."

Riley nodded back at him.

The courtroom was markedly less congested now, so Riley made her way out into the hallway. Reporters had surrounded Murawski and also Mullins's defense attorney and were badgering them with questions. Riley was grateful that the reporters didn't seem to notice her.

But as she looked back and forth, she wondered where her partner had gone. She didn't see Crivaro anywhere inside the building. When she went out onto the courthouse steps, she still couldn't see him.

Where is he? she wondered.

She walked over to the lot where they'd parked their BAU vehicle. She had her own set of keys, so she opened the door and got into the driver's seat and sat waiting.

Surely he'll show up soon, she thought.

But as long minutes began to pass, she started to wonder.

She knew that this verdict had hit Jake especially hard.

Maybe he just couldn't face me, she thought.

She tried to phone him, but he didn't pick up the call. She didn't want to alert the BAU that her partner was missing. Crivaro would certainly return when he was ready.

Riley sat in the car waiting for a full hour before she decided it was time to leave. Finally, she pulled out of the parking lot and drove back to Quantico alone.

CHAPTER TWO

Julian Banfield felt like he was waking up from some terrible dream.

Or maybe not waking up at all, he thought.

He still felt foggy and barely conscious. And he had a splitting headache.

He opened his eyes—or at least he thought he did—and found himself surrounded by complete blackness. When he tried to move, he found that he couldn't. He knew that this sort of immobilization was a typical symptom of his infrequent nightmares, likely caused by the constriction of blankets he was lying under.

But this feels different, he realized.

Even though his limbs were immobilized, he wasn't lying down.

Breathe, Julian instructed himself as he had so often instructed patients. *Slow breaths, in and out.*

But his spirits sank as the reality of his situation began to dawn on him. He was bound in a sitting position in complete darkness. Even after several deep breaths, the calm he was trying to generate escaped him.

Think, he told himself. *What's the last thing I remember?*

Then it came back to him. He'd been looking for Sheila in her office when someone had seized him from behind, and he'd been forced to breathe through a piece of cloth that was wet with some thick, sweet liquid.

Chloroform, he remembered, his thoughts skittering wildly toward a state of panic.

Then Julian heard a voice speak gently in the darkness.

"Hello, Dr. Banfield."

"Who's there?" Julian gasped.

"You don't recognize my voice?" the voice said. "Well, I guess that's not surprising. It's been a long time. I was much younger. My voice is different."

Suddenly a light snapped on, and Julian was momentarily blinded.

"There," the voice said. "Is that better?"

Julian squinted as his eyes struggled to adjust to the light. A face came into view—a smiling man with a long, lean face.

"Surely you recognize me now," he said.

Julian stared hard at him. He thought the shape of his chin looked vaguely familiar, but he couldn't place it. He didn't recognize him, and the truth was, he didn't much care about that at the moment. He was just now starting to grasp his situation, and from what he could tell, it was very, very bad.

He and the strange man were in Julian's wine cellar, surrounded by shelves containing hundreds of bottles of wine. Julian was somehow tied or strapped into one of the heavy and elegant wooden chairs that were part of the wine cellar decor.

A stranger was sitting in another of those chairs, staring at him and still smiling.

The stranger was holding a glass and a newly opened bottle of wine.

Pouring some wine into the glass, he said, "I hope you don't mind—I took the liberty of opening a bottle of Le Vieux Donjon Châteauneuf-du-Pape from just a couple of years ago. I suppose it was rather presumptuous of me. For all I know, you might have been saving it for a much later date. I understand that this vintage is expected to mature very nicely."

He held the glass up to the light and peered at the wine sagely.

He said, "I was tempted to crack open a 1987 Opus One, but of course that would have been way out of line. Besides, I'm very curious about *this* vintage."

The stranger took a sip and swished it in his mouth.

"It definitely lives up to its reputation," he said. "Hints of crushed juniper berry, blackberry, raisin, roasted chestnut. Quite a large, bold, bountiful flavor. Not that I'm any expert, but I'd say this was a good buy for the money."

Julian was still feeling muddled and confused.

Don't scream, he cautioned himself. No one could hear him, and it would only agitate this man. Instead, maybe he should use some of his skills as a therapist. Above all else, it was important to stay calm—or at least *appear* to be calm.

"Well," he said, "now that we're here, perhaps you would like to tell me a bit about yourself."

The stranger chuckled. "What would you like to know, Doctor?" he asked.

"Surely," Julian replied, "there's something you'd like to tell me about why...um...what led us to this particular situation."

The stranger let out a raspy sound that wasn't quite a laugh. "I'm afraid that's a rather long and complicated story," he said. With that, he suddenly stood up and threw the delicate wine glass so that it shattered against the wall. Then he set the wine bottle down on a decorative little table.

Realizing that his professional tactics weren't going to work, Julian began to grasp for another approach.

"My wife will be home soon," he blurted.

The stranger sounded unfazed.

"Will she? Well then I should get on with the business at hand."

"Who the hell are you?" Julian demanded.

A hurt expression crossed the stranger's face.

"Oh dear. I'd hoped you would recognize me by now. Well, that would have been a lot to expect. But I'm sure you'll remember me before long. I've got a surefire way of reminding you."

Again, Julian thought he noticed something slightly familiar about the man's chin. But he certainly didn't recognize him. The only reality that he could focus on was that he was a prisoner in his own wine cellar and at the mercy of a man who was quite mad.

Just how he'd been strapped to this chair he didn't know, but he felt most uncomfortable. Something tight was fastened all the way around his chest, making it difficult to breathe. Now he realized that his feet were bare and cold and wet.

He peered downward. Although his knees were strapped together, he could see that one of his big silver platters was on the floor. When he moved his feet a little, he felt them swish through shallow water.

"Yes," the stranger commented. "I brought a silver platter down from your lovely china cabinet. It's perfect for the task at hand. It holds about a quarter inch of water, and both water and silver are excellent conductors."

Excellent conductors? Julian wondered.

His eyes darted around, trying to take in as much as he could of whatever was happening around him. He could see that the stranger was wearing what appeared to be rubber-soled boots.

Then the stranger began to pull on a pair of heavy rubber gloves.

What on earth … ? Again Julian cautioned himself not to scream.

The stranger stepped out of Julian's range of vision for a moment. After some rattling from the direction of the cellar's breaker panel, the stranger reappeared with a length of heavy-duty insulated cable in his hand. The cable was cut short to expose the wires within.

Julian felt his body beginning to process genuine terror.

The stranger came close to Julian and peered into his eyes.

"Are you sure you don't recognize me, Dr. Banfield?" he asked with that unfading smile of his.

Julian stared hard the stranger's face, again noticing an odd familiarity about the shape of the chin. He thought hard, trying to place that face while a stream of thoughts rushed through his head.

Electricity … electrodes … conductor …

Then the truth hit him in a flash. Although he couldn't bring the name to mind, the face was unmistakable even after many years.

"Yes!" he murmured with surprise. "Yes, I do know who you are!"

"Oh, good!" the stranger said. "I knew I could jog your memory."

Julian's heart was pounding painfully.

"My wife will be home soon," he said again.

"Yes, I'm sure she will be," the stranger said. "And won't she be surprised!"

The stranger carefully dropped the bare wires onto the silver platter, and Julian screamed as his consciousness exploded into a blaze of scorching whiteness.

CHAPTER THREE

R iley clutched the cordless phone in her hand as she paced the floor of the little basement apartment she shared with her fiancé, Ryan Paige. She was trying to call Agent Crivaro.

And once again, he wasn't picking up the call. His phone just kept ringing and ringing.

I can't even get his machine, she thought.

Ryan said, "Still can't reach him?"

She hadn't realized that Ryan was paying any attention to what she was doing. He was sitting at the kitchen table poring over case materials that he'd brought home from Parsons & Rittenhouse, the law firm where he was working as an entry-level attorney.

"No," Riley said. "I feel like I'm going to lose my mind. Maybe I should drive back to Quantico and—"

Ryan interrupted gently. "Riley, no. What good would that do?"

Riley sighed. Ryan was right, of course. After the trial and Crivaro's disappearance, she'd driven their FBI vehicle back to Quantico, hoping to find him at BAU headquarters, but he hadn't been there. Special Agent in Charge Erik Lehl had left his office for the day, which had probably been just as well. If Crivaro hadn't checked in, Riley didn't want to be the one to tell Lehl her partner had gone AWOL.

Ryan asked, "How many times have you tried to call Crivaro?"

"I don't know," Riley said.

Ryan chuckled sympathetically.

"Remember Einstein's definition of insanity," he said.

Riley shrugged. "Yeah—it's doing the same thing over and over again and expecting different results."

13

She plopped herself down on the couch in the living room area where she'd been pacing.

"Maybe I am kind of losing my mind about this," she said.

Ryan got up from the table and went to the kitchen cabinet and took down a bottle of bourbon and a couple of glasses.

"I'd hate to have you committed to an asylum," he said. "Maybe a stiff drink is what you need to restore your sanity."

Riley laughed resignedly.

"It couldn't hurt," she said.

Ryan poured drinks for both of them and sat down on the couch with Riley and put his arm around her shoulder.

"Do you want to talk about it?" he said.

Riley sighed. They'd talked about the trial a lot since she'd gotten home earlier today, and they'd continued talking about it over dinner just a little while ago. Ryan knew how upsetting the verdict had been to her. And of course, they'd also talked about Crivaro's mysterious disappearance.

"I don't know what else there is to say," she said, putting her head on Ryan's shoulder.

"Maybe I can think of something," Ryan said. "Maybe you could answer a few questions for me."

Riley snuggled closer to him and said, "Yeah, let's give that a try."

Ryan took a sip of bourbon and said, "Exactly *why* are you worried about Agent Crivaro?"

"Because he took off without telling me," she said.

"Do you think he's in some kind of danger?"

Riley scoffed. "Agent Crivaro? I don't think so. He's tough. He can take care of himself."

"Are you worried that he's mad at you?" Ryan asked.

Riley squinted with surprise. It was actually a pretty good question. She lifted her head from Ryan's shoulder and took a sip of bourbon. It felt very comforting to swallow.

"I ... can't imagine why he would be," she said.

"So what do you think is going on with him?" Ryan asked.

She remembered his furious expression as he'd charged out of the courtroom.

"He's mad at himself," Riley said. "He feels like he failed."

"Riley, I'm not sure why you were both so unhappy with the verdict. Thirty years is a long sentence. And Mullins is going to have to wait fifteen years for the possibility of parole. That sounds pretty tough to me."

Riley flashed back to her confrontation with the angry parents of the two victims.

She remembered the promise she'd made to them.

"I'm never going to let him get parole or early release."

Now she couldn't help but wonder—would she really be able to keep that promise?

"We wanted more," Riley said. "The victims' families expected more. But…"

Her voice faded away.

"But what?" Ryan asked.

Riley gave him an affectionate shove.

"You're acting like some kind of a shrink," she said.

"No, I'm not," Ryan said. "I'm acting like a lawyer."

"So you're cross-examining me?" Riley said.

"Exactly."

"Then I object," she said. "You're asking me a lot of leading questions."

"Tell it to the judge," Ryan said.

"What judge?" Riley said.

She and Ryan both laughed and huddled together.

Then Ryan asked in a more cautious tone, "What about you, Riley? Are you happy?"

Riley felt a flood of warmth rising inside her.

"Oh, yes," she said.

"Not just with your job, I mean," Ryan said.

"I know," Riley said. "I'm really happy—with everything."

She meant it with all her heart.

She and Ryan had had some tough times since they'd first gotten together, and there had been moments when neither of them had thought their relationship could last. Ryan's new job had put him under enormous pressure, and Riley's caseload had been frantic for a while. She'd spent far too much time away from him.

But Ryan was now settled comfortably into a position with a law firm that gave him lots of upward mobility. And Riley's caseload had thinned out considerably. She and Crivaro hadn't worked a case in the field for more than six weeks now, when they'd closed a case in Kentucky and Tennessee of a serial killer who targeted women who were virgins.

Since then, they had both been working mostly from the Quantico offices on research and information that Jake fed to other agents in the field. Riley found the work boring at times. But she had to admit to herself, it was a relief not to be far away from home and in danger so much of the time.

And it had been a relief to Ryan as well. At long last, he seemed to be getting used to the idea of her being a BAU agent. At least he wasn't trying to talk her into quitting anymore, and they hadn't had a fight in weeks.

Riley hoped maybe her work would continue at this slower, more manageable, and less life-threatening pace. She felt sure that if she could be home more, things would get better and better between her and Ryan.

And at times like now, she appreciated how thoughtful and caring Ryan could be.

Handsome, too, she thought, glancing at him.

Then he asked, "Do you want to keep talking?"

"Huh-uh," Riley said.

"What do you want to do?"

Riley turned his face toward hers and kissed him.

"I want to go to bed," she said.

The next morning when Riley drove to Quantico, the day was as bright and clear as her spirits. Her lovemaking with Ryan last night had been passionate and perfect. And now, they both were on their way to jobs that they really cared about.

Could life be better? she wondered.

Now that she thought about it, maybe it could. In fact, it almost certainly would. Someday soon, she and Ryan would get married, and when they both felt ready, they'd start a family.

As for Agent Crivaro, Riley was sure he'd feel better about everything today.

Yesterday was surely just a passing thing, she thought.

As she pulled into her BAU parking spot, her heart leapt with joy to see Crivaro standing near his car, waiting for her arrival as he often did on mornings like this.

Everything is back to normal!

She parked her car and jumped out.

Don't hug him, she told himself. *He wouldn't like that.*

But her spirits sank as she walked toward him. His arms were crossed and he was gazing down at the pavement, as if he hadn't noticed her arrival.

Definitely not in a hugging mood, she realized.

And whatever he was about to tell her, she was sure she wasn't going to like hearing it.

CHAPTER FOUR

A s Riley approached Crivaro, he barely glanced up at her. Leaning against his car and gazing downward, he said, "I'm sorry about what happened yesterday. I was an asshole."

Riley wanted to assure him that he wasn't an asshole. But somehow the words wouldn't come out.

I guess I'm mad at him, she realized.

That possibility hadn't really occurred to her until just now.

Taking a place next to him, she leaned against the car, too.

"Why did you run out on me like that?" she asked.

Crivaro shrugged tiredly.

"I wasn't running out on you," he said. "At least I don't think so. It was more like..."

His voice faded for a moment.

Then he said in a choked voice, "I just couldn't face those parents. I just couldn't. Not after we'd let them down like that. I felt like I...just had to get away."

Riley was startled. She'd just assumed that it was *her* he hadn't wanted to talk to. Now that she thought about it, her assumption seemed awfully self-centered.

"Did you talk to them?" he asked Riley.

Riley nodded.

"How did it go?"

Riley inhaled sharply.

"About like you would have expected," she said.

"That bad, huh?"

Riley nodded and said, "They were angry about the judge's decision. And yeah, they were angry with us, too."

"I don't blame them," Crivaro said. "What did you tell them?"

"I told them I was sorry, and..."

Riley hesitated a moment. It suddenly seemed difficult to repeat what she had said to the two couples.

Finally she said, "I promised...to make sure Mullins never gets out of prison until he's served his whole term. I told him I'd never let him get parole or early release."

Crivaro nodded slightly.

Stifling a sigh, Riley said, "I hope I didn't make a promise I couldn't keep."

Riley hoped that he would say something encouraging in reply, but he remained silent.

"So what's going on?" she demanded a little impatiently.

"I wanted to tell you myself," Crivaro said, his voice catching with emotion. "I didn't want you to hear it from anybody else."

Riley felt a wave of dread. She just stood there silently until he spoke again.

"I'm quitting," Crivaro told her.

"You can't do that," Riley blurted.

"I already did," he said.

She scrambled for words. "You said if I joined BAU you'd stay..."

"For a while to help you get started," he finished the line for her. "That was nearly a year ago, Riley. I told you back then I was already eligible for retirement."

"Can't you wait...?"

"No, it's already final. I just came here from Erik Lehl's office. I turned in my badge and gun to him and signed and submitted my formal resignation."

"Why?" Riley cried sharply.

Crivaro let out a slight groan.

"You know perfectly well, Riley. Can you honestly say I've been at the top of my game lately? I'll never again be the agent I used to be. I've outlasted my expiration date. In fact, I've had to get special extensions to stay on the job this long."

A silence fell between them. They both stood there for several long moments, not looking at each other.

Finally Crivaro said, "The whole thing really hit me after the verdict. It was one thing not to get Mullins a tougher sentence. But I couldn't make myself talk to those parents. I've never felt that way before, never skipped out on that part of the job. Right then and there I knew it was over. How can I keep on fighting bad guys when I can't even look at their victims? That's why I ran off like that."

"I'm going to talk to Lehl," Riley muttered.

As soon as the words were out, she wondered whether she really meant them. Was she really going to try to talk Special Agent in Charge Erik Lehl into ignoring Crivaro's resignation? Did she imagine she could succeed?

"I think you should do that," Crivaro told her. "In fact, Lehl wants to talk to you. He asked me to tell you to check in with him first thing. It sounded like maybe he's got a case for you."

Riley's mouth fell open, but no words came out.

How could she even put her feelings into words?

Finally she stammered, "Agent Crivaro, I … I don't think I'm ready."

"You're right," Crivaro said. "You're not ready."

Riley looked at her partner with surprise.

Crivaro said, "Look, *nobody's* ready when they're first out on their own. You just have to get yourself ready. You're the most talented agent I've ever worked with. Your instincts are as good as mine ever were, and that's saying a lot. Nobody can get into a killer's mind like the two of us can. And you're developing skills to match your raw abilities. But I'm holding you back. You're depending too much on me. You've got to learn to trust yourself. And I never thought I'd ever say this about a partner but…"

He chuckled quietly.

"You're getting too comfortable with me."

Riley couldn't help laughing as well.

"You're kidding, right?" she said.

"I know it sounds crazy, but it's true," Crivaro said. "I'm not sure what you need next, but it's not me. Maybe you need to go it alone for a couple of cases. God knows, I've had to do that a lot. Or maybe you need to work with a partner who's really hard to get along with."

Shaking her head, Riley said, "I've had that with you."

"Maybe at first, but not anymore. You're the only partner I've ever had who could stand me. I'm a cranky old bastard, and you know it."

Riley smiled a little.

I can't disagree with him about that, she thought.

They fell silent again.

Riley found herself flashing back to cases they'd worked on together—especially the one in Arizona, where she and Crivaro had gone undercover as father and daughter. It hadn't felt like pretending at all, at least as far as Riley was concerned.

And now she wondered—should she tell him he'd been more of a real father to her than her biological father?

No, I'll start crying, she thought. *And that would really piss him off.*

Instead, she said, "What will you do with yourself?"

Crivaro laughed again.

"It's called *retirement,* Riley. What does anybody do? Maybe I'll take up playing bridge—if I can find a partner, which I guess is kind of unlikely. Or maybe I'll go on a Caribbean cruise. Or start playing golf. Or do volunteer work. Or get involved in community theater. Or maybe I'll join a quilting circle."

Riley laughed again at the image of Crivaro sewing a quilt with a bunch of women his age.

"You're not being serious," she said.

"No, and maybe I'm getting kind of tired of being serious. And maybe I *like* the idea of having no idea what I'm going to do with the rest of my life. Whatever else it'll be, it'll be an adventure."

Riley heard a note of uncertainty when he said that word—"adventure."

He's not sure about this, she thought.

He's trying to talk himself into it.

But did she have any business trying to sway his decision?

Crivaro looked at his watch and pointed to the building.

"You've got to get in there," he said. "You don't want to keep Lehl waiting."

Then he put a comforting hand on Riley's shoulder.

"I won't be a stranger, kid," he said. "I'll probably stay in touch more than you want me to."

"I doubt that, Agent Crivaro," Riley said.

Crivaro wagged his finger at her.

"Hey, I'm retired, remember? No more of that 'Agent Crivaro' stuff. It's time for you to start calling me Jake."

Riley felt a knot in her throat.

"OK ... Jake," she said, almost in a whisper.

As he opened the door to his car, he spoke again. "Now get in there, get back to work."

As Riley started to walk away, she turned at the sound of his voice.

"Hey, that promise you made in the courtroom yesterday ... that was the right thing to say, and I wish I'd said it. I know it's got you worried, but you'll keep that promise. I know you will. In fact, if I live long enough, I'll do everything I can to help you keep it."

Crivaro started his car and pulled out of his parking place.

Riley watched after him as he drove away, still determined not to cry.

Then she made her way inside the BAU building to talk with Lehl.

CHAPTER FIVE

E ven though the BAU building was full of the usual bustle of activity, the place felt strangely empty to Riley. She was sharply aware that Jake Crivaro wasn't here. Was it really possible that her mentor would never set foot in this building again? And if he was really gone, how could everybody else here just be going on with their daily routines as if nothing had changed?

Of course, she realized, almost nobody else yet knew that Crivaro had resigned.

Then Riley had to admit that even when they did know, maybe nobody else would care as much about it as she did. Although Jake Crivaro was something of a living legend at the BAU, everybody knew that all legends had to end sometime.

Everybody except me, she thought.

She came to a stop in the hallway, unsure where to go since she couldn't report to her partner's office for instructions. Then she remembered Crivaro had said Lehl was expecting her, possibly to assign her to another case.

As she headed on toward the elevator, she remembered how Crivaro had first come into her life. Back when she'd still been a student at Lanton University, after two of her dorm mates had been murdered, Crivaro had shown up to work on the case. Just when Riley couldn't have felt more terrified and helpless, he'd recognized her unusual instincts and put her to work helping him find the killer.

She'd found the killer, all right. It had turned out to be a favorite professor of hers. And he would have killed her too if Crivaro hadn't saved her life.

Since then, Riley's world had never been the same. After college, Crivaro had gotten her into the FBI's summer honors program and then into the Academy at Quantico. Until the last few weeks without field cases, life had been a constant rush of excitement and danger.

She got into an elevator and pushed the button for the floor she wanted. The elevator car was crowded, which made Riley feel all the more alone.

None of these people know what's happened, she thought again. *And I sure don't know what's going to happen now.*

Part of her harbored some wild idea of turning in her badge and gun herself to protest Crivaro's leaving.

Of course that would be crazy, she reminded herself. She'd put far too much into this career to give up on it now.

Still, she remembered what Crivaro had said to her when she'd told him she was going to talk to Lehl about his decision.

"I think you should do that."

What had he meant? Did Crivaro hope that Riley might keep him from retiring?

She also remembered something else he'd said.

"It's time for you to start calling me Jake."

That certainly hadn't sounded as if he intended to end their relationship, professional or otherwise. And she was sure that he had meant a lot by that decision. After all, who else in the world ever called him just "Jake"? He was estranged from his ex-wife and his son, and he had no close friends that Riley knew of.

To the best of her knowledge, he was a lonely man, and retirement wasn't going to make that any better.

She got off the elevator and headed straight toward Lehl's office. When she got there, she saw that the door was open. Still, she hesitated outside the door.

Then, almost uncannily, she heard Lehl's voice speaking from inside.

"Come in, Agent Sweeney."

She walked on in to find the lanky Special Agent in Charge standing behind his desk. As usual, he seemed almost too outsized for his office, let alone his desk.

She couldn't help but smile as she remembered what Crivaro had said when she'd observed that Lehl looked like he was always on stilts.

"No, he looks like he's made *of stilts."*

"Have a seat, Agent Sweeney," Lehl said in his daunting baritone.

Riley sat down, and so did Lehl. He got on the phone and asked someone to come to his office immediately. Then he steepled his fingers together and peered at Riley and said, "Perhaps there's something you'd like to discuss."

Riley gulped hard.

It's now or never.

But did she dare voice her protest at her partner's departure?

After all, Erik Lehl was probably the only man in the world who could actually intimidate Jake Crivaro.

Even so, she forced the words out of her mouth.

"Sir, I just talked with Agent Crivaro."

Lehl nodded silently.

Riley swallowed again.

"I don't think he should retire, sir," she said.

Lehl nodded again.

"He told me you'd say that," Lehl replied.

Riley was startled. This was about the last thing she'd expected to hear. Apparently Jake and Lehl had already discussed how she was going to react to this.

"Would you like to explain why you feel that way?" Lehl asked.

Riley panicked and almost felt like fleeing the room.

What kind of answer could she possibly give to that question?

She said, "He thinks his abilities are declining, sir."

"And you think otherwise?" Lehl said.

"I do, sir," Riley said.

"Are you quite sure that you know what's best for him?" Lehl said.

Riley suddenly had no idea what to say. After all, it was a good question. *Was* she really sure that Jake was as sharp an agent as he'd ever been? She remembered his recent words.

"Can you honestly say I've been at the top of my game lately?"

She hadn't contradicted him then. Could she honestly say she'd changed her mind in the meantime?

Lehl's eyes narrowed as he looked at her in what felt like a keenly analytical manner.

He said, "I guess what I'm asking is…on whose behalf are you telling me this? Yours or Agent Crivaro's?"

Riley slumped a little in her chair.

"I—I'm not sure," she admitted.

Lehl leaned across his desk toward her.

He said, "Agent Sweeney, you and I have had some differences since I've known you."

"I know," Riley said.

Indeed, that was putting it mildly. Last fall, when she'd still been at the Academy, Crivaro had pulled her away from her studies to help him on a case. Without approval from anybody, she'd posed as a reporter and asked a U.S. senator questions that had led to the exposure of his past sexual misbehavior. She'd been following a hunch, as usual, but the revelation had proven to have nothing to do with the case she was working on.

Without even really meaning to, she'd ended the senator's political career. Worse, the incident had caused a serious stir at the BAU. The senator had been a high-ranking member of some prestigious committees, and he had a lot of pull over the BAU's purse strings.

Lehl had been beyond furious. He'd personally seen to it that Riley was expelled from the Academy, relenting only after she'd done some brilliant work with Jake. But he'd been wary of her ever since she'd graduated from the Academy and officially joined the BAU.

Now Lehl asked her, "Where does this leave us—you and the agency, I mean?"

"I'm not sure what you mean," Riley said.

But she was afraid maybe she did understand. She knew that her status at the BAU was somewhat probationary. Maybe now Lehl considered this a good time to get rid of her

The expression on his face didn't bode well.

"I'll be honest with you, Agent Sweeney," Lehl said. "Your partnership with Crivaro was always productive, sometimes remarkable. Nevertheless, I've always felt that the two of you had a tendency to be…how should I put it? Bad influences on each other. I worked with Crivaro for years, and despite all his brilliance, he was always something of a maverick, and he gave me and the agency a good deal of trouble. He was always bending rules, sometimes breaking them outright. Can you deny that you've got the same tendencies?"

Riley didn't dare lie about it.

"No," she said.

Lehl drummed his fingers on his desk. He said, "I want you to answer my next question as honestly as you can. Your rebellious streak—did you pick that up from Crivaro? And now that he's gone, can I expect you to change your ways? Or...?"

He left the thought unfinished.

But Riley knew all too well what he was asking.

Was she a rebellious maverick by nature?

Would her ways never change, with or without Crivaro's "bad influence"?

He wants an honest answer, Riley reminded herself.

And she knew that an honest answer might end her BAU career right here and now.

But she didn't seem to have any choice.

She took a long, slow breath.

"Agent Lehl, I...can't change who I am," she said.

"I see," Lehl said, frowning.

"I can only promise to do my best—that is, if you keep me on. I don't go out of my way to be difficult. I always try my best to stick to the rules. But sometimes my instincts get the best of me."

She paused for a moment, then added, "But I've been told that my instincts are pretty good. Exceptional, in fact. And maybe... well, maybe there's a price to pay for those instincts. Maybe a bit of a rebellious streak comes with those abilities. And..."

She struggled to think of the right words to say next. But the truth was, there was no tactful way to put it.

She said, "And maybe you just have to decide whether you think I'm worth the trouble. It's really up to you."

Lehl's expression changed a little, but Riley found it hard to read. Was that a smile she saw playing ever so slightly on his lips? And was that grunt he made just a hint of a chuckle?

He said, "I can remember a time when Agent Crivaro sat right where you are, saying much the same thing to me. I thought it was a pretty good answer then, and I guess it's a pretty good answer now."

Then he wagged a finger and added sternly, "But don't make any presumptions about the limits of my toleration. I run a tight ship. And *any* rule-breaking will lead to consequences. And I fully intend to keep you on as short a leash as possible."

Riley breathed a little easier.

"Yes, sir," she said. "Thank you, sir."

Lehl wrinkled his brow.

"What are you thanking me for?" he asked.

Riley stammered, "Well, uh ... for not firing me, I guess."

Lehl shrugged slightly. He certainly wasn't smiling now.

"Oh, that," he said. "Don't take it for granted—and don't get too comfortable. I could change my mind at any moment."

"I understand, sir," Riley said.

Lehl picked up a folder from his desk and began to skim through its contents.

He said, "When Agent Crivaro came here this morning, I'd intended to assign him to a case in Utah. I expected him to take the case, and to ask for you as a partner, but—"

Riley felt her heart sink at the idea of taking on a new case right now. She couldn't work without her partner, her mentor.

Then it was as though she could hear Jake's gravelly voice again.

"Nobody's ready when they're first out on their own. You just have to get yourself ready."

Without another thought, Riley blurted, "I want to take the case, sir."

With a slight growl, Lehl replied, "That's good. But I hope you don't think I'm going to let you go solo. You need adult supervision."

Riley couldn't help cringing at those words.

At that moment, a youngish man with a crew cut and a smooth complexion stepped into the office. Riley remembered Lehl calling for someone to join them when she'd first arrived.

"Thanks for coming, Agent Johnson," Lehl said, rising to his feet. "I'd like you to meet Special Agent Riley Sweeney."

Then he said to Riley, "This is Special Agent Cliff Johnson. Although he's new here in Quantico, perhaps you've heard of him. He did some excellent work in the Boston Field Office, and he asked to be transferred here."

In fact, Riley had heard of Cliff Johnson. He'd come here with an impressive reputation.

Lehl added to Riley, "He'll be working as your senior partner."

Senior partner! Riley thought.

That meant this young man would be giving her orders. Although she knew he was highly thought of, he'd just started working here in Quantico, and he didn't look much older than Riley. But she knew she was definitely in no position to object to the situation.

Lehl said to Riley and Johnson, "A county sheriff in Utah has asked for BAU's help. There have been a couple of deaths by electrocution out there—probable homicides, he says."

He handed the folder to Johnson and said, "He faxed me this information. It's not much to go on, but I'm sure he'll go into a lot more detail when you get there."

Glancing back and forth at Riley and Johnson, Lehl said, "There's a plane waiting on the tarmac right now to fly the two of you to Utah. Get your go-bags and head on out right now."

As Riley left the office and she and Johnson hurried away to fetch their go-bags, something Lehl said kept echoing in her ear.

"You need adult supervision."

She was starting to have a bad feeling about this assignment.

And she desperately wished she was still working with Jake Crivaro.

CHAPTER SIX

A s the plane took off from the tarmac, Riley looked carefully at her new senior partner. Special Agent Cliff Johnson was sitting across a folding table from her staring out the window.

From what she'd heard about him, she knew she should be grateful for the chance to work with him. Although Johnson seemed to be only two or three years older than she was, he'd apparently impressed everyone in the Boston Field Office. In fact, he'd pretty much single-handedly solved the case of a child murderer-rapist.

Riley didn't know the details of that investigation, but she knew that Johnson was regarded as something of a prodigy—a bit like herself when she'd gotten to the BAU. But while Riley had arrived in Quantico with a reputation for gut instincts, Johnson was known for his keen analytical skills.

Maybe we'll complement each other, she thought.

So why did she have her doubts about that?

As she thought it over, Riley realized that her qualms grew from a suspicion that the new agent might not really be all that impressive. She knew that analytical skills were easier for BAU officials to understand and appreciate than the more nebulous gut instincts that had made Jake Crivaro such a successful agent. After all, Johnson hadn't actually worked on any cases since he'd arrived in Quantico. In fact, it was possible that he'd never even worked as many major cases as Riley had with Jake.

The more she thought it over, the more she felt irritated at the idea of him giving her orders.

When the plane reached cruising altitude, Johnson opened up the folder Lehl had handed to him and shared its contents with Riley.

"OK, then," he said. "Let's have a look and see what we've got to deal with."

Riley stifled a giggle. A regional manner of speaking didn't normally amuse her, but Johnson's Boston accent was so thick, it almost sounded like a parody. Along with his clean-cut appearance and military bearing, that exaggerated sound of authority indicated that he was accustomed to privilege, probably from an Ivy League pedigree.

His voice startled her each time he spoke, and she told herself she'd better get used to it fast.

Pointing at the brief report between them, Johnson said, "We've got two deaths by electrocution. A man named Andy Gish was electrocuted just a week ago in Prinneville, Utah. The second victim was a psychiatrist, Julian Banfield, who died last night in Beardsley. Both Beardsley and Prinneville are in Hannaford County. The county sheriff, Collin Dawes, called in for the BAU's help."

"And Dawes thinks both deaths are homicides?" Riley asked.

Johnson shrugged slightly. "Well, there's not much to go on here. But we know that both victims were strapped to chairs before they were killed."

Riley's brow knitted with curiosity.

"I can't recall studying any cases of homicide by electrocution at the Academy," she said. "I wonder how common they are."

Johnson leaned back in his seat and stroked his chin.

"Not common, but no one can say exactly how uncommon," he said. "I suppose you can guess the most common method for murder by electrocution."

Riley was startled—and a little annoyed—by his professorial manner, as if he were quizzing a student. Nevertheless, an answer popped into her mind from movies she'd seen.

She said, "Um, probably dropping some electrical appliance in a bathtub while the victim is taking a bath."

Johnson nodded. "That's right. Not that there's any reliable record for how often it's done. That kind of electrocution doesn't leave any signs of injury—not even burns. If the killer just goes to the trouble of removing the appliance afterwards, the victim can appear to have died by natural causes—a heart attack, perhaps. So who knows how often that kind of homicide ever happens?"

He smiled wryly and added, "You'd have to be a pretty stupid killer to get caught at it. But some do. There was a case of a man killing his wife by throwing a fan heater into the bathtub with her. He might have gotten away with it, except the day before, he'd checked a book out of the library—*The Do-It-Yourself Home Electrician.* That kind of tipped off the cops."

Gazing out the window thoughtfully, Johnson continued, "Otherwise, electricity is pretty hard to use for murder. I can think of a handful of cases—one where a husband wrapped a bare electric cord around his wife's neck. It was a thirty-amp cable stripped of insulation."

He tilted his head and added, "But that kind of crime is rare as well. Not many people are willing to let you wind electrical cables around their neck or bare limbs. There are lots of easier ways to kill people."

Riley's mouth dropped a bit at this little lecture.

How does he know this stuff? she wondered.

She said, "Didn't the most recent murder happen just last night?"

"Yeah."

"And weren't both of us assigned to this case just a little while ago?"

"Yeah, why?"

Riley said, "Well, you sound like you've already been studying pertinent case histories."

Johnson looked a bit surprised.

"It's just stuff I've picked up from regular reading," he said. "Haven't you ever read *Simpson's Forensic Medicine*?"

Riley made a vague, noncommittal gesture. She knew the textbook from forensic classes at the Academy, and she'd read all the assigned parts. But she'd never supposed that anybody not really into forensics would read it from cover to cover.

This guy seems to know it by heart, she thought.

Apparently impervious to Riley's reactions, Johnson kept right on talking.

"Sometimes electrocution is used postmortem to disguise some other method of homicide. For example, I can think of a case where the killer smothered his victim to death, then electrocuted the corpse to make it look like a household appliance accident. Of course, that doesn't sound like what we're dealing with here. I'm curious to find out what this case is all about."

She'd heard that Cliff Johnson was a bit of a know-it-all as well as keenly analytical. But she hadn't expected him to be some kind of walking encyclopedia.

Who does this guy think he is, Sherlock Holmes?

If so, she didn't look forward to playing the sidekick role of Dr. Watson.

Looking at the paper herself, Riley said, "Strapping them down like that would suggest somebody of considerable strength, probably a man."

She thought for a moment, then added, "The big question is—*why?*"

"Huh?" Johnson said, squinting at her.

"Well, first there's the question of motive. The police don't seem to have found any connection between the two victims. Does that mean there won't be any more killings, or that he's just getting started?"

Riley leaned forward in her chair and said, "But more than that— *why* would anybody go to the trouble of killing anyone in this particular manner? You said yourself, electricity is pretty hard to use to murder someone. It's not exactly convenient. There are lots of easier ways to kill people."

She looked into Johnson's eyes and said, "I guess what I'm asking is—what's this killer's obsession? What makes him tick? Just why does he have a thing about electricity?"

Johnson looked rather puzzled. Finally he said, "Well, obviously, we don't yet have enough data to know that." Then he put his hands behind his head and leaned back in his chair and gazed out the window.

Riley tried hard not to stare at her new partner.

Data? she thought.

Did Johnson really think they could get into a killer's mindset by using *data?*

Riley herself had connected with many murderous minds, but always through pure gut instinct. Was her talent already obsolete? Was Johnson right in thinking that cold numbers and stats could reveal a killer's personality?

Maybe he's even smarter than he seems to be, she thought.

It was almost a four-hour flight from Quantico to the airport in Provo, Utah. Once they crossed the Appalachian Mountains, Riley got bored by the monotony of the Midwestern landscape and dozed off and on.

Riley was seized by a weird, icy feeling of déjà vu as she fastened the handcuffs behind the murderer's back.

This has happened before, *she thought.*

I've done this exact same thing before.

Then the man she was arresting turned his babyish face toward her and smiled with an expression of malicious evil.

"Good luck," he murmured.

With a violent shudder, Riley remembered.

Larry Mullins!

Not only was she was arresting this loathsome, child-murdering monster all over again, he was mocking her exactly the same way he had before.

And once again, she reached for her Glock.

She expected Crivaro to touch her warningly on the shoulder, the same as he had the last time this had happened.

Instead she heard him say, "Go ahead. We made a mistake last time. Go right on and kill him. It's the only way to get rid of the bastard. If you don't do it, I will."

Riley seized the handcuffed man by the shoulder and spun him around to face her. Then she pulled out her pistol and fired a single shot square in the center of his chest at pointblank range. She felt a surge of satisfaction as he collapsed to the floor. But as she looked down at him, his body and face went through a sickening transformation.

The person lying at her feet was no longer the pudgy, baby-faced monster, but an innocent-looking young girl. Her eyes were wide open, and her mouth worked silently as she gasped her final breaths. Her eyes locked on Riley's with an expression of terrible sadness, and then she fell completely still.

Heidi Wright! *Riley realized with horror.*
Riley had killed Heidi Wright earlier this year in New York state.
And now she was killing her again ...

Riley awoke with a gasp to find herself in the airplane cabin.

"Is something wrong?" Agent Johnson asked, still sitting directly across from her.

"No," Riley said.

But something was very wrong. She'd just had a dream about her first and only use of lethal force. Back in January during the course of a gunfight, a young woman named Heidi Wright had raised her own pistol to shoot Riley from only a few feet away.

Riley had had no choice but to shoot first.

The shooting had been justified, and nobody had questioned that. Nevertheless, Riley had been haunted by guilt for weeks afterward. As far as she was concerned, poor Heidi Wright had been a victim of circumstances who hadn't deserved to die because of some unwise youthful choices.

Riley thought she'd worked through this trauma with a BAU therapist. But apparently it was still gnawing at her deep down. Riley guessed that her troubled feelings about the result of the Larry Mullins trial were stirring up this recent trauma.

But she couldn't let it get the best of her. Not now that she was on a new case with a new partner, who surely wouldn't understand her feelings about either Heidi Wright's death or the Mullins verdict.

Just deal with it, Riley told herself.

Riley was now fully awake, and the plane was crossing the Rocky Mountains into Utah. Although there was now little snow except on the mountain peaks, the terrain brought back memories of the last time she'd been in this state, just last December. She'd been here working with Crivaro on her first case as a full-fledged BAU agent.

Was this case going to be as grisly as the case they'd solved then—the case of a serial killer who stalked campgrounds? It didn't seem unlikely, given the method of the murders. But maybe this time, they could stop the killer before he claimed any more victims.

And maybe at least the weather will be nicer, she thought.

As the plane came to a halt on the tarmac, Riley realized there was a small matter that was nagging at her. She was used to working with a man who called her "Riley," while she'd always called him "Agent Crivaro"—at least until earlier this morning. It had felt perfectly natural for both of them.

What kind of formality should she expect with her new partner?

As she and Johnson got out of their seats and made their way to the exit, she said to him, "I just want to settle one thing between us before we start working together."

"What's that?" Johnson said, putting on his overcoat.

"What should we call each other?"

Johnson shrugged and said, "Well, I like to keep things professional. I guess I'd prefer that you address me as Agent Johnson. What do you want me to call you?"

Riley appreciated that he was giving her a choice. Unlike Crivaro, she doubted that she was going to look up to this guy as some kind of mentor. She sure didn't want him calling her "Riley."

She said, "I'd like you to call me Agent Sweeney."

"OK, then. I'll do that."

As they stepped onto the tarmac, a slouching man smoking a cigarette was waiting for them. Riley thought he looked like some old-time, hard-boiled movie detective. But then he opened his rumpled trench coat and showed his badge.

"I'm Sheriff Collin Dawes," he told them.

"You're the one who call for BAU's help?" Johnson asked.

Dawes nodded, and Johnson introduced himself and Riley.

The two men turned and walked together toward the sheriff's waiting vehicle.

Johnson told Dawes, "It sounds like you have an unusual situation here."

"Like nothing I've ever seen before," Dawes replied. "If we didn't have photos it would be hard to even describe."

Tagging along behind the two men, Riley felt oddly left out.

This might get to be normal, she told herself.

Maybe I'd better get used to it.

CHAPTER SEVEN

After Riley and Johnson got into Sheriff Dawes's waiting vehicle, she again had to fight down her impulse to complain. She found it pretty disagreeable to be sitting in the back seat listening to the two men talk as if she weren't even there—or worse, as if she were a child excluded from an adult conversation. Although she was still making an effort to adjust to her new partner, she forced herself to keep quiet and listen.

In his low, growling voice, Dawes commented, "I thought I'd seen the last of cases like this since I'd come out here to Utah. I've been here for five years, and things have been pretty ordinary until now. I liked it that way."

"Where were you before?" Johnson asked.

"Los Angeles," Dawes said. "A homicide detective. I saw more than my share of murders there, believe me. The truth is, though—well, homicide by electrocution is a new twist even for me. Call me old-fashioned, but stabbing and shooting is what I'm used to. I guess things are getting ugly all over these days."

Riley could well imagine why a homicide detective would want to get away from Los Angeles. Dawes had surely expected Utah to be more laid back. She also realized that Dawes's hard-boiled manner wasn't just some affectation. He'd seen his share of ugly stuff, and he had the demeanor to prove it.

Dawes said to Johnson, "You sound like you're from out east somewhere."

"Boston," Johnson said.

Dawes looked at him in surprise.

"Boston? And your name is Johnson? Hey, I think I've heard of you. Didn't you solve that child murderer-rapist case a year or so ago?"

"So they tell me," Johnson said, with a grin that wasn't exactly modest.

"I'd love to hear how you pulled it off," Dawes said.

But as soon as Johnson started to tell him, Riley suspected that Dawes probably regretted his request. Based on his own account, Johnson seemed to have cornered his prey by dint of sheer statistics, by breaking the city down into zones and analyzing them for the presence of registered sex offenders until he'd cannily spotted the whereabouts of the actual murderer.

She had to admit that using mathematics to catch a murderer was an impressive achievement. But Riley couldn't help but wonder—had Johnson ever had to leave his desk to process all those masses of data, at least until he'd led a team of cops to what sounded like a fairly routine house arrest?

She couldn't help comparing what he'd done to her own field work. By comparison, her own career seemed like nonstop mayhem, danger, and sheer messiness. She couldn't imagine pulling off what she and Jake had achieved without going out into the field to track down those killers.

Does this guy even know what it's like to get his hands dirty? she wondered.

How was he going to cope if this case got as ugly as most of the ones she had worked on? This new one already sounded as nasty as the rest.

And, she wondered, how would she manage taking orders from a guy who struck her as both a know-it-all and a green rookie?

In spite of her efforts to pay attention, Riley found herself tuning out of Johnson's increasingly tedious, data-driven account of his only major case. She wondered if Sheriff Dawes wished he had that option.

Getting stuck in the back seat actually has its advantages, she thought wryly.

She spent the rest of the short drive south from the Provo Airport to the scene of the second crime looking out the window. The wide level valley they passed through was flanked by two ranges of snow-topped mountains. She still found the landscape stark and spare in comparison with that of Virginia, but it wasn't as grim as it had been when she was here in December. There was no snow at this altitude, and the temperature was cool and pleasant. Spring buds were appearing everywhere.

Soon they pulled into Beardsley, a modest-sized but upscale town picturesquely positioned between the mountain ranges and near a lake. Finally the sheriff parked in a broad driveway in front of a large, fairly new-looking Spanish-style house fronted by a three-car garage.

As they walked inside, Riley noticed a couple of suitcases by the door. She wondered what they were doing there.

Indicating the alarm system, Johnson asked, "How did the intruder get past the electronic security?"

"We haven't had time to check it out."

Johnson peered closely at the device.

"I'm familiar with this system," he said. "It's pretty state of the art. If somebody hacked it, they must have a good bit of tech savvy. It would have been quite a trick. What about the other house where the other victim was killed?"

"It didn't have a system," Dawes said. "No sign of break-in, either. It's possible that both victims simply let the killer inside."

Johnson looked at Riley and said, "That suggests two possibilities. Either the killer had excellent break-in skills, or the victims knew and trusted him."

Riley winced a little at the self-assuredness in his statement, as if he'd come to some truly astute conclusion. At this point in a case, she figured just about everything had multiple possible explanations that required narrowing down.

They followed Johnson through an open hallway with a high ceiling. A staircase led upward, and one door appeared to be a coat closet. On one side of the hallway, an open door revealed a study. There was yellow tape across the door, and a forensics team was inside gathering evidence.

"The victim's office?" Johnson asked.

"No, his wife's," Sheriff Dawes said. "But there are signs that a struggle took place in there, including a broken desk lamp."

Pointing into the office at the floor, Dawes added, "You can see some scuff marks on the floor. It looks like the victim was attacked here and dragged away to the basement. As you read in the report, the first victim was apparently subdued with chloroform."

Johnson nodded and said, "There's a good chance that's what happened here as well."

Riley couldn't disagree, but his tone continued to annoy her. She wished she could duck under the police tape and try to get a sense of how the killer had felt during the attack. But she doubted that either Dawes or Johnson would like that—and maybe for good reason. Disrupting the forensic team's delicate work probably wasn't a good idea.

As they continued on into the house, Riley found it to be a lot more tasteful than many expensive homes she'd been in, but it still struck her as dauntingly, uncomfortably large. From the brief case report she and Johnson had read, Riley was under the impression that the Banfields had been a childless couple. She wondered what two people could want with so much living space.

Dawes escorted them into a large open area, with a living room on their right and a large dining room on their left. Cheerful sunlight poured in through large windows.

There was no clutter. Everything appeared to be in its place. Riley could tell that the people who lived here had lived a tidy and well-ordered life.

In the living area, two women were seated on one of a facing pair of chocolate brown leather sofas. One of the women got up to greet them.

She said, "I'm Elaine Bonet, and I live next door. I'm here to watch over Sheila for a while. Her neighbors are planning to take care of her in shifts. We don't want her to be alone."

Elaine Bonet was wearing a jogging suit, as if she'd recently been running or exercising. The victim's wife was well-dressed by comparison, looking as if she'd been on her way to or from some formal event.

As Riley and her two colleagues started to sit down, something about victim's wife's face struck Riley as eerily familiar. Was it possible that she'd met her when she and Crivaro had been out here in December?

No, that can't be it.

Glancing around for some clue as to this familiarity, Riley noticed a book lying on the coffee table with the woman's face on the cover. Then it quickly hit her.

Of course! That *Sheila Banfield!*

She was a family therapist who had written this book, *The Analog Touch.* It was a nonfiction bestseller about raising families in the digital age. Riley had read some of the glowing reviews, but she'd figured she had plenty of time to get around to parenting books. Now she felt oddly embarrassed, as if she was going to have to admit to the woman that she hadn't read it.

Realistically, of course, she knew that was nothing to worry about. It was hardly likely to be a topic of conversation under these circumstances. Sheila Banfield had other things on her mind at the moment.

While the face on the cover looked bright and smiling, Sheila herself looked stunned and numb. When Dawes finished his introductions, Sheila spoke in a near whisper.

"The BAU. That's good. Thank you for coming."

Leaning toward her, Agent Johnson said, "We're terribly sorry about what has happened, Dr. Banfield. We'll do everything we can to find whoever did this."

Sheila Banfield nodded mutely.

Riley noticed that her eyes kept darting around, as if her surroundings were unfamiliar and she had no idea how she had gotten here. Riley had seen this kind of reaction among bereaved family members on other occasions.

There was a box of tissues at Sheila's side, but it appeared to be almost full. Sheila didn't look like she'd done a lot of crying yet, but Riley knew that part was yet to come, after the shock began to wear off. It was good that she had friends to help her through all that.

At Johnson's request, Sheila began to give her own account of what had happened.

"I'd been in the Northwest for a few days doing book signings," she said. She nodded toward the book and added awkwardly, "I, uh, wrote that. Maybe you've heard of it. I've been doing a lot of traveling to promote it. I'd been gone for several days this time."

She took a deep breath and continued.

"Last night after I finished my tour, I took a flight back from Seattle. My car was parked for me at the airport in Provo. When I first started doing all this traveling, Julian…"

She paused at the mention of her husband's name.

Then she continued, "Julian used to drive me to and from the airport whenever I did a book tour. But it got to be a lot of bother, especially since we have more than one car, and I...I suggested that I just do the driving myself. He seemed to like the idea. Anyway, last night..."

Her voice faded for a moment.

"I got home pretty late last night—around twelve thirty or so. When I came through the door, I saw that the alarm system wasn't activated for some reason. That worried me. It wasn't like Julian not to set it earlier at night. All the downstairs lights were on, so I figured Julian was still awake, and I came on inside."

And you left your suitcases at the door, Riley thought, mentally filling in details.

"I saw that my office door was open and the light was on inside," Sheila continued. "I thought that was odd, because he seldom goes in there. I looked inside, and I saw that the lamp was broken, and it looked like something...bad had happened in there, and I started getting scared."

She trembled, and for a moment, Riley wondered whether she was going to slip into an overdue emotional collapse. But then Sheila kept on speaking in an eerily detached voice, as if she were talking about something that had happened to someone else.

Riley was familiar with this kind of emotional dissociation from some similar interviews. She wondered whether Agent Johnson understood what the woman was feeling—and not feeling.

Sheila said, "I called out to him. He didn't answer. I wandered around downstairs looking for him. I didn't bother looking for him upstairs. The lights were off up there, and I was sure he hadn't gone up to bed after leaving the downstairs lights on and the alarm system not set."

Pointing on into the house, she said, "I went into the kitchen and saw that he'd fixed himself something to eat." For a moment the bereaved woman's mouth twisted oddly as if she was remembering something, then she continued, "I noticed the basement door was open and the light was on and..."

She shuddered and froze.

Riley sensed that she couldn't bring herself to describe what had happened after that.

It's time to change the topic, she realized.

She said, "Dr. Banfield, did your husband have any enemies? Was there anybody who might have meant him any harm?"

Sheila sighed and said, "Yes, I'm sorry to say, possibly so."

Riley's felt a surge of surprise.

"Can you tell me who?" she said.

Sheila shrugged and said, "That's harder to say. As a therapist, he specialized in working with criminals, from juvenile delinquents to hardened murderers. His work involved helping them process past traumas and to cope with severe mental issues. He found it to be gratifying work, and much of the time he was really able to help his patients in their rehabilitation process. Other times…"

She paused and took a long, slow breath.

"Other times it didn't work out too well," she added. "Sometimes his patients only descended into deeper anger and hostility—and sometimes they directed it against him. But… I don't believe he mentioned any cases like that recently. And most of those patients are now in prison or otherwise institutionalized, I believe."

Riley said, "Could you give us access to his patients' medical records?"

Sheila squinted and said, "I'll do everything I can—legally, I mean. But it might be difficult. He worked for a number of facilities over the years—sometimes more than one at a time. Those places would hold the records."

Riley asked, "Could you make a list of those records and email or fax them to the sheriff's office?"

"Yes, I could do that," Sheila said.

Johnson said to Riley, "You should stay and continue with the questioning while the sheriff takes me downstairs to look at the murder scene."

Riley winced sharply with annoyance. Two things upset her. One was that the Johnson would use the phrase "murder scene" in front of a grieving widow. But more importantly, Johnson just seemed to assume that he could exclude Riley from viewing the scene where the murder had taken place.

What's he thinking? she thought.

Was he trying to protect her from viewing such a grisly scene?

Didn't he have any idea of the sort of horrors she'd already witnessed?

Of course, she knew she mustn't get into an argument about it right here and now...

But I'll be damned if I'm not going into that basement right now.

She spoke in an exaggeratedly soft voice that she hoped signaled her disapproval to him.

"We should give Dr. Banfield a rest. I'll come down with you."

Johnson shrugged slightly, apparently oblivious to Riley's unstated annoyance.

"OK, then," he said. "Let's go."

Sheriff Dawes led them through the kitchen, where Riley saw that there was a frying pan still on the stove. When they got to the basement door, Dawes led them downstairs.

Riley's eyes widened at what she saw.

She'd seen plenty of shocking scenes during her short career, but she'd never seen anything quite like this.

CHAPTER EIGHT

T he scene in the basement was more than simply disturbing—Riley found it grotesque. Two heavy, elegant wooden chairs stood facing each other, just a few feet apart. An open wine bottle was sitting on a decorative table near one chair. The other chair still had the tattered remnants of duct tape from where the victim had been strapped to it. An elegant silver platter was on the floor in front of that one.

More than a quick and simple murder must have occurred here. Some sort of scene had played out, but Riley couldn't get any sense of what that might have been. Not yet, anyhow.

She wasn't surprised that the victim's body had been removed. She figured the county coroner had naturally wanted to take it away for an autopsy as soon as possible. But she doubted that Crivaro would have approved. As grisly a sight as the electrocuted body would be, it would have given the agents a clearer sense of exactly what had happened here.

"Have you got any pictures?" she asked Dawes.

"Right here," Dawes said, opening a folder with some black-and-white photos. "We took these this morning."

Riley and Johnson passed the pictures to each other. They showed the murder scene fresh after the police had arrived. The body was still strapped to the chair, his head slumped forward as if the victim had fallen asleep.

As Riley stepped nearer the chairs, Sheriff Dawes pointed down at the silver tray and explained, "The soles of the victim's feet were held in place in the water here."

Referring to the photographs, Riley could see the naked feet in the shallow water. Looking at the tray itself, Riley could see that it had a little water in it. Then the sheriff indicated a heavy insulated cable on the floor near the tray. The end had been cut off, leaving the internal wires exposed.

Dawes added, "The killer rigged this wire to the breaker box, then threw the exposed end into the water. That closed the circuit, and the victim was immediately electrocuted."

The word "immediately" struck Riley as wrong somehow. The victim might or might not have died a quick death, but there had been more to it than that. There had clearly been some sort of interaction between the killer and his victim, and the murder hadn't happened "immediately."

Just what sort of exchange had taken place was a riddle that Riley wanted to unravel.

"I get the picture," Johnson said, nodding sagely and putting on a pair of gloves. "Water is an excellent conductor of electricity, and so is silver. The killer must have been wearing rubber soles to protect himself. I take it the circuit got blown when the electrocution happened."

Sheriff Dawes nodded.

"Then this is safe to handle," Johnson said, delicately picking up the cable and eyeing it carefully. "It's eight gauge, heavy-duty enough to handle one hell of a current."

The other end of the heavy cable was still attached inside a big metal breaker box on the wall. Johnson walked over and inspected it.

He said, "The circuit is labeled 'laundry room,' and it's got a 240-volt, 30-amp circuit. The poor guy probably didn't know what hit him."

Riley was both impressed and annoyed. Obviously Johnson knew a fair amount about electrical circuits. But he was very wrong to say that the victim hadn't known what hit him. She was certain that Julian Banfield had spent some long, agonizing moments knowing he was going to die.

Across the room, the wall was stained with wine, and pieces of shattered crystal were lying on the floor. Without touching the wine bottle that remained on the table, she read the label—Le Vieux Donjon Châteauneuf-du-Pape. The name didn't mean anything to her.

She said to the sheriff, "I take it this bottle was open when you found the body."

The sheriff grunted slightly and said, "Nobody on my team opened it, you can be sure of that."

Johnson stepped toward Riley and looked at the bottle.

"I don't know much about wines," he said.

Riley held back a slight smirk.

At least there's something *he doesn't know about,* she thought.

"I don't either," she admitted.

Johnson squinted at the bottle thoughtfully. Then he pointed upward and murmured to her, "Do you think...?"

His voice trailed, and for a moment Riley didn't catch his unspoken meaning.

Then it dawned on her. Johnson was wondering whether Sheila Banfield herself had opened the bottle, either before or after her husband was dead.

He thinks she might be a suspect, Riley realized.

Somehow, the possibility that Sheila herself had killed her husband hadn't occurred to Riley. She tried to imagine the woman she had just talked to gloating over her dead or soon-to-be-dead husband, enjoying a glass of wine that had a fancy name, then throwing the glass against the wall.

"I don't think so," she said.

"How do you know?"

Riley wasn't sure just why she felt that way. But somehow her gut told her that Sheila's grief was genuine, and that she didn't have the makings of a killer.

"I just really don't think so," she repeated.

Johnson shook his head and stepped away from her. Talking with the sheriff again, he took out a tape measure and checked the distance between the two chairs. As he kept on talking, he started moving around the room, taking other measurements that didn't make any real sense to Riley. He seemed to be writing all the numbers down in a little notebook.

He's liable to measure everything in sight, she thought.

And maybe that was a good thing, at least as far as she was concerned.

Normally, this would be the moment in an investigation when Jake Crivaro would coax her into trying to get a sense of the killer's mind.

Of course, Jake wasn't here, and Riley didn't suppose either Johnson or the sheriff would understand what she was doing. But the two men were talking while Johnson kept randomly measuring things. Now that they were thoroughly ignoring Riley, she figured she could at least give it a try.

She knew that the police had already checked for prints and any other evidence on the chairs, as well as the wine bottle and anything else the killer might have touched. Still, she was careful not to disturb anything as she sat down in the large chair next to the table that held the wine bottle, where she assumed the killer had sat. She faced the chair where the murdered man had been bound and electrocuted, then closed her eyes and took a long, slow breath. Then Riley opened her eyes and began to imagine things from the killer's point of view, as he might have sat here pouring himself a nice glass of wine while gazing at his bound victim, waiting for him to regain consciousness after being dosed with chloroform.

Then he saw Julian's eyes flicker open, and...

And then what?

She guessed that the killer greeted him in a mock-friendly manner, perhaps raising a toast and taking a sip.

But what did he say?

And did he and the victim know each other?

What had happened here struck her as intensely personal. She had a strong feeling that the killer at least knew Julian Banfield, and that he harbored some fatal grudge against him.

She imagined the killer chatting away about trifles, perhaps the quality of the wine, cruelly taunting and teasing his prey.

Yes, the killer definitely knew his victim.

But did that necessarily mean that Banfield recognized the killer?

Maybe not, she thought. *Maybe that was part of what the teasing was about.*

But the killer's feigned light-heartedness hadn't lasted. For some reason, he had gotten angry. And then he'd thrown the glass against the wall...

And then?

Riley could imagine that the victim was pleading for his life by now. And his every word only added to the killer's determination. Finally the killer had reached down and picked up the cable and...

"What are you doing, Agent Sweeney?"

Riley's snapped out of her reverie at the sound of Agent Johnson's voice.

"Sorry," she said, getting to her feet.

Of course, she wasn't sorry—merely annoyed. Was she going to have to explain to her partner that she *needed* these moments of intense meditation in order to be of any use at all?

"We've got work to do," Agent Johnson said in critical tone.

Then he turned to Sheriff Dawes and asked, "Could we get a look at the other murder scene?"

Dawes nodded and said, "Sure. I'll call Heck Berry, the police chief over in Prinneville."

As Dawes took out his phone and made the call, Johnson whispered to Riley.

"What was going on with you just now? You could have contaminated the crime scene."

She whispered back, "It's just something I do."

"What do you mean, it's something you do?"

Riley stifled a sigh, then said, "Look, this isn't the time or place to get into all that. Let's just say that you've got your methods, and I've got mine. Can't we both just respect that?"

Johnson said, "Not if your methods involve plopping yourself down and vegging out at a crime scene."

Riley rolled her eyes.

"I'm *not* vegging out," she said.

"You'd better explain it to me," Johnson said.

Riley had no idea how she was going to tell him.

Fortunately, Dawes finished his phone call and said to them, "Heck Berry will meet us at the house where it happened. Let's get going."

As Riley and Johnson followed Dawes upstairs and back through the house, Riley saw the two women sitting in the living room. They were watching TV now. Sheila's friend, Elaine, was almost smiling, as if she were amused by what she was watching. By contrast, Sheila seemed to be in a completely different world, staring right through the TV.

Riley remembered how Johnson had suggested that Sheila might be a suspect.

Is that possible? Riley wondered.

She really hadn't thought so, at least not when she was glimpsing the killer's mind. He'd seemed male to her, and of a very distinct personality.

But after all, a glimpse was all she'd gotten.

Still, it had felt very real.

She really needed to find a way to put her particular abilities to work. If she couldn't, she might as well head on back to Quantico for all the use she'd be in this investigation.

Chapter Nine

A lthough Sheriff Dawes said that Prinneville was only a half-hour drive south, Riley was finding that hard to believe. Once they drove out of Beardsley with its manicured lawns, all she could see ahead was the highway stretching straight in front of them, seeming to converge in a distant vanishing point at the base of snow-capped mountains.

Like everything out here just goes nowhere, Riley thought.

She was starting to feel the same way about this case. She couldn't remember being this discouraged about a case this early on, and she knew that it wasn't just the landscape that was getting her down. Partnering with someone who didn't have a clue about what made her tick was a new and demoralizing experience.

And of course, she was again relegated to the back seat of the car, like a child.

Up front, Dawes was speaking to Agent Johnson. "So what have you got so far?"

Johnson stroked his chin and asked, "Do you know of any wine-tasting clubs or groups in the area?"

Dawes said, "Now that you mention it, I think there's a group like that back in Beardsley."

"Do you happen to know whether Sheila Banfield belongs to it?" Johnson asked.

"I've got no idea," Dawes said. "Do you really think she might be a suspect?"

Johnson seemed to think for a moment.

"I kind of doubt it," he admitted. "It seems like a long shot."

Yeah, it sure does, Riley thought.

Now that she had a chance to mull it over, she couldn't think of any likely scenario in which Sheila could be the killer. How could it have happened? Had she crept up behind her husband in her own office with a rag soaked in chloroform, physically struggled with him before he lost consciousness, then physically dragged him down to the basement and bound him up and toasted him with a glass of wine when he started to come to his senses and then …?

It doesn't make sense, Riley thought.

"The conditions indicate that it's a man," Johnson added. "And a pretty strong man at that."

At least we're thinking along the same lines about that, Riley realized.

Sheila Banfield wasn't exactly a small woman, but she wasn't an especially large or strong one, either.

Johnson continued, "Also, it's a man who knows something about electricity. And he's got an interest in wines. We need to put together a list of people who belong to that wine group, find out if any of them are trained electricians."

"Good idea," Dawes replied, sounding rather impressed.

Riley said nothing, but she figured it wasn't exactly a bad idea.

Maybe kind of lame, though.

For all she knew, the killer had picked a random bottle out of the wine racks and opened it up in a mood of perverse glee. That didn't necessarily make him some sort of connoisseur. And mightn't the smashed wine glass almost suggest the opposite?

Unless he really didn't like the wine.

Of course, Riley realized an analytical guy like Johnson would want to comb through lists of one kind or another. That was just his style. But it sure wasn't the sort of thing she was used to from working with Crivaro. And she hoped Johnson wasn't going to get too fixated on the wine-tasting angle.

After what felt like longer than a half hour, a town did come into sight up ahead. As Dawes drove through Prinneville, Riley saw that it was considerably smaller and less upscale than Beardsley. It seemed old-fashioned, actually kind of picturesque, although it looked as though it had seen better days.

At the far edge of town, Sheriff Dawes finally pulled up to a simple bungalow with a wide porch. Beyond the house, which had a lived-in sort of look, the scenery was much as it had been before—more empty fields reaching to more snow-capped mountains. A couple of vehicles were parked in front of the house. One was an SUV, the other a cop car with a uniformed man leaning against it.

When they got out of their car, the man hurried toward them, and Dawes introduced Riley and Johnson to Prinneville's police chief, Heck Berry. He was a short, stocky man who reminded Riley a little bit of Jake Crivaro. When he spoke, he seemed to be even more hot-tempered than Crivaro.

"BAU, eh?" he growled. "It's about time. Where the hell were you a few days ago?"

Riley was startled by his accusatory tone.

Does he think the decision was up to us? she wondered.

Sheriff Dawes delicately tried to explain how help from the BAU had to be specifically requested, and even then only under special circumstances. Those circumstances hadn't existed until there had been a second murder. But Chief Berry didn't seem to be mollified.

"Special circumstances, huh?" he echoed bitterly. "In my book, one of my former cops getting killed right here in Prinneville is pretty damned 'special.'"

Riley was startled.

The victim was a cop?

She'd known almost nothing about the first victim except his name— Andy Gish.

Chief Berry continued, "But I guess it takes a rich shrink also getting killed to stir up enough of a fuss about some poor cop. Well, I sure hope you make yourselves useful now that you're here. Come on inside."

As they walked toward the house, Riley felt worried over the newly revealed fact that this victim had been a cop. This could make the investigation more difficult. Local cops—Chief Berry especially—were likely to be thirsting for justice and any kind of vigilante zealousness might well be more a hindrance than help. She wondered whether Johnson was up to the task of dealing with angry and impatient local lawmen.

I hope I'm up to it, she thought.

She, Johnson, and Dawes followed the chief into a cozy living room with comfortable-looking, though well-worn, furniture. Two women were standing in the room, and one of them was snapping pictures of the fake stone wall behind the fireplace.

Not crime scene photos, Riley thought. Surely that had been taken care of days ago.

The woman taking the pictures was middle-aged, slim, and well-dressed. The other was a stout woman, probably in her sixties, who was wearing a housecoat.

When Chief Berry introduced Riley and Johnson, the woman with the camera explained, "I'm Grace Hamilton, Lyda's friend and also a real estate agent. Lyda wants me to help her sell this place."

Chief Berry shook his head and said, "Lyda, are you sure you want to do that?"

Now Riley knew that the stout woman was the widow, Lyda Gish. She smiled a warm, sad smile.

"Now, Heck, how many times do we have to talk about this?" she said. "Andy and I had a lot of wonderful years here, and I want to remember this place that way. It's time to move on, before those memories turn sour on me, and I think of this place where something awful happened."

His voice choking a little, Berry said, "I've got a lot of memories of this place too. I've got half a mind to buy it myself. I'd hate for it to wind up belonging to some total strangers."

Lyda's eyes glowed.

"Why Heck, do you really mean that?" she said.

Chief Berry tilted his head and shuffled his feet.

"Let me talk to the missus when I get home, find out what she thinks," he said.

"Well, I hope you'll do that. That would be just wonderful."

Riley felt a pang of emotion. The sight of old friends quietly supporting each other through a terrible ordeal wasn't something she was especially used to. At most crime scenes, things were usually much more tense, and tempers were often frayed.

She thought back to Sheila Banfield's blank demeanor at the house in Beardsley. Riley had sensed that Sheila hadn't even begun to process her grief. But Lyda was obviously a different case. During the last few days, she'd cried a lot of her grief out of her system.

Not that she still doesn't have a lot more crying to do.

Then Lyda said to Riley and Johnson, "Now you folks have a seat. I'm sure you've got a lot of questions for me. I'm not sure how many of them I'll be able to answer, but I'll do my best."

As the group sat down, Lyda's friend Grace politely asked the group, "Would anybody like coffee? Lyda's got a fresh pot ready."

Dawes, Berry, and Johnson all declined, but Riley said yes. She'd found that accepting little gestures of hospitality sometimes tended to break the ice before interviews.

Sitting right next to Lyda, Chief Berry gently patted her on the knee.

"Lyda, I'm afraid these folks want to hear the whole story from your point of view. I know you feel like you've told it a thousand times, and I hate for you to have to go through it all again—"

Lyda interrupted, "Now, Heck, you know I'll do anything I've got to do to help find out who did this. It's especially important now that there's been another victim. This has got to stop."

With a stern nod of her head, she added, "I'm a policeman's wife, after all. I've got a sense of duty." Glancing at Riley and her partner, she added, "Where would you folks like me to start?"

"Wherever you like," Riley said.

Grace came back from the kitchen with Riley's coffee and took a seat with the others.

Lyda tilted her head thoughtfully.

"Well, I'd been away for a short while. My son and I had driven down to Phoenix to visit my mother. She's in a rest home down there, and the poor thing really doesn't have any idea what's going on anymore. I guess … when it comes to what happened to Andy … maybe it's just as well …"

Her voice faded away for a moment. Riley sensed that some of the pain of what had happened was welling up inside her a bit. Then she continued bravely.

"Anyway, my son Denver and I stayed down in Phoenix for a couple of days. Tuesday we drove back here, arrived at the house about two in the afternoon, I believe. The door was unlocked, which wasn't so unusual. We don't have a lot of reason to keep the house locked up here. Andy didn't seem to be at home, which didn't seem all that unusual either. He oftentimes went into town to spend time with old friends."

Chief Berry added, "He liked hanging around the station, too. Sometimes I think he missed his old job."

Lyda continued, "Well, when I'd left, there was a load of laundry to be done, and Andy had promised to do it and ..."

She smiled sadly.

"Well, he hadn't done it, which wasn't so unusual either, at least not anymore. He'd been getting a tad forgetful recently. We'd both been worried about that."

Lyda gestured toward the back of the house.

She said, "When I tried to start a load of laundry, I found that the power was out in the laundry area. I figured a breaker circuit had just gone out. It happens a lot here, things get overloaded easily. Our wiring isn't the best in the world. So I asked Denver to go downstairs and switch the circuit back on. And he went down ... and he found ..."

Lyda's voice faded. When she spoke again, it was almost in a whisper.

"Denver was white as a sheet when he came back from the basement. 'Something's happened to Dad,' he said, and then he got on the phone to Heck right away. Denver wouldn't let me go down there and have a look for myself. And it's just as well. Heck and Denver have told me everything about it that I need to know."

Riley nodded sympathetically.

Then Johnson asked, "Ms. Gish, did your husband happen to know the most recent victim?"

Lyda tilted her head thoughtfully.

"Somebody mentioned he was a psychiatrist," she said. "Wasn't his name Julian ... something?"

"Julian Banfield," Johnson said.

Lyda shrugged a little.

"The name doesn't ring a bell," she said. "And besides, he lived over in Beardsley, didn't he? Andy and I never knew anybody who lived there. No, I'm sure he never knew him."

Johnson asked, "Can you think of anyone who might have wanted to kill your husband?"

Lyda scoffed slightly.

"Goodness, no," she said. "He was a policeman, of course, so he ruffled some feathers. But there's hardly ever any serious crime here in Prinneville, just an occasional burglary, or someone gets drunk and disorderly, little things like that. Anyway, folks here don't tend to hold a grudge. I can think of only one really serious case Andy ever had anything to do with."

Chief Berry nodded in agreement and said, "Yeah, and that wasn't even a local case, really. He arrested a guy—Quincy Harris was his name—who was wanted for murder over in Nebraska. Harris got extra-dited and sentenced to the death penalty. The last I heard, the sentence had been carried out. That was six months ago, I think."

Riley asked, "Doesn't Nebraska use the electric chair?"

All three of the men looked at her curiously.

"Yeah, the last I heard," Chief Berry said. "But I don't know what that's got to do with anything."

Sheriff Dawes added a bit sarcastically, "To the best of my knowl-edge, dead men aren't inclined to seek revenge."

Johnson didn't comment, but Riley could see by his expression that he agreed that it was a ridiculous question. He even looked a bit embarrassed.

And maybe for good reason, she thought, flushing a little.

She certainly couldn't think of any reason why Nebraska's method of capital punishment might matter to the present situation.

The group fell silent for a couple of moments.

Then Lyda said to Riley and Johnson, "I guess you Federal folks need to go down and have a look for yourselves. I hope you'll excuse me for not joining you. I haven't been down there once since this happened. I guess that sounds cowardly of me, but …"

She shrugged and said, "I've got my reasons."

Chief Berry got to his feet and said to Riley and her colleagues, "Come on, I'll show you what you need to see."

Riley, Johnson, and Dawes followed Berry into the kitchen, where Riley paused to look around. There was a small wooden dinner table with chairs at one end of the kitchen. At the other end was a wide, wood-burning stove. Riley had seen similar stoves in the mountains of Virginia. In fact, her father still had a smaller one in his backwoods cabin. He used it for cooking as well as heat.

This is a nice house, Riley thought.

She was just starting to wonder whether she and Ryan could be happy in a place like this when Johnson tapped her on the shoulder.

In a low voice, he commented, "The wife seems awfully detached, don't you think?"

Riley looked into the living room and saw that the two women were back on their feet discussing the possible sale of the house.

The words Lyda had said just now rattled through Riley mind.

"I've got my reasons."

Riley felt like she was just starting to understand Lyda Gish. She thought she had some idea of things the woman had left unsaid. There was a reason Lyda Gish was wearing her housecoat. She probably hadn't left the house since her husband had died. And of course, she hadn't been down to the basement.

Riley also remembered what Lyda had said when they'd first arrived.

"It's time to move on, before those memories turn sour on me, and I think of this place where something awful happened."

She'll be leaving here soon, Riley thought.

In the meantime, Riley sensed that Lyda wanted to drink in all the best memories she could.

Riley said to Johnson, "She's innocent."

"How do you know?" Johnson demanded.

"I just know," Riley told him.

Ignoring her partner's skeptical stare, she followed the sheriff and the police chief into the basement.

CHAPTER TEN

A s Riley followed her colleagues down the stairs, she found herself wondering how these two murders could possibly be connected. The two houses they had visited today indicated nothing in common between the two families. Their incomes, backgrounds, tastes, and needs were far apart by any measures of how people lived.

The murderer had entered the Banfield home late at night, possibly by hacking an expensive security system. He had entered here in broad daylight, either through an unlocked door or let in by the victim.

Even the basement that came into view was nothing like the Banfields' rather posh and well-furnished wine cellar. This one was just an ordinary, musty space with a concrete floor and some storage boxes on wooden pallets. The shelves on these cinderblock walls held an array of home-canned vegetables and a few store-bought supplies.

These victims have nothing in common, she thought.

But of course two basement homicides by electrocution within a few days of each other and within a small geographical area had to be related in some way.

As the group gathered at the base of the stairs, Chief Berry told them, "There's not much to see. Of course we broke down the crime scene before we had any idea there might be a serial in the area, and Lyda's son cleared everything out. But I've got some pictures…"

He opened a folder and showed Riley and Johnson some crime photos.

And there it was, a murder matching the other in every important detail.

Sheriff Dawes said, "You can see Gish was also strapped into a chair—an ordinary kitchen chair in this case. And instead of a silver platter, the killer put a simple baking pan with water under Gish's feet. But the method of electrocution was exactly the same. The killer hooked up a power cable to the breaker box, then threw the exposed wire into the water."

Seeming to notice something of interest, Johnson took one of the photos and knelt down on the floor.

"Look here, Agent Sweeney," he said.

Riley squatted down beside him. Sure enough, she saw that Johnson had spotted a partial boot print. The soles had left tread marks.

"Rubber soles, I bet," Johnson said. Pointing the photo, he added, "You can see right here—a bit of water got spilled out of the pan. The killer stepped in it and made this mark."

He handed the picture back to Chief Berry.

"I think this is important, Agent Sweeney."

Riley hoped he was right, but she had her doubts. The footprint was only partial, after all, and she thought the tread looked fairly ordinary.

Then Johnson went right to work with his tape measure. He took a photo of the of the tape measure next to the footprint to indicate its size. Then he began to move around taking measurements that Riley couldn't make much sense of, but which surely meant something to him.

As he did so, he said to Chief Berry and Sheriff Dawes, "Are there any industries in the area that use chloroform?"

Berry and Dawes glanced at each other.

"What kind of industries do you mean?" Berry asked.

Johnson said, "Well, we know that the killer obtained some chloroform to subdue his victims. But he didn't get it from any medical facility. I know that because chloroform isn't used as an anesthetic anymore. It can be dangerous, and there are now safer methods of anesthesia."

Johnson got to his feet and wiped his hands.

He continued, "But chloroform is still used for industrial purposes, like construction and the manufacture of paper and pesticides. It's also widely used as a solvent for paints and lacquers and such, and it's also used to make refrigerants. But its use is strictly regulated, so my guess is the killer works in an industry that uses it. Are there any industries like that in this area?"

Sheriff Dawes said, "There's a paint-manufacturing plant over in Jellicoe. That's in the same county."

"Great!" Johnson said. "We need to look into that."

"You think we could pin down somebody stealing it?" Sheriff Dawes asked. "But how?"

How indeed? Riley thought.

Aside from the difficulty of determining who might be stealing relatively small amounts of chloroform at a paint factory, Riley saw another serious flaw in Johnson's theory—the killer didn't have to steal it at all.

Not wanting to embarrass Johnson in front of Dawes and Berry, she just tugged him gently by the arm and coaxed him away from the sheriff and the police chief.

"The killer probably just made the chloroform," she whispered to him.

"Huh?" Johnson said.

"He made it himself," Riley whispered. "He made it from a recipe."

Johnson's eyes widened.

"How do you know?" he asked.

"Because this isn't my first case where chloroform was used as a knockout drug," Riley said. "Last fall, Crivaro and I hunted down a killer who subdued his victims with chloroform. He made the stuff in his lair."

Johnson looked skeptical.

"Look, it's really easy to do," Riley whispered. "It's made out of bleach and acetone, and you can find recipes for it just about anywhere."

"But isn't it dangerous to handle?" Johnson asked.

"Oh, yeah, and volatile too," Riley said. "The killer we caught accidentally broke a bottle and knocked himself out with it. Almost knocked out Crivaro and me as well. We had to stay away until the air cleared. It's dangerous even to make, much less put it to any kind of use."

Johnson said, "In that case, isn't it more likely that the killer is stealing it ready-made?"

Riley didn't know what to say.

To her, it seemed obvious that the simplest explanation was that the killer was making the stuff by himself—and she knew that the simplest explanation was usually best.

But of course Johnson could be right, she told herself.

She felt certain that he wasn't. But then, she was sure Johnson felt the same about what she'd suggested.

Then she realized something really unsettling. The differences between the two of them went much deeper than she'd realized. It was more than a matter of technique and training. They actually seemed to see the world in such different ways that they didn't even know how to talk to each other, much less actually sort out who was right and who was wrong.

As she and Johnson stood looking at each other, she could see annoyance in his face. Even though she'd tried not to embarrass him, he clearly didn't like being taken aside and having his theory questioned.

Johnson shrugged, then turned away and walked back toward Dawes and Berry.

He said to Berry, "Let's go to your station and see what we can do with the information we've got."

Information? Riley thought.

Do we actually have information?

But it was obvious that Riley felt alone in her skepticism. Both Dawes and Berry seemed to think this was a good idea. As they climbed the stairs out of the basement, Riley looked back at the spot where the man had been killed.

Electrocution, she thought.

It was such a singular method of murder—unique among even her own grisly experiences with human monsters. She'd never even heard any Academy lecturer or any other agent mention it.

But why had the killer chosen it?

She wished she could lag behind for just a few minutes to try to get a sense of the killer, even a fleeting impression like what she'd gotten back at the Banfields'. Crivaro would understand. In fact, Crivaro would insist that she try.

But that wasn't an option right now—not with a partner who didn't seem to have any idea of what her methods were.

I've just got to deal with it, she told herself. *Or figure out some way to work around this guy.*

Feeling defeated, she followed Agent Johnson out of the house.

CHAPTER ELEVEN

Riley was struggling with her own inner turmoil. When she and Johnson got back into Dawes's vehicle, she tried to psych herself into a more positive attitude. As the sheriff drove behind Berry's car back into Prineville, she kept silently lecturing herself...

Be a team player. Is that so hard?

But right now, nothing seemed easy to her.

After Dawes parked at Prineville's storefront police station on a corner of Main Street and she followed her colleagues inside, Riley was still trying to picture herself as part of that team.

A female receptionist wearing horn-rimmed glasses and a necklace of fake pearls looked up at them anxiously. The only other person visible was a uniformed cop who seemed to be trying to make himself look busy doing paperwork at his desk.

Berry introduced Riley and Johnson to the receptionist, Joyce Raffin, and the cop, Forrest Banks.

The receptionist blurted, "What happened to Andy Gish... well, it was terrible, and everyone who knew him is taking it very hard. Please find whoever killed him."

The cop at the other desk looked up and nodded in agreement.

Riley followed Johnson, Dawes, and Berry into a small conference room, where they sat down at the table.

"First things first," Johnson said to Berry. "You knew Andy Gish, and you know his wife well. Do you think she might have had any reason to want him dead?"

Berry's mouth dropped open.

He stammered, "I … well, no, I just don't think that's possible. I mean, I've known them both for years. They've always been happy together, and they raised a great kid. They're good people."

Johnson drummed his fingers on the table and said, "I don't doubt that you're right. All the more reason to eliminate her as a suspect as fast as we can. We'll need to do some checking in order to rule her out."

Berry replied, "Well, I'm … sure we can do that without much trouble."

Johnson then took out his camera and set it in front of him.

Patting it, he said, "I need to get these digital photos I took of the boot prints printed out. Then I'll send them to Quantico. The tech guys there should be able to find the exact make and size so we can start contacting shoe retailers in the area to find out who might have bought them."

Dawes nodded, and Berry was taking notes.

Johnson said, "Also, I want to check out that paint company you mentioned. We need to find out if there have been any missing supplies of chloroform. If so, we need to know if they suspect any employees of stealing it or who else might have had access."

Still taking notes, Chief Berry said, "I'll have to call in my cops from their beats to help with this. Even then, we might be short of manpower."

"That's OK," Sheriff Dawes said. "I'll get our guys at the county office working on it."

Riley listened as the three men discussed the logistics of their upcoming efforts. The sheriff and the police chief seemed to be getting enthusiastic over Johnson's plans. As for Riley, she kept quiet and tried her best not to show her own skepticism. Unfortunately, that effort seemed to have failed.

Johnson glared straight at her and said, "Do you have something on your mind, Agent Sweeney?"

Riley gulped hard.

She said, "It's just that … we're kind of short of personnel and resources, and I'm not sure we're talking about putting them to the wisest use."

Johnson asked, "And what would that be?"

Riley felt a surge of embarrassment. The truth was, she really had no idea. And now, the tension she'd been feeling around Johnson had clearly come to a head.

A silence fell over the little room.

Then Johnson said to Dawes and Berry, "Could you give Agent Sweeney and me the room for a moment, please?"

Looking embarrassed at the obvious unease in the room, Dawes and Berry both stepped outside.

Riley sat there dreading whatever might be coming next. When the others were gone, Johnson leaned across the table toward her.

He said, "Back at the crime scene, I asked you *how* you felt sure that Lyda Gish was innocent. Do you remember what you said?"

Riley nodded. "I said, I just know."

"And why do you think you knew?"

Riley stifled a sigh.

"It was a gut feeling," she said.

"A gut feeling," Johnson repeated. "And tell me—back in the Banfield wine cellar in Beardsley, what was going on when you vegged out on me?"

Riley replied sharply, "I told you. I wasn't vegging out."

"What were you doing, then?"

Riley twisted uncomfortably in her chair.

"It was something Jake Crivaro taught me to do," she said. "I get into a certain … mental state. And I …"

Riley paused, knowing that what she was about to say might sound ridiculous to Johnson.

"I get a sense of the killer's mind."

Johnson's eyes widened.

"What are you talking about?" he said. "Something like ESP or—?"

"No, it's nothing like that," Riley interrupted. "There's nothing supernatural about it. It's instinct, that's all. Crivaro does it himself. And the reason he recruited me as an agent was because he thought I had a talent for it. Sometimes I get strong insights. Sometimes I don't. Sometimes I'm right, and sometimes I'm flat-out wrong. But …"

She said with a shrug, "It's what I do."

Johnson stared at Riley, and they both fell silent for a long moment.

Finally Johnson said, "Agent Sweeney, I haven't said anything about this so far, but I've heard a lot about you. Even in Boston, there was a lot of talk about you. You're Jake Crivaro's protégé, which is a big deal. And now that Crivaro's gone, I guess people will think you'll be able to fill his shoes, but "

His voice faded for a moment.

Then he leaned back in his chair and said, "Look, I know that Crivaro's got one hell of a record for solving cases. He's a living legend. But from what I've heard about his methods, and from what you've just told me..."

He shook his head and added, "It's not my place to say."

Riley felt shocked. What was her new partner thinking about Jake Crivaro? She was finding it harder to keep her anger in check.

Unable to keep a note of sarcasm out of her voice, she said, "Oh, no, you're my senior partner. It's definitely your place to say. In fact, it's kind of an obligation. So go right ahead. Spit it out."

Johnson frowned and hesitated. Then he spoke sharply.

"OK, then. I think—and I'm not alone in thinking this—that Jake Crivaro is kind of a relic. The younger agents say he's 'Old BAU,' the kind of profiler the unit started out with back in the 1970s. Times have changed, Agent Sweeney. We're at the start of a new century. We've got better tools than instincts. We've got computers, and ways to share information nobody ever imagined."

Riley felt strangely fascinated. She hadn't realized this sort of talk had been going on in law enforcement circles.

I guess it's about time I found out, she thought.

She said, "What you're telling me is—the future belongs to data."

"Well, doesn't it?" Johnson said with a shrug.

Riley hesitated.

He might well be right, she thought. *And yet...*

She said, "Look, data can tell us about a lot of things, but as far I know, it still can't tell us what makes people tick. I don't think it could tell us why you and I are butting heads like this. That's something no computer is ever going to figure out."

She took a deep breath and added, "And data sure as hell can't tell us why someone is killing people in makeshift electric chairs, and why he's choosing the victims he's choosing, or who he's going to choose next. That's something deep and personal, and more twisted than we even know how to think about just yet. All the numbers and statistics in the world won't explain it. And until we start understanding the killer, we've got no chance of catching him."

Johnson glowered at her.

Then he said, "You seem awfully sure of yourself."

Riley was startled. She didn't feel that way at all—not the least bit cocky or overconfident.

"No, that's not what I meant, it's just that—"

Johnson interrupted, "Agent Sweeney, I'm sure you learned a lot from Jake Crivaro. But he didn't teach you everything there is to know. Maybe you'd like to work on this team and learn something new. Or maybe not. As far as I'm concerned, it's entirely up to you."

Without another word, he got up from his chair and walked to the door and called for Sheriff Dawes and Chief Berry to come back inside. Barely glancing at Riley, they took their seats again and in a matter of seconds, the three men were talking about what they might learn from the boot print.

Riley sat there trying to pay attention. But she kept thinking of all the reasons this might be a waste of time. Johnson had some idea that he could track down the store where the boots had been bought, and then find out who had bought them. But how likely was that to happen?

What if the killer had bought the boots in some other state?

What if he had bought them many years ago?

It would be like finding a needle in a haystack.

And yet she had the feeling Johnson would stubbornly stick to his methods until he found that needle.

And who else might be dead by then?

One thing he'd said just now echoed sharply through her mind.

"It's entirely up to you."

Without a word, Riley got up and walked out of the room.

Chapter Twelve

R iley realized that she was hyperventilating. She sat down on a wooden bench in the police station hallway and tried to bring her breathing under control.

But her anxiety kept rising.

What did I just do? she asked herself.

She knew that the meeting was still going on without her, right on the other side of the door she'd just closed behind her. The two law officers and her own partner would be discussing the case she was also assigned to. And she had just walked out on them.

And what could she expect to happen now?

It seemed pretty obvious. As soon as Agent Johnson got a chance, he'd put in a call to Erik Lehl to report Riley's insubordinate behavior. She remembered what Lehl had said just this morning when he'd assigned Johnson to be her senior partner.

"You need adult supervision."

There was no doubt about it. This would be the last straw as far as Lehl was concerned. He'd fire her from the BAU once and for all.

Unless ...

She might still be able to salvage her career. She could swallow her pride and walk back into that room, sit back down, listen nicely, and do whatever she was told to do. After all, maybe Johnson was right. Maybe he did have things to teach her.

But somehow, she couldn't bring herself to do that.

Why not?

She quickly realized—this wasn't just a matter of pride. She hadn't walked out of there only out of personal pique. She'd walked out mostly because she really and truly questioned Agent Johnson's methods. At least, she questioned his use of those methods to the exclusion of all others, including the instincts that she and Jake Crivaro had always found essential.

Which means I'd better make good use of what I can do, she thought.

She was feeling a little calmer. More importantly, she could think much better now that she was alone. She wished she could have had a moment alone like this when she'd still been in Andy Gish's basement.

She closed her eyes and thought hard. Some vague worry had been nipping at her thoughts ever since they'd left the Gishes' house. Now that it was starting to come into focus, she remembered Lyda and Chief Berry mentioning one of the dead policeman's past cases.

They said that Gish had arrested a criminal named Quincy Harris, and he'd been extradited to Nebraska where he'd been sentenced to the death penalty—a sentence that Berry said had been carried out some six months ago.

She also remembered what Dawes had said about that.

"To the best of my knowledge, dead men aren't inclined to seek revenge."

It was true, of course.

And yet, that conversation was still replaying in Riley's thoughts. Her gut told her that there was still some kind of connection. It had something to do with the method of execution in Nebraska—the electric chair. Whoever had committed the two murders was somehow fixated on electricity. And he didn't seem to be merely *murdering* his victims. It seemed more like he was *executing* them in those jury-rigged electric chairs.

But how could a dead man be seeking revenge? Obviously, that was impossible. But might someone be seeking revenge on Quincy Harris's behalf? Who might want to do that?

A single word flashed through Riley's mind.

Family.

For a moment, she thought again about going back into the conference room and ...

Telling them what?

Whatever her instincts were trying to tell her, it wasn't even a theory yet.

She stood up and walked down the hall to the front area of the police station, where the receptionist and the cop were still at their desks.

Riley said to receptionist, "Ms. Raffin, I wonder if you could help me with something. Where do you keep your case files?"

"Do you have a particular case in mind?" Ms. Raffin said.

"Yes, I'd like to find records about Quincy Harris. Officer Gish arrested him some years ago."

Ms. Raffin nodded and tilted her glasses down on her nose.

"Oh, yes, I remember," she said. "That was an odd case. When Andy first arrested him, we had no idea he was wanted for murder. Mr. Harris was on death row in Nebraska, the last I'd heard."

Riley didn't mention that his sentence had been carried out.

"Could I see the file on that case?" Riley asked.

"Certainly," Ms. Raffin said, getting up from her chair. "But I'm afraid we're going to have dig through some paper. All that happened before we started storing case reports digitally."

Riley followed Ms. Raffin over to a filing cabinet.

The receptionist rummaged among the musty-smelling files, some of them yellowing with age, until she pulled one out and handed it to Riley.

"Here's what you're looking for," she said. "I hope it helps."

Riley thanked Ms. Raffin, who went back to her desk. Riley sat down at an unoccupied desk and opened the file. Most of it dealt with how Officer Gish had arrested Quincy Harris and his then eighteen-year-old son Ayers for attempted burglary right here in Prinneville.

Aside from the peculiar novelty of a father and son burglary team, nothing had seemed especially odd about the case. Quincy and Ayers were drifters traveling across the country, and when they'd run short of funds in Prinneville they'd resorted to theft. They'd probably done the same thing in several other towns along the way.

But it was procedure to alert law enforcement institutions nationwide even about routine arrests like this, to make sure the culprits weren't guilty of serious crimes elsewhere in the country.

Sure enough, Quincy was wanted for murder in Nebraska. The state authorities called for his extradition, and he went back to Nebraska and stood trial for homicide.

Riley skimmed through the information about the Nebraska case, which was rather skimpy because it didn't directly pertain to the crime here in Prinneville. But she saw that Quincy Harris had been a long-divorced man who apparently found it impossible to hold down a job or maintain a relationship.

One day he came home early from his current job to find his live-in girlfriend in bed with a friend of his. He'd shot them both dead, then had gone on the lam with his son heading westward.

Riley shuddered as she read about the shooting.

She actually felt dizzy.

She couldn't help flashing back to the gunfight in New York in January. She could see the life fading from Heidi Wright's eyes after she had fatally shot her...

Snap out of it, Riley scolded herself.

Still, the memory wasn't easy to shake off.

But this has got to stop, she thought.

If she had any hope of salvaging her career from the mess she was in right now, she couldn't allow herself to get thrown off track by past traumas.

I've got to be better than that.

She kept reading about the trial. In an attempt to plead manslaughter instead of homicide, Harris's lawyer had argued that the murders were a crime of passion. According to Harris's account, the gun had actually belonged to the male victim, and Harris had grabbed it off a nearby piece of furniture and shot the victims in a fit of fury.

But that defense had crumbled. Not only was it proven that Harris had bought the weapon himself, he'd been seen carrying it at work earlier that day. The prosecution then had no trouble convicting Quincy and sentencing him to death.

Riley remembered what Berry had said back at the Gish home.

"The last I heard, the sentence had been carried out. That was six months ago, I think."

And now Riley wondered—what had happened to the son?

Riley read on and learned that Ayers Harris hadn't been extradited back to Nebraska along with his father, Quincy. Nothing in the Nebraska case had indicated that he had anything to do with his father's double homicide. Neither side had even called him in as a witness. Instead, he'd been tried and convicted right here in Utah of much less serious crime of attempted breaking and entering. He'd served a short prison sentence and...

And then what? Riley wondered.

The records didn't say. But again, that single word flashed through Riley's mind.

Family.

Was it possible that Ayers Harris had killed Andy Gish in revenge for his father's arrest, conviction, and execution?

Following a growing gut feeling, Riley reached for a phone book on the desk where she was sitting. She saw that it covered not only Prinneville but the rest of Hannaford County.

She opened the book to the letter H and scanned down the names. She quickly saw that there was no Ayers Harris listed.

Of course not, she thought with a sigh.

That would be too easy.

But her eye was a caught by another name farther down on the page.

Ayers Hamby.

Riley felt a surge of excitement.

It's him! she thought. *It's got to be him!*

She couldn't remember ever hearing "Ayers" used as a first name before. It was surely no coincidence that such a singular and unusual name would show up right here in this phone book and on this page. Riley also took note of Ayers Hamby's address, which was in Kedgwick, a town closer to Beardsley than to Prinneville. The young man actually lived near where the psychiatrist had been killed.

Things suddenly started making sense to Riley. She started playing out a scenario in her head. When Ayers Harris had finished his short stint in prison, he'd decided not to leave the area and had quietly disappeared into his surroundings, perhaps hoping to start his whole life over. He'd changed his last name in an attempt to sever himself from his father.

But he didn't succeed, Riley thought.

Instead, he'd been brooding about his father's arrest and conviction all along. When his father had been executed a few months back, something inside him had snapped, and he began to mull over revenge.

But what about Dr. Banfield? she asked herself.

Why would Ayers have wanted to kill him as well?

Riley realized that Dr. Banfield could easily have also done something that led to Quincy Harris's conviction, perhaps as an expert witness.

It was all starting to gel as a theory. But what should she do next? Under normal circumstances, the first thing Riley would do was share her thoughts with her partner.

But these weren't normal circumstances, and Riley didn't feel like talking to Agent Johnson about this. Not that her wounded pride was a good excuse to leave him out of the loop. She knew she really *ought* to tell him.

And yet—what could she expect if she did share this idea with him? Would he take it the least bit seriously?

Probably not, she thought. *And that would be the end of any investigation into the matter.*

After all, her theory wasn't the least bit data-driven. Once again, she was following her instincts. Johnson would surely not approve. In fact, he'd probably shut her right down. And if she was right, that could set the whole case hopelessly behind. Meanwhile, Ayers might be plotting revenge against yet another person he held responsible for his father's death.

I need to pay this guy a visit, she decided.

And she needed to do it alone.

Riley got up from the desk and walked over to the receptionist.

She asked, "Ms. Raffin, I wonder if I…uh, if we could borrow a vehicle for a little while. I need to follow up on a lead while Agent Johnson is working on a different matter."

It wasn't an unusual request. Local police were often glad to lend a visiting BAU team a car to use during the duration of the case. Of course, it *was* unusual for a team member to borrow a vehicle without telling a senior partner about it. But Riley simply had to improvise.

Ms. Raffin nodded toward the cop at the other desk.

"Maybe Officer Banks could help you with that," she said.

The cop looked up from his work and shrugged.

"That might be kind of tough," he said to Riley. "We're just a little outfit, and all our cruisers are currently on patrol. There's a car rental place a few blocks away. Maybe you could walk over there and pick up something."

Riley stifled a discouraged sigh. Actually renting a car on the BAU account without Agent Johnson's knowledge might really be pushing things.

Then Officer Banks added, "Hey, I can think of one possibility. We impounded a car a couple of months ago. The owner hasn't come to claim it or pay the fine, so it pretty much belongs to us now. I could lend you that one if you like."

"Thank you, that would be great," Riley said.

Grabbing a key from a nearby rack, Officer Banks scoffed and said, "Don't thank me till you get a look at the vehicle. Sure, we'll let you use it for free. Even so, you might still want to turn it down."

Riley followed Banks out of the station. They walked around the building to the alley in back. Parked behind the building was a decrepit-looking Ford hatchback. It was at least fifteen years old, Riley guessed. It had been poorly repainted an ugly shade of brown, probably in an effort to make its many scratches and dents less noticeable.

Officer Banks asked, "Where are you planning to drive to?"

"Kedgwick," Riley said. "Could you tell me how to get there?"

"Sure," Banks said, pointing. "It's over that way, close to Beardsley. Not much of a drive."

Then with a chuckle he added, "I can't make any guarantees this heap will get you there, though."

I'll just have to take my chances, Riley thought.

Banks gave her directions, and Riley took the keys and thanked him again.

She climbed into the driver's seat and turned the key. The ignition made a horrible rasping sound.

Banks said loudly from outside the car, "I hope the battery isn't dead."

I hope so too, Riley thought.

For one thing, it didn't look like there were any other vehicles handy to help out with jumper cables.

Riley turned the key a couple more times, and finally the engine grumbled to life. Banks smiled and flashed Riley an "OK" sign and walked back toward the station.

Riley glanced at the gas gauge. At least the tank seemed to be fairly full.

She backed up the car and drove out of the alley onto a side street. Then she headed down Main Street on her way out of Prinneville and out onto the open road—the same highway she and Johnson had driven on coming from Beardsley.

The automatic gears struggled as Riley picked up speed, and the engine made suspicious sputtering, knocking noises. She could barely accelerate to the legal speed limit.

Meanwhile, that seemingly endless highway spread out in front of her. Of course, Riley knew that the distance to Kedgwick wasn't nearly as far as it looked. But would this miserable vehicle get her to her destination?

It damned well better, she thought.

But she couldn't help imagining herself stranded somewhere on this highway with a white handkerchief on an antenna, desperately signaling for help. How would she explain *that* to Agent Johnson?

Oh, well, my career's probably over anyway, she thought with a groan.

Besides, it's just turning out to be that kind of a day.

CHAPTER THIRTEEN

The man who liked to call himself Sparky walked around the block yet again, watching for his next victim to arrive back at her home. It was late in the afternoon of nice, cool spring day, and he didn't mind the wait or the walk. He had plenty of time on his hands, and he enjoyed strolling through this charming little family neighborhood with its neat suburban houses.

Sparky.

Nobody called him that anymore—at least nobody but himself in the privacy of his own high-voltage brain circuitry. But he had fond memories of being called Sparky when he was a kid. It was his dad's nickname for him whenever he got wound up and too full of energy for teachers and other adults to handle.

Sparky.

He smiled sadly at the bittersweet memory. Dad had been taken away from him too soon—much too soon. If Dad were still around, he'd understand everything Sparky was doing these days, like he always had.

Understanding had been a rare thing in Sparky's life. For the most part, he'd long since gotten used to living without it. He no longer expected any recognition for things he'd learned, such as knowing fine wines, appreciating excellent cuisine, and enjoying a comfortable lifestyle. He'd learned to live without a lot of things, like family, friends ... even memories.

His past was mostly a blur in his mind. But he *could* remember how Dad had helped him conquer his fear of electricity by teaching him how to make a shocking coil made out of wire, pieces of steel tubing, a battery, and a wooden block.

The shocks he'd gotten from it were so mild, he'd come to believe he had nothing to fear from electricity. He'd even come to enjoy it.

Neither he nor his father had ever envisioned electricity as a tool of torture, or as a weapon of death.

Sparky dismissed even that memory from his past. He had to keep his mind focused on the task at hand.

On these necessary executions.

He'd had his trepidations when he'd been working out his scheme to kill the policeman, Officer Gish. Was he going to be able to go through with it? He wasn't sure until he'd actually walked into the man's house and stood face to face with him. Officer Gish had recognized Sparky pretty much right away, and he hadn't seemed unhappy to see him—at least not at first.

Of course, he'd been much less happy when he'd understood what Sparky was going to do to him.

Dr. Banfield had been a different story. Even when he'd come to his senses in the basement, he hadn't recognized Sparky at all—not until the very last possible moment.

Maybe that was what made me angry, Sparky thought, remembering when he'd thrown the wine glass against the wall.

Odd, the things I can *remember,* he thought.

So much of his past was murky, but those two executions were seared into his memory.

He remembered with satisfaction the two men's anguished expressions as they writhed in agony when the current was closed and the electrical charge passed through their bodies.

He even vividly recalled the berry-like taste of the wine he'd opened in Dr. Banfield's basement—the Le Vieux Donjon Châteauneuf-du-Pape. It had been quite good. He felt a little pang of regret at not having opened the other much older bottle—the 1987 Opus One. Perhaps he should have loitered for just a few moments after Banfield's electrocution to try it out. Perhaps he should have taken a bottle home with him.

But no, he reminded himself, *I want nothing from them.*

He wanted nothing more than what they deserved to lose—nothing more than to take their lives in a way that reflected how they had lived them.

As Sparky rounded the street corner and Mrs. Pugh's house came into sight again, he saw that her car still wasn't in the driveway. He felt a slight, nagging worry. She was taking longer buying groceries than usual.

That didn't present him with a real problem, of course. The equipment he needed was safely stashed in a satchel in his car, which was parked nearby. He could grab it at a moment's notice. But the sidewalks weren't vacant, now that the weather was getting nice. Some children were out playing, and grown-ups were walking their dogs. How long could he keep walking around the block without somebody in the neighborhood noticing his presence?

Pretty much forever, he told himself.

He felt pretty sure nobody who saw him would give him a second look, no matter how many times he walked past them. He had an uncanny way of disappearing into his surroundings, whether he wanted to or not. Nobody paid him the least bit of attention anymore. The idea that anybody could describe him from memory seemed perfectly laughable.

And of course, there were advantages to that.

With some luck, he could keep right on doing what needed to be done. And those murders were what kept him going these days, gave him a sense of purpose that he'd lacked too long.

They keep my batteries charged, he thought with a smile.

When he was finished with his tasks, it wouldn't much matter whether he would be caught or not.

But in the meantime…

I've got work to do.

As he came around the corner again, his heart quickened when he saw Mrs. Pugh's car approaching from down the street.

He kept walking toward her house as she parked in her driveway, then got out of her car and took two bags of groceries out of the trunk. He noticed that Mrs. Pugh looked more frail than she used to look, and she tottered a little under the weight of the bags. It seemed a shame that she lived alone and had no one to help her with such things.

Should I stop and give her a hand? he thought.

It would be a nice gesture, especially considering what he was going to do to her later on. But then—what if she recognized him on the spot?

He might have to act immediately, and he didn't have his satchel of equipment with him.

He kept walking down the sidewalk toward her house as she managed to lug the bags up onto her front stoop and took out her key to unlock her front door. Then, for just a second, her eyes met his. A quizzical look crossed her face, as if she thought he looked familiar.

With a surge of boldness, he waved and called out, "It's a nice day."

She smiled and nodded and called back, "Yes, it is."

She opened the door and picked up her bags to take them inside.

Sparky considered his options. He could fetch his satchel right now, come back to Mrs. Pugh's house, and take advantage of her curiosity about him to talk his way into her house, or ...

His thoughts were interrupted as a couple of small children rushed by him, almost colliding with him.

Not yet, he thought.

Not while there are people around.

Not while it's still so light outside.

He'd go away for a while, then come back here later on after it got dark.

As Mrs. Pugh carried the groceries into the house and shut the door behind her, Sparky thought about her smile.

She seems like such a nice lady, he thought.

Indeed, his murky memories of her were mostly pleasant ones.

But he knew from experience that some of the nicest people could do truly terrible things.

Sometimes the nicest people sent other people to hell.

And those nice people deserved to die.

CHAPTER FOURTEEN

Twilight was setting in when the borrowed car began to sputter anxiously.

Maybe this wasn't such a good idea, Riley thought. She was driving alone in a decrepit vehicle on an errand she wasn't sure she really understood herself.

"Don't give up on me," she urged the car, patting the dashboard. As if in response, the engine resumed its normal clatter.

She turned off the highway onto a smaller road that led to Kedgwick, the town where Ayers Hamby lived, at least according to the phone book. She hoped the vehicle would make it the rest of the way to her destination. But even if it got her there, what did she expect to happen next? What did she expect to actually do?

In fact, she couldn't really think of anything really about it at the moment.

Her phone had started buzzing a few minutes ago, and although she hadn't looked at it, much less answered it, she was sure that the caller was Agent Johnson, wanting to know where she had taken off to and why.

It's a pretty good question, she thought.

But she couldn't bring herself to take Johnson's call. What would be the point? He'd be furious at her for what she'd done. And he wouldn't have any use for her hunch that an executed killer's son was now committing murders out of revenge for his father's execution.

The truth was, Riley was starting to question her own thinking. She'd gotten awfully upset with Agent Johnson a little while ago, and maybe she'd let her emotions get the best of her when she'd hatched her theory.

Maybe my judgment's shot, she thought.

Or maybe she simply couldn't do this job without Jake Crivaro's guidance.

She hated that possibility.

But at the moment, she felt like she had no choice but to see her hunch through.

As she drove along the dusty road, she heard a speeding vehicle coming up behind her. She could see in her rearview mirror that the car was a nice-looking Dodge sedan.

Riley was driving exactly at the speed limit, and the approaching vehicle was moving way above it. The driver seemed to be in more of a hurry than she was. She signaled for the driver to pass, and the Dodge accelerated and zoomed past her. She briefly saw that the driver was a young man looking straight ahead as if she weren't even there. Then the car left her in a momentary cloud of dust.

I hope he gets caught speeding, she thought as the dust cleared and she continued on her way.

Riley soon came to a sign announcing that she was now entering Kedgwick, an unincorporated town with a population of only a few hundred people. As she drove on into Kedgwick, she saw that it was as different as it could possibly be from the much more upscale nearby town of Beardsley.

It was a working-class area with well-ordered streets and small, box-shaped houses. For a moment, Riley thought about stopping and asking somebody for directions. Then she noticed a sign on a cross street. She'd found the one she was looking for.

As she drove down that cross street, she reached an area on the outskirts of the little town where the residences were mostly double-wide mobile homes on permanent foundations. Riley guessed that most of the residents were renters.

At the very end of the street, she was surprised to see the nice-looking Dodge sedan that had roared past her. It was now parked right next to a markedly more rundown Volkswagen in front of a double-wide with a porch. There was rubble in the yard and an untidy little pyramid of beer cans on the porch. She was musing about how weirdly out of place the Dodge looked when she noticed the number on a post next to the street.

This was the address Riley was looking for. She pulled up next to the Dodge and stopped her car.

Now what? she wondered.

She had no idea whether the suspect was dangerous—or for that matter, whether he was really a viable suspect.

Was she here to arrest him, confront him, or just talk to him?

And what was she doing out here all by herself, anyway?

Maybe she needed to call Agent Johnson after all, try to explain to him what was going on, see if she could get him and maybe a cop or two to come out here and join her …

No, that's impossible, she realized.

She was on her own now, and there was nothing she could do except follow her instincts.

And right now, her instincts didn't tell her much—except that she needed to walk right up to the door of that trailer.

Her heart pounding uncomfortably, she got out of her car and went up onto the porch. Her footsteps on the floorboards made the stack of beer cans rattle and threaten to fall over.

She pushed the doorbell button, but she didn't hear a bell. She figured maybe the bell wasn't working, so she rapped on the door.

A man's voice called out from somewhere far inside, "Who is it?"

Riley replied, "Are you Ayers Hamby?"

"Who wants to know?"

Riley took out her badge so she'd have it ready to show him when he came to the door.

"I'm Special Agent Riley Sweeney, with the FBI. I just want to come in and talk to you."

She heard profanity from inside.

Then she heard a loud clattering noise.

This isn't good, she thought.

In fact, she felt pretty sure the man was leaving by what must have been the nearest exit—a window on the end of the unit.

Putting away her badge, she darted off the porch and ran to the back of the unit. Sure enough, she saw a pushed-out screen lying in the grass under an open window. A man wearing jeans and sneakers and a sweatshirt was clambering over a tall fence that separated his yard from an open field beyond it. It was the same guy she'd seen driving the Dodge a few minutes ago.

"Halt!" Riley called out.

Straddling the fence now, he turned to glare back at her.

Then he lost his balance and fell off the fence on its far side.

He struggled to his feet and staggered away, limping as he ran.

Riley didn't doubt that she would be able to catch him. Ayers Hamby was heading off into a flat, barren terrain that that appeared to be interrupted by nothing except the mountains in the distance. There was no place for him to hide. However, it was getting dark now and she knew there was no time to waste.

She went over the fence considerably more deftly than the young man had. She dropped to the other side and chased after him.

Despite his limp, Ayers Hamby understood this terrain well, and he dodged and weaved among the bushes and clusters of weeds. But his limp slowed him down.

Riley soon caught up with him.

"You're under arrest," she cried, grabbing him by the arm and spinning him around.

He yanked himself away from her and took a swing at her with his fist. He was clumsy but strong, and he clipped her hard to the side of the head.

Riley was momentarily dizzy and Ayers was about to break into a run again.

She drew her weapon and pointed it at him.

"Stop or I'll shoot," she commanded sharply.

He froze in his tracks, then turned slowly with his hands raised.

Riley's brain was still slightly foggy from the blow to her head. For a moment, the look in his eyes reminded him of Heidi Wright staring at Riley in the moments before her death.

Stunned by the flashback, Riley almost dropped her weapon.

Although his hands were still raised, Hamby's lips formed a sneer.

"You're not going to use that," he snarled.

"Don't test me," Riley said, unable to keep her voice from shaking a little.

Hamby shook his head and said, "You can't do it. I know a few things about the law. You can't use lethal force."

Riley's heart sank. She knew this was truly a gray area. Lethal force was only a legal option when a suspect presented a serious threat to her or someone else. Riley certainly didn't feel as though her life was in any imminent danger from this guy. And there was no one else in sight.

Besides, it was vital that she bring in this suspect alive. Drawing her Glock had been little more than a bluff on her part.

So why is the gun shaking in my hand? she wondered.

And why was she still having flashbacks to killing Heidi Wright?

Riley lowered her weapon and took a deep breath.

Slowly and patiently, she said, "Look, there's no point in this. You're limping, and I'm not. I'll catch up with you again, and fast. And I don't think you want to match your personal combat skills against mine."

"I might still get away," the man said.

"And I might shoot you in the leg," Riley said.

"Wouldn't that be excessive force?"

Riley smirked a little. "I don't know. I'm not sure I care. And anyway, where are you going to run? This looks like pretty much nowhere to me. And you won't be able to go back home."

Hamby looked around for a moment, as if trying to gauge his chances. Then he shrugged with resignation, and turned around with his hands behind his back, obviously familiar with this procedure.

Riley put her gun back in her holster and handcuffed him.

She said, "Ayers Hamby, you're under arrest for—"

Hamby interrupted, "Yeah, yeah, yeah, I know what I'm under arrest for. And don't waste your breath reading me my rights. I know all about it. I've got the right to a lawyer, yadda yadda yadda, and since I sure as hell can't afford one, you'll get me one for free. I've got the right to remain silent—and you can bet I *will* keep silent. I've got nothing to say to you."

He sounds kind of used to this, Riley thought.

He also didn't sound very worried.

Then, as they started back across the field, he muttered, "How did you get on it so fast anyhow?"

Riley wasn't sure what he meant. Before she could answer, something seemed to dawn on him. "FBI? You said you're FBI?"

"Right."

"Why is the FBI arresting me, anyway?"

Riley said, "We do get called when there are multiple murders."

Hamby stopped in his tracks.

"Murders?" he gasped.

Then he broke into a smile.

"Oh, man," he said. "You are making *such* a mistake, lady. You've got no idea."

With a laugh, he turned and walked quietly toward a gate that was off to one side in the fence they had just climbed.

His casual attitude worried Riley, and so did his sudden docility. Didn't he understand how serious his situation was? Or did he know something she didn't know, some reason why this arrest was pointless and he'd be going free soon?

After they went through the gate, she took out her cell phone and called Agent Johnson. He sounded furious, and she wasn't surprised.

"Agent Sweeney, what the hell are you doing? A cop here says you took a car. Where did you go? What's going on?"

"I'm making an arrest," Riley said.

"You're *what*?"

"I've got a suspect," Riley said. "I found him in Kedgwick, over near Beardsley. He goes by the name of Ayers Hamby, although his original name is Ayers Harris. He's Quincy Harris's son."

"Quincy who?"

He's forgotten already, Riley thought, suppressing a growl of annoyance.

"Ask Chief Berry, he'll remind you," she said.

"What are you arresting him for?" Johnson asked.

"Resisting arrest, for starters," Riley said. Then, remembering the punch to the side of her head, she added, "Oh, and assaulting an officer."

"You've lost your mind, Agent Sweeney."

"Yeah, well, we'll see about that," Riley said. "Send somebody out here to help me bring him in."

"I'm doing nothing of the kind," Johnson said. "We're all busy here doing real investigative work. Now get back here right now—with or without your so-called 'suspect.'"

Agent Johnson ended the call without another word.

Riley stared at the phone as she and Hamby continued across the yard. She was surprised at the tone she'd used with Agent Johnson right now.

I sure sounded arrogant, she thought.

And she knew that wasn't good, for several reasons.

For one thing, it wasn't a good idea to antagonize Agent Johnson, especially since she was on his bad side already. No good could come of that.

But maybe more importantly, she was learning a few important things about herself as she got older and more experienced. And she knew that she tended to act sassy and cocky when her confidence was actually shaky, when she wasn't at all sure of what she was doing.

And it didn't take a lot of introspection for her to realize that she wasn't really all that confident right now—far from it, in fact.

She could only hope that this arrest wouldn't blow up in her face.

When they reached the beat-up Ford hatchback, Ayers Hamby's mouth dropped open.

"What the hell is this?" he asked. "An official FBI vehicle?"

As she opened the passenger side door, Riley replied, "Mind your own business and get in," Riley said.

Hamby shook his head. "I don't know. How do I know you're even really FBI?"

Riley suddenly realized—in all the confusion, she hadn't gotten a chance to show him her badge. For all he really knew, she was just some crazy woman with a gun. She took out her badge now and displayed it for him.

Hamby squinted at the badge as if trying to decide whether it was real.

"Just get in the car," she said.

"I don't trust this heap." He nodded toward the Dodge and added, "Are you sure you don't want take my nice new car?"

For a moment, Riley was tempted. But she quickly decided that borrowing a suspect's vehicle to take him into custody was just too weird an option to even consider.

"Get in," she said, giving him a shove.

Hamby got into the car and sat there quietly,

Riley got into the driver's seat and turned the ignition. She was relieved that the car grumbled to life again. It was getting dark now, so she turned on the headlights. Soon she left Kedgwick behind and was driving on the open road again.

She was feeling tired after a long day, and the side of her head ached from where Hamby had punched her. Remembering all that had just happened, again she flashed back to Heidi Wright's eyes as she lay dying at Riley's feet, and how her lips had moved wordlessly with her final breaths ...

Riley shuddered and shook off the image.

She realized she was lucky she hadn't had to use lethal force just now.

But if her career wasn't over, someday she would surely face that choice.

Will I be able to do it? she wondered.

CHAPTER FIFTEEN

When Riley escorted her suspect into the Prinneville police station, she found Agent Johnson pacing the floor angrily. Sheriff Dawes was standing nearby, looking a bit anxious. Chief Berry was nowhere in sight but the receptionist and the cop named Banks were at their desks, trying to look busy.

Riley had been feeling relieved that the borrowed heap she'd been driving made it all the way back from Kedgwick. Ayers Hamby hadn't said a word during the drive, but he hadn't given her any trouble, either. But now she felt somewhat deflated by the expression on her partner's face.

Johnson strode toward Riley and whispered rather loudly, "You've got some explaining to do, Agent Sweeney."

"First I've got a suspect to interrogate," Riley told him.

She called out to the others present, "I need to get this man into an interrogation room right now."

Looking quite puzzled, Dawes and Banks stepped forward and led the prisoner away. Before Riley could follow them, Johnson blocked her way. Livid with rage, he leaned toward her, still making an effort to keep his voice low.

"Agent Sweeney, I wanted to cover for you, but I had no idea what to tell Dawes or Berry."

"Didn't you tell them I was bringing in a suspect?" Riley asked.

"Yeah, but it didn't make any more sense to them than it did to me. And I sure didn't know how to explain why you'd taken a police vehicle."

Bristling, Riley said, "It's not a police vehicle. It's impounded. I asked Officer Banks if I could borrow it."

"Did you tell him I was good with that?"

Riley stopped short. She remembered how evasive she'd been with the receptionist and Officer Banks.

"I wonder if I ... uh, if we could borrow a vehicle for a little while."

No, she hadn't been fully upfront about the matter.

Trying to sound calmer than she felt, Riley said, "I was following up on a theory. And I made an arrest. What were *you* doing all this time?"

Johnson nodded a bit defensively.

"We've been busy here. Right now Chief Berry is at the paint factory checking out possible chloroform thefts. Sheriff Dawes and I have been here coordinating with the tech people at Quantico, working through data."

I'll bet you have, Riley thought sarcastically.

She figured a guy like Johnson could fritter hours away dealing with details like boot prints.

Johnson continued, "Then when you called a little while ago, Dawes and I looked up this Ayers Hamby character you've just dragged in. He's no killer. He's a nobody—a petty thief, that's all."

Riley said, "Like I told you over the phone—he's also the son of a convicted murderer who was electrocuted over in Nebraska."

"So what?" Johnson said.

Riley's eyes widened with disbelief.

What could she possibly say to shake Johnson's belief that she was always wrong about everything?

Nothing—at least not yet, she thought.

"I'm going to interrogate Hamby right now," Riley said.

"Knock yourself out," Johnson said, pointing toward the hallway where they'd taken the prisoner.

With Johnson right behind her, Riley hurried to the interrogation room, where Banks was standing outside the door. When she went inside alone, Ayers Hamby was already sitting at the table in handcuffs. The room had the usual two-way mirror, and Riley was sure that Johnson was on the other side of it, and possibly Sheriff Dawes and Officer Banks as well, all of them watching and listening.

I'd better get this right, she thought.

He said, "So I'm wanted for murder, huh? That's a new one for me."

She didn't reply. Instead she stood silently staring at him, trying to see whether she could psych him out. He reacted with a smirk and a shrug, obviously not in awe of her authority.

Then she said, "Where were you yesterday, between nine p.m. and midnight?"

"I was at home in my trailer," Hamby said.

"Can anyone confirm that?" Riley asked.

Hamby chuckled a little.

"You mean like some hot little bedmate? No such luck. I live a solitary life. I don't get laid a lot. Although if you're free later on ..."

He was goading her, and she knew it.

She also knew better than to take the bait.

Instead, Riley asked him the same question about the hours when Andy Gish had been killed.

"Huh—I'd have to check my social calendar," he said. Then with a snap of his fingers he added, "No, wait. I don't keep a social calendar, because I don't have a social life. So I can't remember for sure. I don't work regular hours—just odd jobs whenever I can pick them up. Maybe I was painting somebody's house. Yeah, that might be it. I was painting a house."

"No doing any *electrical* work?" Riley said snidely.

"Now that you mention it, maybe so," he said. "I do a little wiring from time to time. I've taught myself a thing or two about electricity over the years. I don't have a license, though. Is that what you brought me in for?"

So he is interested in electricity, Riley thought.

But was he *obsessed* with it, the way she felt sure the killer must be? Riley found it hard to imagine this ordinary-seeming jerk being obsessed with anything. He seemed too apathetic for that. But then, even his apathy could well be an act.

Riley leaned across the table toward him.

"You don't seem to be taking this very seriously," she said.

"How'd you guess?" he said.

Riley held his gaze again for a moment.

Then she said, "What can you tell me about Julian Banfield?"

"Only that I've never heard of him," Hamby scoffed. "Who is he?"

"A psychiatrist in Beardsley."

"Well, that explains it. I don't do any business over in Beardsley, and no socializing either. The likes of me aren't exactly welcome there."

"Next you'll be trying to tell me you've never heard of Andy Gish," Riley said.

Hamby squinted at her.

"You mean *Officer* Andy Gish?" he said. "Yeah, the name kind of rings a bell."

Riley tried to gauge his reaction. She wasn't sure what to make of it. He certainly didn't seem alarmed by the mention of Gish's name. But then, if he was the cold-blooded killer she believed him to be, he'd know how to cover up any alarm. And of course he would have known she was going to mention Gish.

"Can you tell me why the name rings a bell?" Riley asked.

"Maybe you can tell me," Hamby said.

Riley said nothing. She knew better than to supply a suspect with any information that would be more useful coming from him.

Hamby fidgeted a little in his chair.

"Andy Gish is a good guy," he said. "We didn't meet under the best circumstances. But I don't hold anything against him."

"What circumstances do you mean?" Riley said.

Hamby chuckled a little nervously.

"He arrested me, OK?" he said. "Me and my dad both. We were traveling, and we stopped right here in Prinneville, just passing through town, and we..."

Hamby rolled his head and said, "Aw, you know what happened. Stop playing games with me."

"I'm not the one playing games, Mr. Hamby," Riley said.

Hamby looked at the ceiling.

"Officer Gish arrested us, OK?" he said.

"Arrested you for what?" Riley asked.

"He caught us trying to rob a liquor store," Hamby said. "It was no big deal, not even armed robbery, we were just trying to break into the place during the night. Officer Gish just happened to show up and..."

He shrugged and added, "Well, the rest is history."

Riley shook her head.

"Oh, there's a lot of history you're leaving out," she said.

"For example?" Hamby said.

Again Riley fell silent, but she had to keep some doubts in check as she waited for him to reply. She realized that whoever rigged those chairs must have a specific obsession, a strong reason for going to that much trouble to kill in that particular way. This man didn't seem that focused.

She also felt sure that the killer had a higher-than-average IQ. Smart-ass though Hamby might be, he didn't come across as especially bright. But of course, all of that might be an act.

Hamby looked her directly in the eye.

He said, "As it happened, Dad was wanted in Nebraska."

"For what?" Riley asked.

"A murder charge. A *double* murder."

He snickered a little and added, "And in case you're wondering, Dad was as guilty as hell. And he got extradited back to Nebraska. And he was tried and sentenced to die."

Seemingly almost amused now, he continued, "And, oh, did he ever die—just last year, on his birthday I believe. They shot two thousand volts of electricity through him. That ought to have done the trick. I'd like to have seen the expression on his face. Of course, I guess he was wearing a hood."

He chuckled grimly.

"You know, when they pass that much electricity through you, it roasts you alive, and smoke comes out of you. Sometimes your eyes pop out of their sockets. And it sucks up so much power, whole neighborhoods get blacked out. Of course, you're supposed to lose consciousness before you can feel anything. But how would anybody know? Whoever knows, they're not talking."

He added with a sigh, "It's all pretty awe-inspiring, when you think about it. Sure, people can get electrocuted around the house, but nothing like that. The guy who throws the switch must feel like God or something. I wouldn't mind feeling like that at least once in my life."

Riley's attention quickened at his grim fascination with electrocution. The real murderer might feel exactly this way. At the same time, she was startled by his gleeful attitude.

"You don't sound too broken up about it," she said.

"Why should I be?" Hamby said. "He was a bastard, treated me like shit ever since I was a baby. The only reason I was traveling with him and helping him rob places along the way was because he bullied me into it, like he did with everything else. I thought about going to his execution, but I guess my invitation got lost in the mail. Truth is, I would have liked to have thrown the switch myself. Good riddance to the prick."

Riley felt a prickle of worry.

Was he feigning his hostility toward his father? If not, how did it fit with her theory that he'd committed the murders out of revenge?

She found that she couldn't read him at all.

Drumming his fingers on the table, Hamby said, "Anyway, after I did my time, I changed my name and started life all over again over in Kedgwick. And I've got Officer Gish to thank for getting Dad out of my life. Sure, I wound up doing time for attempted burglary, but it was worth it in the end. Besides, I don't mind spending a little time in the slammer now and again. It's just part of my lifestyle, I guess."

Then he tilted his head and asked, "How's Officer Gish doing, anyway? I haven't seen him in years. He must be getting close to retirement age. Is he around the station maybe? If he is, send him on in here, I'd like to say hi."

Riley observed how his eyes sparkled as he said that.

Is he playing me? she wondered.

She couldn't feel sure one way or the other. And she really wished Jake Crivaro was here helping her. It occurred to her that she'd never conducted an interrogation completely by herself before. She felt seriously out of her depth. But getting help from Agent Johnson wasn't an option.

She said, "I think you know why I'm bringing up Officer Gish."

"I'm not sure I do," Hamby said. "Unless he's …"

Hamby's voice faded and his eyes widened.

"Jesus, did something happen to him?" he asked. "Is that what you're thinking I …?"

He fell silent again and sat there with his mouth open. Riley tried to assess his apparent surprise. She couldn't tell whether it was feigned or not. Hamby shook his head with a worried expression.

"I'm not sure I should answer any more questions," he said.

Keep the pressure on, Riley thought.

She knew that was what Crivaro would tell her to do.

Crivaro would also tell her to distract him with another topic, try to put him off his guard.

She pointed to the side of her face.

"See this bruise?" she said. "Are you going to sit there telling me you don't know how I got this?"

Hamby shrugged.

"Maybe you tripped and fell," he said.

"Oh, you know better than that," Riley said. Pointing to the two-way mirror, she said, "My partner's back there watching and listening. So is the sheriff. And probably Officer Banks too. You don't want to keep lying in front of four officers of the law."

"OK, I hit you," Hamby blurted. "It was self-defense and you know it."

"Self-defense? How?"

"You were using unnecessary force. You were beating the hell out of me."

Not only was he lying, he was getting defensive and nervous. That was exactly what Riley wanted. If he was guilty, he'd be blurting out a full confession in just a few seconds.

"You're lying, and you know it," she said.

Nodding toward his leg, he said, "It is so true. I've got a sprained ankle to prove it. In fact, I demand to see a doctor. It might even be broken."

"You sprained that ankle jumping over a fence running away from me," she said. "You punched me when you were resisting arrest."

Leaning sharply toward him, she said, "Why *were* you resisting arrest, anyway? Why did you try to run away from me?"

"Why do you think?" Hamby asked.

He said it as if she really ought to know the answer.

Riley thought hard and fast.

She flashed back to that moment on the road near Kedgwick when that nice-looking Dodge sedan sped past her own decrepit vehicle, leaving her in a momentary cloud of dust. Then she remembered seeing that car in Hamby's driveway, and how odd she thought it had looked next to his beat-up Volkswagen.

Suddenly, things made sense.

She said quietly, "You stole a car."

"No comment," Hamby replied, with a smirk.

"You know I can run the plates," Riley told him.

Hamby gave a shrug.

When Riley just kept staring silently at him, he finally said, "Well, it ain't murder, is it then?"

Before Riley could decide what to do next, the door to the room flew open and Agent Johnson charged in. Riley saw Sheriff Dawes and Officer Banks standing behind him in the doorway.

Agent Johnson said in a snarl, "That will be enough, Agent Sweeney."

Then he looked at Hamby and said, "Ayers Hamby, it looks like we've got you on car theft, assaulting a law enforcement officer, and resisting arrest. It's a pretty hefty list. I hope you enjoy your jail cell while we decide how much of it we're going to charge you for."

He turned to Officer Banks and said, "Take this man into custody."

Officer Banks obediently led Hamby out of the room. Johnson gave Sheriff Dawes a sharp look that clearly communicated he wanted to be with Riley alone again. The sheriff left the room and shut the door behind him.

Riley didn't know what was going to happen next, but she knew it was going to be unpleasant. She hoped that Dawes wasn't watching behind the one-way glass.

"Sit," Johnson said to Riley.

Riley obediently sat down at the table where Hamby had been sitting just moments before.

Johnson began to pace back and forth. Through gritted teeth, he said, "Congratulations, Agent Sweeney. You just caught a car thief."

He leaned across the table toward her and added, "Unless you still think he's a serial killer."

"No, sir," Riley murmured.

She realized it was the first time she'd called Johnson "sir." She hated the sound of it. But under the circumstances, she didn't feel like she had much choice.

Johnson said, "Now suppose you tell me just how you came up with this crazy idea."

Riley haltingly told him what she had done since she'd walked out on that meeting earlier. She explained how she'd found out that Quincy Harris had been arrested by the slain policeman, and was then extradited to Nebraska where he was eventually executed. She told him how she'd found out his son was living in Kedgwick. Finally she explained her theory that Hamby was taking revenge on people he blamed for his father's death.

Johnson was aghast.

"And that was it?" he said. "On the basis of that, you grabbed a vehicle and drove over to Kedgwick and arrested some dork all by yourself?"

Riley hung her head.

It seemed to make sense at the time, she wanted to say.

Johnson demanded, "Did you happen to find any connection between Hamby and Julian Banfield?"

"No," Riley said.

"Did you even try?"

"I didn't feel like I had time for that, sir," Riley said.

Johnson jabbed his finger in her face.

"You should have *made* time. You should have come to me with your idea."

"But you would have told me..."

Johnson interrupted, "I'd have told you it was a stupid idea. And I'd have been right.

More than anything else you should *never* have left this station without telling me exactly what you were up to."

Johnson stood for a moment panting with anger.

He shook his head and said, "I sure as hell don't know what to do with you right now. All I know is, we can't work together as partners. I can't have you running amok like this every time my back is turned."

He thought for a moment, then said, "I want you to stay put right here."

Riley said, "But what do you want me to do?"

"I don't want you to do *anything*! That's exactly the idea. I've got work to do, and I don't need you to distract me."

He stormed out of the room.

Riley sat there, feeling limp with shock and humiliation.

How long is he going to leave me in here? she wondered.

She hoped it wasn't going to be until Johnson solved the case. That could be a long time—especially considering his meticulous methods.

But she didn't dare take off on her own again.

She had no choice but to stay put.

If only Crivaro was here, she thought miserably.

Chapter Sixteen

N ow that he had a few spare moments, Sparky looked around Mrs. Pugh's basement with almost childlike curiosity. Everything seemed to be exactly the same as when he'd last been here—the same boxed items on the same wooden shelves, the same gas furnace, the same lawnmower. From his glimpses of the rest of the house, the same seemed to be true everywhere. Even the swing set in the well-kept back yard hadn't changed.

It was as if life had passed Mrs. Pugh by—and now here she was, living all alone.

Sad, he thought.

Perhaps if he hadn't been taken away so quickly, he might have brought some excitement into her life. Perhaps things would have turned out differently for both of them.

He remembered what she used to say about him when he got rambunctious.

"Full of beans."

He'd never bored her, at least.

He'd liked her, and she'd always seemed to like him.

It was sad to consider what might have been.

But it had been her fault—her fault among other people's—that things had turned out the way they had. If he had stayed, perhaps some of the things he'd learned would have brightened up this place. For a moment Sparky pictured a small collection of fine wines in a neat cupboard over by one wall.

Or ...

His mind wandered through all the interests he had cultivated in secret over the years. Maybe this would have become an art studio or a little reading room with nice books in glass-door cases and comfortable furniture and good light to read by…

His thoughts were interrupted when his eyes fell on one familiar sight—a pegboard with garden tools hanging from it. The tools were neat and well organized, but there were telltale bits of soil on some of the diggers and trowels and such. Earlier, when he'd been outdoors stalking about, he'd thought the small beds of flowers and vegetables looked to be still in use, although it was hard to tell for sure this early in spring.

But the condition of the tools confirmed that Mrs. Pugh was still using them.

He murmured aloud, "At least you're still gardening. Good for you."

But she didn't seem to hear him. Her head was still hanging forward, her chin resting on her chest, and her eyes were closed. It worried him a little. She was taking an unusually long time recovering from the chloroform, maybe because she was older and frailer than his other two victims.

What if she never snaps out of it?

Everything was ready. She was strapped into the chair with her bare feet in a pan of water, and the hefty length of cable attached to the breaker box was right at hand. If she'd slipped into some sort of ongoing coma, he couldn't do what he meant to do.

He tapped her on the shoulder.

To his relief, she jerked slightly, then tilted her head up and opened her eyes.

Her eyes widened with alarm at the sight of his face.

Does she recognize me? he wondered.

She couldn't tell him whether she did or not, of course—not with the duct tape over her mouth. But he knew it wasn't a good idea to pull the tape off, at least not yet. If she started screaming in this close-knit neighborhood, someone was liable to hear.

As he looked into her eyes with a smile, he put on his rubber gloves.

"It's good to see you, Mrs. Pugh," he said. "I just observed that you still seem to be gardening."

Mrs. Pugh's brow knitted with confusion.

Then she nodded yes.

Sparky said, "I knew you wouldn't give that up. I remember how much pleasure it always gave you. Do you still share the flowers and vegetables that you grow with your neighbors?"

She just stared at him.

In a sharper voice, Sparky demanded, "Well, do you?"

Trembling all over now, she nodded yes.

His voice gentle again, Sparky said, "That's good. You always were such a kind soul. Do you recognize me?"

Her eyes bulged as she stared hard at him.

"I know it's been a long, long time," Sparky said. "But I thought you'd recognize me. You used to say you never, ever forgot a face, no matter how many years went by. Don't you recognize me?"

She stared hard for a moment.

Then she breathed in sharply and let out a groan of realization. Somehow, he felt sure he could ungag her now and she wouldn't scream. She winced with pain as she pulled the duct tape off her mouth. She stared at him again and murmured in a voice still foggy from the chloroform.

"Full of beans."

Sparky let out a melancholy chuckle.

"Yes, that's right," he said. "I knew you wouldn't forget."

Her eyes filled up with tears.

"I'm sorry," she whispered.

Sparky stroked her hair with his gloved right hand.

"That's all I need to hear," he said.

Then he lowered the cable into the water.

CHAPTER SEVENTEEN

Riley was pacing the interrogation room, feeling isolated and depressed. She wondered how long Agent Johnson was going to leave her alone in here.

For all she knew, she might be stuck here all night while Johnson kept working with his team. And what if, by some chance, Johnson managed to solve the case soon?

Would he maybe just fly back to Quantico without saying a word to her?

No, that would be ridiculous, she told herself.

Even so, she could be in here for a very long time.

She kept asking herself, *Couldn't I just leave?*

It wasn't as if she was being held prisoner. She could walk right out of here if she wanted to. She still had the keys to the impounded car she'd borrowed, so it was probably still parked in front of the police station where she'd left it. She could drive it to a motel and check in alone and at least get a good night's sleep, then come back here tomorrow morning and return the vehicle and see if she could get back into Johnson's good graces.

What harm would it do? she wondered.

She certainly wasn't doing any good where she was.

But she kept hearing Agent Johnson's words as he'd walked out the door.

"I want you to stay put right here."

It had been a simple, straightforward order from a senior partner. But was Johnson even her partner anymore? Was he through with her? For that matter, was her whole BAU career now over? If it was, did she really need to keep on taking anybody's orders? Maybe not, but what else was she going to do? She'd already learned the hard way not to try to solve the case on her own.

Riley interrupted her internal tirade with a long sigh.

"Maybe this is where I belong," she whispered aloud.

It seemed ironic and almost appropriate that she would find herself stranded in an interrogation room—the same room where she had just questioned a man who had turned out to be obviously innocent.

On impulse, she sat down in the chair where Ayers Hamby had been seated. Looking around the small, rather dingy space, she wondered briefly if anyone was watching her from behind that mirrored wall, waiting to hear what excuses she would give for her behavior. Of course she knew that they all had better things to do than to watch her sitting there alone, doing nothing, just as Johnson had commanded. Even so, it felt as if an eager interrogator sat there in the empty chair across the table from her.

Time for a few hard questions, she thought.

Riley asked herself, *Do you think you deserve this?*

She couldn't help thinking maybe she did. If Agent Johnson didn't understand her work methods, she should have tried to explain herself this morning, back when they'd been on the plane flying out to Utah and before they'd gotten at odds with each other. By the time she'd tried to make him understand, he was already beyond frustrated with her. He hadn't been in the mood to listen.

And was that his fault, really?

He wasn't the first law enforcement officer to be mystified by the methods she'd learned from Jake Crivaro. Everywhere she and Crivaro had traveled together to work on cases, the local cops had been puzzled by the trance-like reveries she slipped into at crime scenes, and also by the hunches and theories that came from those reveries. It was small wonder that Johnson was puzzled as well.

And yet—what other abilities did she have to draw on?

Could she even learn the kind of analytical skills that Agent Johnson regarded as so important—as the way of the future, even?

She'd had considerable training in investigative techniques at the Academy, but that kind of analysis had never been her strong suit. On real cases, she'd had much more success following her gut feelings. And now she had to face the possibility that gut feelings weren't enough to continue in this kind of work. The only person who'd ever encouraged that skill was Jake Crivaro, and she desperately wished she could talk with him right now.

She took out her cell phone, thinking she could call him, explain what was going on, get his advice about what to do now. Of course it was a couple of hours later back in Virginia, but Riley suspected that Crivaro might still be up. He might even be glad to hear from her.

But then her throat tightened with sadness. Could she really bring herself to tell Jake, of all people, how badly she had failed today? How would it make him feel?

She sat there remembering how Jake had come to her college graduation and recruited her directly into the FBI Honors Internship Program. He'd told her right then and there that she'd make a fine BAU agent.

She remembered the expectations Jake had for her back then.

"I'm eligible for retirement," he'd told her, *"but I might stay on for a while to help someone like you get started."*

Jake had done just that. He'd kept working until he'd felt like he couldn't do the job anymore—and until he thought he'd outlasted his usefulness as Riley's mentor.

"I'm holding you back," he'd said this morning. *"You're depending too much on me. You've got to learn to trust yourself."*

He'd harbored such hopes for Riley, and he'd believed in her more than anyone else ever had in her entire life. He'd even hoped she could carry on his work for him when he retired. But now Riley wondered if maybe he'd been wrong. Had Jake seen too much of himself in her, tricked himself into believing she had more potential than she really had?

She hated the thought of letting him down.

But maybe she simply couldn't help it.

Maybe I'm just not good enough.

She only knew for sure that she couldn't call Jake right now. In fact, maybe she'd never be able to talk to him or look him in the face ever again.

Riley fingered her cell phone restlessly. She still felt the need to talk with someone. If she couldn't call Jake, she knew one other person she might be able to talk to.

And that was Ryan.

She remembered how kind and understanding he'd been last night when they'd talked together about her disappointment with the Mullins case and her concerns about Jake. And when she'd called Ryan this morning to tell him she was going away on another case, he'd actually sounded pleased for her.

But unlike Jake, Ryan probably wouldn't be disappointed to hear that she'd flamed out on this case. In fact, he might be greatly relieved. They'd been through some rough times, and things had been better between them for a few weeks now partly *because* she hadn't been doing any fieldwork.

She sat staring hard at her cell phone, trying to decide what to do.

It was late, of course. But Ryan might still be up working on a law case.

She breathed deeply for a few moments, trying to settle her nerves.

Maybe it would do me good, she thought.

Maybe she herself would feel relieved to tell Ryan—to tell *anybody*—that her time as a field agent was almost certainly over, and that she could get on with whatever else she found to do with her life.

I'll do it, Riley thought. *I'll make the call.*

But before she could punch in the number, the interrogation room door opened

Agent Johnson was standing there. He just stared at her for a moment, as if in a slight state of shock.

What's the matter with him? she wondered.

Then she realized what had happened.

"There's been another murder," she said.

Agent Johnson nodded.

"Right here in Prinneville," he said. "A woman this time. It happened just a little while ago."

"Are we sure it's the same killer?" Riley asked.

"It was another electrocution," Johnson said, still standing as if frozen there in the doorway.

Riley realized what was restraining him. He had gotten too confident about his methods, too sure that his data-driven approach would lead to the killer's capture before he had the chance to murder anyone else.

But Johnson had been wrong.

And he's not used to being wrong.

In fact, she thought, this might be the first time in his budding career that he'd felt truly out of his depth.

Finally he said, "Sheriff Dawes and Chief Berry and I are going to head over to the crime scene right now."

"Do you want me to come with you?" Riley asked.

Johnson hesitated. Swallowing his pride obviously wasn't easy for him. But Riley knew that one of them had to make a decision as quickly as possible.

"Look, you need my help," she said. "I promise not to go AWOL on you again. I'll do as I'm told."

"Good," Johnson said. "Let's go."

Chapter Eighteen

A s she followed her partner and the local lawmen out the door, Riley was thinking about what she'd just promised Johnson.

"I'll do as I'm told."

She intended to keep that promise ... if she could.

She realized that, like her, he was intent on using the skills that he knew best. That's what had worked for both of them in the past. But what if she got worried that Johnson's methods were putting more lives at stake? What if his plodding techniques seemed to be missing the most important clues?

Riley hoped they wouldn't butt heads again, but she couldn't help feeling that the case mattered much more than getting along with a partner.

Outside the station, she was glad to see that the clunker car she had borrowed was still parked where she had left it. Fingering the keys in her pocket, she wondered if she might need that little hatchback again soon.

For now, she climbed into Dawes's vehicle along with her three colleagues. As they pulled away from the station, Chief Berry told them all about the phone call he'd just gotten from a hysterical woman who'd found her neighbor dead in her basement. Electrocuted, the caller had told him between her gasps and sobs.

"The victim's name was Stacey Pugh," Berry added. "That's all I know just yet. I called some of my people out on patrol, told them to get straight over to the crime scene. They'll be there ahead of us."

"We'll find out more shortly," Johnson said, sounding as though he was recovering from his momentary lapse in self-confidence.

They soon reached a sleepy-looking working-class neighborhood, where the flashing lights of police vehicles came into view. A couple of patrol cars were parked in the driveway of a modest, ranch-style house. As Berry parked his vehicle, Riley could see that the small police team was already efficiently at work, warding curious and gawking neighbors away and putting up police tape to isolate the area. The streetlights shed some illumination on the outdoor scene, but there didn't seem to be any lights on inside the house.

"The house is still dark," Berry commented. "The woman who called said she came over because she saw her neighbor's lights go out."

As they got out of the car, Riley and her colleagues readied their flashlights. They walked past two figures sitting on the front steps, a female cop and a distraught-looking woman in curlers, slippers, and a bathrobe.

Riley guessed that the woman was the hysterical neighbor who had called Chief Berry about Stacey Pugh's death. The night was getting chilly and the woman was obviously still in shock, but the female cop seemed to be taking good care of her. Shivering deeply, she had a blanket wrapped around her shoulders, which Riley guessed that the policewoman had considerately obtained for her.

Berry stopped and crouched in front of the cop, whose nameplate identified her as Officer Tori Hayworth.

He said quietly, "Is this the woman who called?"

Officer Hayworth nodded and said, "I don't think she's ready to talk to anybody yet."

In fact, the woman's eyes looked glazed and her teeth were chattering. She seemed to be barely conscious of where she was or what was going on. Glad that there was a kindly female officer helping out, Riley paused to introduce herself to Officer Hayworth.

Then she turned on her flashlight and followed Berry, Dawes, and Johnson on into the house. The four flashlight beams darted about, giving an eerie impression of the living room. It appeared to be a cozy little place, comfortable but not ostentatious, rather like Andy Gish's home but not at all like the Banfields' place in Beardsley. Still, Riley knew that all three victims must be connected in some way.

If only I can figure out what it is, she thought.

As she flashed her light around the room, it fell upon a portrait of a smiling man wearing some sort of uniform. There were also a lot of framed pictures of children arranged on tables and the fireplace mantel.

Her kids? Riley wondered. *Her grandkids?*

She looked more closely at one group photo. The children seemed close together in age and quite varied in appearance.

Probably not blood relatives, she thought, her curiosity aroused.

Dawes, Berry, and Johnson were moving on through the house, so Riley hurried to catch up with them. She followed them down the basement stairs.

A pungent smell greeted them on their way down.

Roasted flesh? Riley wondered, remembering what Ayers Hamby had said about execution by electric chair. But that couldn't be it. From what little she'd learned about electricity so far today, the power from a household circuit passing through a human body via water might not leave any physical traces at all.

As if in reply to Riley's curiosity, Agent Johnson said, "I smell burnt-out electrical wiring. I guess this time the flow of electricity was enough to blow out the whole circuit board in this old house."

As they reached the bottom of the steps, their flashlight beams bobbed eerily on the victim—a woman dressed in slippers and a housecoat, strapped to a kitchen chair.

Riley felt unsettled for a moment.

She'd visited the two other crime scenes today, but the victims had been removed from both places. Especially in the jittery light, the woman was a disturbing sight even for Riley.

The woman had short gray hair and her head was hanging forward as if she had fallen asleep. But she was obviously dead. Like Andy Gish, her bare feet had been placed in a shallow baking pan that had water in it.

Riley couldn't help studying Agent Johnson's reaction to this grim spectacle. She wondered, had he ever actually seen a murdered person's body fresh at a crime scene? For all she knew, he'd solved that child murderer-rapist case back in Boston without having to look a corpse.

But he didn't seem to be shaken as he peered closely at the body in the beam of his flashlight.

He said to Chief Berry, "Have you called the county coroner?"

"Yeah, he should be getting here soon," Berry said.

"Good," Johnson said. "Meanwhile, let's be careful not to disturb the body."

He tilted his head down so he could see the woman's face.

"Her mouth is open," he said. "But I can see that it was taped shut. There are telltale marks on her cheeks."

Sheriff Dawes said, "I think I found the tape."

Dawes stooped down and picked up a piece of duct tape off the floor.

"Put it in evidence," Johnson said. "He's been using quite a bit of that kind of tape. Maybe we can trace down where he's buying it."

As Dawes dutifully put the tape in a paper bag, Riley's imagination lurched into gear.

She imagined the terrified woman, who appeared to be in her late sixties or seventies, staring mutely, perhaps not even struggling against the tape over her mouth.

Riley imagined the killer facing her.

What did he say to her?

As she had at the Banfield crime scene, she sensed that there had been some sort of interaction between the killer and the victim before she was electrocuted.

For a while, she'd been gagged. But then he'd pulled the tape off her mouth.

But why?

Hadn't he been worried that she'd scream?

For some reason, that possibility hadn't mattered to him.

A chill settled over her as it dawned on her...

She didn't scream.

Instead she said something to him.

Riley had a weird feeling that she hadn't begged for mercy. Instead, there had been some kind of personal connection during that moment before he'd closed the electrical current that had killed her.

She knew him, Riley thought.

But maybe only at the very last second.

Before she could muse any further, Agent Johnson spoke up again.

"Look here," he said.

With a gloved hand, he reached down to pick up the hefty length of electric cable lying beside the pan of water. Riley almost blurted out a warning not to touch it when she remembered that all the electricity in the house was dead.

Peering closely at the object, Agent Johnson said, "This is the same gauge of cable that was used at the other crime scene. We need to analyze it along with the duct tape, try to find out where it came from."

It didn't sound like a bad idea to Riley. She was also relieved that Johnson seemed to have fully regained his self-assurance. But once again, she felt as though her partner was overlooking the human dimension of what had happened here.

She wondered—should she risk asking him for a quiet moment right here and now to try to get a sense of the killer?

No, of course not.

She'd find herself at odds with him again. Worse, her unusual behavior would puzzle both Chief Berry and Sheriff Dawes. And this time there wouldn't be any way to patch things up. She'd only make things a whole lot worse.

Meanwhile, Chief Berry spoke up from a crouched position on the floor.

"Hey, I've got what looks like another partial boot print here."

Dawes and Johnson clustered close to him for a look.

Taking out his tape measure, Johnson said, "It looks identical to the one at the crime scene in Beardsley—except this print's more complete. We'll fax photos of this to the tech guys in Quantico. They should be able to nail down the shoe size once and for all."

Riley stifled a growl of impatience. Johnson had been excited all day about that partial boot print in Beardsley. Was he still waiting for technicians in Quantico to determine the exact size of the boot, so he could try to track down where it was bought?

She wondered—had he had any better luck finding out about missing chloroform at the paint factory? Since Riley felt pretty sure that the chloroform had been homemade, she doubted it.

While it was true that her arrest of Ayers Hamby had been a thoroughgoing bust, she wondered—was Agent Johnson making even less progress with his team?

He's moving too slowly, she thought.

And the killer's moving a lot faster.

But what on earth could she do about it without making pointless trouble? All Riley knew for sure was that she wasn't doing anything useful here in the basement. She needed to get out of here.

She walked up behind Johnson and spoke to him quietly.

"Excuse me, Agent Johnson—but would it be OK for me to go upstairs for a look around?"

Seeming barely to notice Riley's voice as he snapped pictures of the boot print, Johnson mumbled, "Sure, go right ahead."

Riley turned away and followed her flashlight beam back up the basement stairs. She made her way through the kitchen. Through the window over the sink, she could see a well-kept back yard with a swing set silhouetted against the moonlight. She turned and saw that the kitchen was unusually big and well-equipped for a house this size, as if meals had been made here for a lot of people over the years.

As she continued into the dining room, she noted the size of the dinner table. It was large, and a good many chairs were lined up next to the walls. Perhaps Stacey Pugh had raised an unusually large family. But Riley somehow suspected something different.

Making her way into the living room, she stopped to get a better look at the pictures of children on the tables and fireplace mantel. Now she could see that some of children were actually of different races. Also, many of the pictures seemed to have been taken in the same backyard, with some of the kids playing on the swing set she'd just seen through the kitchen window.

She also took another look at the larger picture of the smiling, uniformed man hanging on the wall. The man seemed fairly young, perhaps about thirty. If the picture was of Stacey Pugh's deceased husband, maybe he'd died quite a few years ago.

Riley walked down the hallway and shined her light into a bedroom. It was a cozy little space with two sets of bunk beds. Everything was tidy and the beds were neatly made—too neatly, Riley thought, to have been recently used. She peeked into a second bedroom and saw an almost identical arrangement of bedroom furniture.

Now things started to make more sense. Stacey Pugh must have kept a foster home here, although it didn't look as though kids had lived here recently.

Riley headed back through the living room toward the front door, which stood slightly open. She shined her flashlight on the latch. She saw no sign of a break-in.

She thought back to how the killer had gotten into the other two houses. While he might have hacked into the security system of Julian Banfield's home, there had been no sign of break-in at Andy Gish's residence. Apparently Gish had either let the man in or had neglected to lock the door.

What about here? Riley wondered.

Gish's murder had taken place in broad daylight, when the murdered man might unwarily let a stranger come into his house. But the killer had arrived here at night, when Stacey Pugh was in her housecoat and slippers.

Riley looked through the door's small window. If the killer had come up onto the porch and simply knocked, Stacey Pugh could have seen his face.

Maybe he wasn't a total stranger.

Maybe there was something about that face, that personality, that Stacey trusted—perhaps something familiar.

For an instant, Riley started to get a feeling of the killer. She imagined him standing on the porch, charming and coaxing Stacey to let him inside.

And then? she wondered.

Her thoughts were jolted as a face appeared in the door window.

A voice said, "Excuse me, Agent Sweeney..."

Riley's flashlight showed the face of Officer Tori Hayworth, who had been sitting on the front porch with the neighbor woman when Riley had arrived. She opened the door the rest of the way and saw that the woman was still sitting there, huddled under a blanket.

Standing outside the door, Officer Hayworth said, "It's kind of chilly out here. Would it be OK for me to either bring her inside or take her home? She lives right across the street."

Riley appreciated Hayworth asking for permission. She saw that the lights were on in the little house that Hayworth was indicating.

"Let's go over there," Riley decided. She told one of the cops in the yard to let her colleagues know where they were and followed the two women to the neighbor's house.

Hayworth guided the neighbor inside and helped her onto the living room couch. Then she asked, "Is there anything I can do to make you comfortable, Mrs. Merrill?"

The woman seemed to be recovering from her deep state of shock.

"Why, yes," she said. "There's some chamomile tea in my kitchen cupboard. There's a teapot on the stove. A cup of tea would make me feel better."

Officer Hayworth went into the kitchen. Riley sat down in a chair facing the woman and reintroduced herself.

"I'm Astrid Merrill," the woman replied. "And I'm the one who found..."

Her voice trailed off.

"Could you tell me how you found your friend?" Riley said.

Astrid nodded and thought for a moment.

"I live alone like she does—did. My husband died five years ago. I was sitting in my living room watching TV, when suddenly the power went out. The lights came back on, but very dim and flickering. I went to the window, and it looked the same in a lot of windows up and down the street. While I was standing there, the power came fully on again all over the neighborhood, except..."

She inhaled sharply.

"Except right there in Stacey's house. That worried me, because I knew Stacey was probably still up, and I didn't like the idea of her being stuck in the dark alone. I got a flashlight and walked on over to see if I could help. When I got up onto the porch, I found that the door was partly open. I went on inside and called for Stacey. She didn't answer, and I got more worried."

She squinted thoughtfully, then said, "I thought maybe she'd gone down to the basement to check her breaker box. She's gotten pretty frail during the last few years, and I was afraid she'd fallen in the dark. So I made my way down the basement stairs and..."

Her eyes widened with alarm at the sound of the teapot whistling in the kitchen. For a moment Riley was afraid she might slip back into a state of shock.

I need to keep her talking, she thought.

As Officer Hayworth brought a cup of tea for Astrid, Riley spoke to her in a gentle voice.

"Astrid, how long did Stacey raise foster kids?"

Astrid looked slightly surprised by the question.

"Why, for a good many years," she said. "She started doing it quite a long time ago, after her husband, Otto, died. He was a fireman. He died while saving a whole family in a burning house. He really was a hero. He and Stacey had only been married for six or seven years, and they'd never had kids. Stacey had taught elementary school, but her heart wasn't in it anymore after he died. So... she started to bring unwanted or orphaned kids into her home."

Astrid shrugged slightly.

"Well, her friends weren't sure that was a good idea at first. It seemed like a lot of effort for a woman all by herself. And of course the financial support was never really enough. But having kids around made a huge difference for her. She stopped grieving, was in good spirits just about all the time. So she kept on raising kids for... oh, years and years. There was a constant stream of them coming and going. She spoiled them, but that was OK. So did all of us who lived around here. Those kids brought us a lot of joy."

Astrid sipped her tea with a sigh.

"A few years ago, Stacey's health started slipping, and she got frailer, and the kids got to be too much for her. So she stopped keeping them. I asked her once if that made her sad. She said no, because her house was full of wonderful memories. And she still felt Otto smiling down on her."

Astrid shuddered.

"I don't understand how this could happen," she said. "Who could want to do this to Stacey? I don't believe she ever said an unkind word to anyone, or about anyone. Everybody loved her. They loved what she was doing for children. Whoever did this..."

Astrid shook her head.

"Whoever did this made a mistake. They couldn't have meant to kill Stacey. They must have meant to kill someone else. They must have gotten... I don't know, the wrong address or something. Whoever did this couldn't possibly have known her."

Riley felt a chill at those words.

You're wrong, Astrid, she thought. *Whoever killed her most certainly knew her.*

More than that, Riley sensed that whoever killed her may well have cared about her as much as Astrid or any of the people who lived in this neighborhood did. It didn't make sense yet, but Riley knew one thing for sure.

I've got to find some connection among the three victims.

And she had to do it before there was a fourth.

CHAPTER NINETEEN

R iley couldn't stop pacing her motel room.
I need to get some sleep, she told herself.

But she'd already tried to lie down and get to sleep. It had been a disaster.

Whenever she closed her eyes, she kept seeing Stacey Pugh's dead body, strapped into that deadly chair, weirdly lit by jittery flashlights.

Worse, she kept hearing Astrid Merrill's words.

"Who could want to do this to Stacey?"

No one at the crime scene had suggested any answer to that question. Nor had anyone offered any clue after the coroner had taken Stacey Pugh's body away and Agent Johnson regrouped his team at the police station.

When the investigators had gotten together in the conference room, Johnson hadn't appeared discouraged anymore. His determination to stop the killer seemed to be heightened now that there was a new victim, and he appeared to be energized and full of new ideas. But the discussion had driven Riley crazy. She'd tried to speak up a couple of times, once to suggest that the fact that Stacey Pugh had run a foster home might be significant. But nobody had listened. She felt as though she'd become invisible as the three men did all the talking.

Johnson was more fixated than ever on the boot print, and he was also obsessing about the electrical cable and the duct tape. And he hadn't given up on tracing the origin of the chloroform, either.

But the neighbor's words were already running through Riley's mind.

"Who could want to do this to Stacey?"

More than once she'd wanted to pipe in and say something like, *"This case isn't about data. It's about people."*

She had to stop herself from breaking into the conversation, because she didn't have any answer to that awful question either.

"Who could want to do this to Stacey?"

Besides, Johnson was sure he'd found some other pertinent data in the basement. He thought they were making good progress in their investigation. And for all she knew, Johnson was absolutely right.

Riley wondered, how could she know one way or another? She and Johnson were on such separate wavelengths, they couldn't seem to comprehend each other.

But no good would have come from complaining about it, especially when Riley didn't have any well-formed theories of her own. Dawes and Berry certainly seemed to be fully on board with Johnson's methods, and it looked like the three of them were ready to pull an all-nighter if need be, right there at the station.

So for what felt like hours, she had just watched and listened in silence. To her relief, Johnson finally noted that she looked tired, and that maybe she should find a place to turn in for the night.

Maybe a little bit of that was thoughtfulness, she realized. *But mostly, he just didn't feel like he needed me.*

And as far as she was concerned, he was right. As long as Johnson was determined to conduct a completely data-driven investigation, ignoring any human aspects of these murders, Riley could be of no use to him.

She had left the station in the clunker of a car she'd borrowed earlier and driven around town until she found a motel. She'd checked in, taken a shower and put on her pajamas, and gotten into the perfectly comfortable bed.

But she hadn't been able to escape the question.

"Who could want to do this to Stacey?"

She'd realized there was no point in trying to sleep.

What she needed to do was think.

She kept the room lights on and played pop music on the clock radio, pacing the narrow space between the bed and the standard motel furniture, trying to force the image and the voice from her mind.

It wasn't working.

Tired of pacing, she plopped herself down in the big armchair beside the bed. She put her feet up on the little ottoman.

Again, she felt desperate to hear a friendly voice—not only friendly, but helpful and guiding. True, it was late, especially in the east, but surely there was somebody in the world she could call.

Ryan? she wondered again.

No, if he wasn't asleep by now, he ought to be, and he had his own work to worry about. Besides, how could he possibly understand what she was going through right now? Calling him would only make him worry about her for no good reason.

Jake Crivaro? she thought.

When she'd thought about calling him earlier this evening, she'd decided against it, ashamed of having to admit her failure.

But would that even be what she was doing?

Was there anything wrong with still wanting help from the man who had recruited her into this kind of work in the first place?

What else are mentors for?

He was a light sleeper, and he might still be up, and he might even be eager to hear from her.

She switched off the radio and reached for her cell phone on the nightstand and punched in Jake's number.

Soon she heard a familiar voice growling with mock annoyance.

"Hello, I don't know who the hell you are or how you got this number, but this is ex–Special Agent Jake Crivaro of the BAU, and I'm retired, damn it. When you hear the tone, leave a message for me, and make it worth my while. If it's not important, I don't want to hear it."

Riley couldn't help but smile at the gruff playfulness of the outgoing message.

Then came the beep, and Riley haltingly started to speak.

"Hey, Agent Crivaro … I mean Jake. I'm still trying to get used to calling you that. It might be easier if you were still around …"

Her voice faded as she wondered what to say next.

Where could she even begin talking about all that had gone wrong today?

It might be easier if he'd simply answered the phone.

She stammered, "I—well, I just thought I'd check in, see how retirement is treating you after—what? Twelve hours or so? Also, I..."

She fell silent for a moment.

"I'd just like to talk...about *things.* Call me back whenever you get a chance."

She ended the message and set the phone back down.

To her surprise, her whole body seemed to melt.

She closed her eyes and waited...

This time she didn't see the corpse in the basement.

At last, she thought with a sigh of relief.

Maybe she could clear her mind and really think about the case.

Riley was shining a flashlight into the darkness, walking down a long flight of creaky wooden stairs.

She couldn't see anything else around her.

Where am I? *she wondered.* Where am I going?

Her flashlight beam didn't seem strong enough to overpower the sheer depth of the darkness. There were only those stairs, which seemed to go down and down and down...

At last she reached a hard floor.

Concrete, *she thought. Is this someone's basement?*

Like the stairs, the floor seemed to go on forever. She could see nothing else in the thick darkness.

She followed the beam of the flashlight until something finally came into view.

It was a human figure sitting in a chair—a man this time—bound hand and foot with duct tape, his head hanging on his chest, his bare feet in a pan of water.

Another murder! *Riley thought with horror.*

But to her relief, the man groaned aloud.

He's still alive!

She rushed over to the man and shined her flashlight on him.

"I'm going to get you out of here," she told him.

The man still kept groaning and rolling his head back and forth as if he were struggling to regain consciousness.

"Did you hear me?" she said. "You're going to be OK."

She reached under the man's chin and lifted up his face.

Even with a strip of duct tape over his mouth, she recognized him immediately.

She could never forget that babyish face with the glint of evil in his eyes.

It was Larry Mullins!

She ripped the duct tape from his lips, enjoying his momentary grimace of pain.

But the pain seemed to last only for a second.

Then he was smiling at her, as if silently asking a question ...

"What are you going to do now?"

Riley had no idea what to do.

But the weight of the flashlight and its metal surface suddenly felt strange in her right hand.

She took a step back and looked at her hands and saw that she was wearing rubber gloves.

And in her left hand, she was holding a length of power cord. She knew what that cord was. She knew how it was connected and what it could do.

Just then Larry Mullins sneered at her and spoke aloud.

"Good luck."

She let the wire fall into the pan of water and watched as Mullins began to writhe ...

Riley was awakened by the sound of her phone ringing. She moved to answer it and groaned at the stiffness in her body. She'd slept in this chair the whole night. The dream was still vivid in her mind, and she felt as though she knew something she hadn't fully understood before. But she couldn't quite get what it was.

Why had she dreamed of Mullins? Of personally executing him?

The phone kept on ringing.

As she picked it up, an answer flickered through her mind.

Justice, she thought.

It's about justice.

She accepted the call and heard Agent Johnson's voice, sounding surprisingly eager and friendly.

"Did you get some sleep, Agent Sweeney? Do you feel rested?"

"Yes," Riley murmured foggily.

"Good," Johnson said. "Because I need you to get over here to the station. We've got work to do."

"Do you have a lead?" Riley asked.

"Better yet. I have an arrest warrant."

Chapter Twenty

When Riley parked her beat-up borrowed hatchback in front of the police station, she soon realized that quite a lot must have happened here overnight. Officer Tori Hayworth, who had taken such good care of the witness last night, came trotting toward the car to greet her.

"Come on inside!" Hayworth called out. "We think we've got him!"

We? Riley wondered, as she got out and followed Hayworth into the station.

Since when had Officer Hayworth become part of the investigative team?

And who did she mean by "him"?

Hayworth led Riley straight to the conference room, where three people with tired faces and bloodshot eyes had obviously pulled an all-nighter. Agent Johnson, Chief Berry, and Sheriff Dawes all looked tired but alert. Forrest Banks, the officer who had lent Riley the car yesterday, was there too, looking fresher than the others.

On seeing Riley, Johnson pointed to a spot on a map that was spread out on the table.

"We've found him, Agent Sweeney," he said excitedly. "We know exactly who and where he is. Now it's just a matter of picking him up. As soon as we fill you in, we're headed right out to do that."

Everyone else in the room appeared to share his confidence.

"Tell me what's going on," she said.

Johnson nodded and said, "We've been on the phone with the tech guys in Quantico off and on all night. They found out everything there was to know about those boot prints, including the size and brand of the boot. Then they did a credit card search of purchases in the area of that brand and that size. They found exactly what they were looking for, a purchase made less than two weeks ago. The store is just a couple of blocks away from here."

Riley's attention quickened, and she couldn't help being impressed. Even though the technicians at Quantico were known for their ever-increasing digital investigative wizardry, these results had come faster than she'd expected—and overnight as well.

Chief Berry said, "The name of the guy who bought the boots is Jared Graves."

Both Banks and Hayworth let out growls of annoyance. The identity of the man was clearly of interest to the two uniformed cops.

Banks said to Riley, "Graves is no stranger to us, believe me."

"Please explain," Riley said.

Officer Hayworth replied, "He's an abusive husband. He has been for years. And he's gotten a lot worse during the last few months."

Banks added, "Tori and I have responded to calls from his neighbors. Other cops have, too. It's always a report of screaming or sounds of violence coming from the Graves house. When we get there, it's always pretty obvious what's been going on. His wife, Sabrina, looks absolutely terrified, and so do his kids, and he's obviously been drinking, and his house looks like a tornado went through it."

"But we can't nail him for anything," Hayworth said.

Riley stifled a sigh. She knew from her training that cops had plenty of good reasons to hate domestic abuse cases worse than almost any other kind.

Riley said, "Don't tell me. Everybody in the family denies that he's done anything bad to them."

"You've got it," Officer Banks said. "Whenever Sabrina or the kids get injured or bruised, they always tell some story about being clumsy and falling or something like that. Child Services keeps trying to investigate what's going on with the kids, but they've never been able to prove anything."

"The whole family is scared to death of him," Officer Hayworth added. "And without their cooperation, we haven't been able to arrest him. But we've always figured we'd nail him sooner or later. Andy Gish hated Graves even more than the rest of us, and Graves knew it and hated him right back. And look what happened to Andy."

Motive? Riley wondered.

Riley sympathized with the local police, but she knew that her skepticism must be showing. She was still a long way from convinced that Graves was their killer.

"There's more," Agent Johnson added in a satisfied voice. "Jared Graves is also a utility lineman with the local power company."

Riley felt a sharp prickle of interest.

"An electrician," she said.

Sheriff Berry nodded and said, "Yeah, but he's not popular with his co-workers. He's known to have a short temper, which can be pretty dangerous when you're doing that kind of work. He's constantly on the verge of getting fired, and he often works alone."

Agent Johnson pointed to the map with his pencil.

"But here's the clincher," he said. "The tech guys in Quantico even managed to track down Graves's work schedule. Graves did line work in the neighborhoods where both of the victims here in Prinneville lived and were killed. He worked on a line in Stacey Pugh's neighborhood three days before she was killed. He worked on Andy Gish's street on the morning he was killed."

It's all starting to add up, Riley thought, remembering Andy Gish's isolated home on the outskirts of Prinneville. A lineman working alone high up in a telephone pole could get an excellent view of that house.

"What about Banfield?" she asked.

"We haven't placed him up in Beardsley yet," Johnson replied. "But this is the kind of guy who might have the know-how to hack the Banfields' security system.'

She asked Johnson, "And you've already got a warrant for his arrest?"

"We sure do," Johnson said, holding up a piece of paper.

Sheriff Dawes said, "I've got a good relationship with Judge McBride, so he didn't mind when I woke him up early this morning with a phone call. He was impressed by the evidence, and he's as anxious as anybody to catch this killer. He faxed a warrant right over."

Riley couldn't deny that the situation looked promising.

And yet ...

Doubt still lurked in the back of her mind.

Agent Johnson said to the whole group, "I hope everybody's ready. Because we're heading out right now to make this arrest."

There was a murmur of excitement from the group, and everybody got ready to leave. On the way out the conference room door, Johnson whispered to Riley.

"This is how it's done nowadays, Agent Sweeney."

Riley felt slightly stung by his superior tone. But maybe he had a right to feel that way. If their team really was about to apprehend the man responsible for the three murders, it would certainly vindicate Johnson's data-driven methods.

It would mean that he was right and she'd been wrong. But the truth was, she'd be happy to be proven wrong for ever doubting him. What mattered was putting this killer behind bars before he could murder anyone else.

As they continued on their way out of the station, Riley overheard Officers Hayworth and Banks speaking quietly to each other.

The female cop said, "Damn it, I wish Andy could be with us. I'd love to see him slap the cuffs on this bastard."

The man replied, "Don't worry, he'll be with us in spirit. And he'll be proud of us."

"I hope so," Hayworth said.

Those words echoed through Riley's mind as she and Johnson got into Sheriff Dawes's vehicle.

This is personal for them, she realized.

And she wasn't at all sure that was a good thing.

The neighborhood where Jared Graves lived wasn't far away from where Stacey Pugh had lived, but the houses here were somewhat smaller and the neighborhood wasn't quite as well groomed. Sheriff Dawes, driving the car with Riley and Agent Johnson inside, parked front of Graves's house, and the other vehicles pulled up behind him.

As they got out of the car, Riley saw that the house was a shabby little bungalow. Two very small children, one a toddler in diapers, were standing in the yard, staring open-mouthed at the arriving vehicles. Judging from the quantity and variety of toys that cluttered the small yard, Riley was sure that these weren't the only children who lived here. She realized that the others might be older and at school already.

Too many children for such a small house, she thought.

As the local cops got out of their vehicles and moved quickly toward the house, they looked more than ready for action. Riley hung back, figuring she could let them make the arrest. Apparently deciding the same thing, Agent Johnson remained standing beside her.

As they watched, a tall, rugged man with uncombed hair stepped out the front door. He looked like he'd just been getting dressed for work when he'd heard the vehicles arriving. He also looked more than a little hung over.

"What the hell?" he shouted at the cops who were converging on him.

Getting his cuffs ready, Chief Berry called out to him, "Jared Graves, you're under arrest on three counts of murder."

"Murder?" Graves snapped back. "What is this, some kind of joke?"

"No joke," Berry said, walking right up to him. "If you thought you were going to get away with it, you were wrong."

"Get away with what?" Graves yelled. "I swear, you cops are harassing me for the last time."

As Berry reached out for his shoulder to turn him around, Graves clenched his fist and took a swing at the chief. Almost as if he had expected this, Berry deftly dodged the blow. In a flash, Officer Banks lunged forward and landed a punch to the suspect's stomach.

Graves groaned and buckled over.

Riley felt a surge of alarm.

This is getting out of hand, she thought.

As she started toward the house to intervene, Banks pulled Graves's head up by the hair and drew his fist back.

She heard Johnson mutter, "Oh, shit."

Poised to slam the suspect in the face, Banks snarled, "This is for Andy Gish, you murderous bastard."

As Riley and Johnson both started forward to break it up, Officer Hayworth's voice interrupted the action.

"Forrest, don't!"

The female cop stepped between Banks and the suspect.

"He's not worth it!" Hayworth told Banks firmly. "He'll get what he deserves, we'll make sure of it. But this isn't the way."

Banks trembled with rage for a moment.

"It's what he wants you to do," Hayworth added.

Breathing heavily, Banks nodded and unclenched his fist. Chief Berry put the cuffs on Graves, read him his rights, and led him away from the house. The two small children still in the yard seemed to be frozen in place, gaping with horror.

Then a lean, tired-looking woman appeared in the doorway of the house. She was holding an infant.

As Graves was marched across the yard, he turned and yelled back to her, "This was your doing, Sabrina."

Sabrina shook her head and called to him, "No."

"Of course it was," Graves said. "You called the cops with lies about me."

Weeping, Sabrina said, "I promise! I didn't!"

"I warned you about this, you bitch!" Graves barked out, just as Chief Berry ducked his head down and Officer Banks shoved him into a police car.

Before Riley could join Agent Johnson and Sheriff Dawes at their vehicle, she heard Officer Hayworth call her.

"Agent Sweeney, wait!"

Riley turned and saw Officer Hayworth standing next to Graves's wife. The woman was weeping silently now and the female cop looked like she wanted some kind of help.

Riley turned and walked back toward the house.

Hayworth requested, "Show her your badge."

Riley did so, and Hayworth said to Sabrina, "This is Agent Sweeney from the BAU. That's an important branch of the FBI. She knows a lot more than I do. You should listen to her."

Riley felt a slight shiver as she realized why Hayworth had called her back. She could only hope she could help.

"But I don't understand," Sabrina blubbered. "Jared didn't kill anybody."

"He did," Hayworth said. "He killed three people. It's time you faced facts about your husband."

"I don't know what you mean," Sabrina said.

The baby was also crying now. Hayworth took Sabrina by the hand. Clearly visible on her wrist were three red, blister-like wounds.

"How did this happen?" Hayworth demanded.

Forcing a laugh, Sabrina said, "Oh, the usual thing. I got clumsy and burned myself on the stove."

Riley knew that the woman was lying and that it was her turn to speak.

"You did not burn yourself," Riley said. "Your husband did this to you."

Sabrina stared silently back at her.

At least she isn't denying it, Riley thought.

Officer Hayworth told Sabrina, "You and I have talked about this over and over again. You never listen to me. You've got to listen to Agent Sweeney."

Riley took a breath and gathered her wits.

She said, "Sabrina, you can't live like this. You don't deserve it."

Sabrina gave her a strange look.

She thinks she does *deserve it,* Riley thought.

It was clear that, like many women, Sabrina had felt unworthy of anybody's love or kindness for her whole life.

For an instant, Riley flashed back to how her own father had blamed her for her mother's shooting death in a botched robbery.

"You let her down," he'd often said.

"You let her die. You can't do anything right, girl."

Riley gulped hard at the memory of the heartless accusation.

It wasn't my fault, she told herself for the thousandth time.

I was only five when it happened.

Over time, Riley had managed to face the truth about her father's cruel, unjustified anger. She had realized that he hated himself more than he did her. And she'd learned not to blame herself for his pain and anger

But this woman hadn't learned that lesson. But both Sabrina and her children had already paid too much for her acceptance of her situation.

"I know how this gets started," Riley blurted out. "You've got to trust me, and you've got to believe me."

Sabrina looked up at her. She wasn't crying now but she didn't look convinced. Riley was sure that the whole ugly family situation would just play itself out again in another day or another week.

"Accepting what he does isn't fair to you," Riley told her. "But most of all it's not fair to your kids. You've got to do the right thing—for them. You've got to report what he's been doing to you so they don't wind up the same way."

Officer Hayworth added, "And you don't have to be afraid of him this time. We've finally been able to arrest him. He's going to be behind bars. He can't hurt you."

Riley could see a slight change in the woman's eyes and a little relaxation in the lines around her mouth.

"Hush, sweetie," Sabrina said to the baby, bouncing it slightly in her arms. "Just hush now. Everything's going to be all right."

The baby stopped whimpering.

Sabrina looked at Officer Hayworth.

"I'll do it," Sabrina said. "This time I'll file a report."

"Are you sure?" Hayworth asked.

The woman nodded silently.

"It's the right thing to do," Hayworth said. "You won't regret it."

"Good for you," Riley added.

Then she heard Agent Johnson call out.

"Agent Sweeney, we're leaving."

Riley turned and walked back to the car where the two men were waiting for her. As the car pulled away, she looked back at Sabrina Graves, who was still standing there with Hayworth, watching them go.

Will she really go through with it? Riley wondered.

But even more than that...

Have we got the right man?

CHAPTER TWENTY ONE

Inside the interrogation room, Agent Johnson was stalking the suspect, who was cuffed and sitting at the table. Watching through the two-way mirror, Riley recognized what her senior partner was doing. She had used the same tactic when she'd interviewed Ayers Hamby yesterday—moving silently around the suspect and maintaining eye contact with him, testing the possibility of psyching him out before asking any questions.

Did Johnson get that idea from me? she wondered.

No, probably not, she figured. She and Johnson shared much the same training, after all, and this was a well-worn approach. Still, she wondered—how often had Johnson even conducted an interrogation? Might he have solved that child murderer-rapist case in Baltimore without ever interviewing a suspect?

How new is he to all this?

Standing outside the interrogation room and flanked on either side by Sheriff Dawes and Chief Berry, Riley made no comment on the proceedings. But as Johnson prepared to question Jared Graves, she found herself wondering about the BAU agent rather than the suspect.

Why is he the one in charge here?

She had speculated before about her partner's position of authority. Jake Crivaro already had many years of service behind him when she first encountered him. When she became his partner, she really benefitted from his expertise.

More than that, she reminded herself.

She had probably only survived in the agency because of his support. Now she was suddenly partnered with a man nearly as green as she was, and whose approach to investigation was much more conventional than hers or Jake's. Would Johnson's by-the-book methods actually work well in a division as unique as the Behavioral Analysis Unit? And if they did, if that was the direction the agency was going to take, would there be any place in it for her?

She did appreciate that Johnson appeared to be perfectly confident—and during an interrogation, the appearance of confidence was more important than the real thing.

Finally Johnson said to Graves, "Where were you last night between nine o'clock and midnight?"

"At home," Graves said with a shrug.

"Can your wife confirm that?" Johnson said.

Graves let out a monosyllabic chuckle.

"Sure, why couldn't she?"

"What about during those same hours the night before last?" Johnson asked.

"Ditto," Graves said.

"Can your wife confirm that too?"

"Hey, I said 'ditto,' didn't I?"

Then, without mentioning Andy Gish by name, Johnson asked him about his whereabouts during the time when the cop had been killed.

Graves drummed his fingers on the table and tilted his head as if thinking it over.

"Hmm ... I must have been working that day or ... No, wait a minute. I called in sick that day. The truth is, I had a hell of a hangover. I know better than to do any line work when I'm feeling that lousy. A lineman can get himself fried that way. So I stayed home."

Johnson opened his mouth to ask him the obvious next question, but Graves interrupted.

"And yeah, Sabrina can confirm that. Or at least she'd damn well better, because she knows it's true. I don't know what to expect from her now that she's telling lies about me. Who did she tell you I killed, anyway? You said that's what I'm under arrest for, right? Well, I didn't kill anybody, and she's crazy for saying so, and you sure can't prove I did it. You've got nothing."

He sounded smug and sassy. Riley could tell that Johnson's attempt to silently psych him out hadn't worked very well.

But smug can be good, she thought.

Killers often tripped themselves up in their own self-assurance. Riley hoped that was what was going to happen this time. And she hoped Johnson would shift his own tactics with that possibility in mind.

As for his alibis, Riley knew better than to take them seriously. He'd always been able to count on his wife to obey him and sometimes to lie for him.

But that could be changing, Riley thought.

Judging from the conversation Riley and Officer Hayworth had had with Sabrina, maybe Jared Graves couldn't be so sure that he was safe and secure no matter what he did.

Maybe this time Sabrina wouldn't confirm any fake alibis.

Graves looked Johnson in the eye and said, "I'm a law-abiding citizen. Why the hell are you feds coming after me? It doesn't make sense. I can't get my head around it. And I'm waiting for you to tell me exactly who you think I killed. If you don't get around to it soon, I'm liable to want a lawyer."

Riley was relieved that he wasn't pushing the lawyer issue—at least not yet. So far, he seemed too sure of himself to worry about it. She figured the trick now was to keep him feeling that way until he tripped himself up answering questions. She hoped Johnson could pull it off.

Johnson asked, "What kind of relationship did you have with Dr. Julian Banfield?"

Graves squinted for a moment.

"I can't say the name rings a bell," he said.

"What about Stacey Pugh?"

Graves tilted his head and glanced upward.

"Hm. Maybe I've heard the name. I don't know her, though. 'Stacey' is a *her,* right?"

Riley's brain clicked away as she processed what she was hearing. Something about the way Graves had answered the last two questions worried her. Guilty killers tended to go a little overboard denying ever having heard of their victims.

But Graves sounded...

Almost honest.

And if he was innocent, both answers would make sense. A working-class guy here in Prinneville wouldn't be likely to know a well-to-do psychiatrist over in Beardsley. And in a small town like this, he might well have heard Stacey Pugh's name without ever getting to know her.

But Johnson's next question triggered an abrupt change in tone.

"What kind of relationship did you have with Officer Andy Gish?"

Graves let out a snort of contempt.

"Why, Andy and I are great pals. Always have been. I'm kind of sorry he's retired, I miss seeing him around. Sure, he used to come over to the house with other cops and pester me about one thing or another. That was his job, and I didn't hold it against him. He never meant it personally, and I always took it like a good sport."

Riley could see that the man's eyes glowing with contempt.

Of course she knew he was lying. She remembered what Officer Hayworth had said a while ago.

"Andy Gish hated Graves even more than the rest of us, and Graves knew it and hated him right back."

Graves said, "So tell me—how's Andy doing these days? How's retirement treating him? Maybe now that he's a civilian, him and me can get together for a few drinks. But I guess you never knew him, being new in town and all. Maybe I should introduce you. You'd like him. Everybody likes good old Andy."

Johnson crossed his arms without replying.

Graves let out an audible chuckle.

"Oh, yeah. I almost forgot. He's dead, isn't he? I heard about it on the radio one day while I was working. That's too bad, I'll miss the guy. So you think I'm the one who killed Officer Andy, right? That's a good one. But the chief said something about three counts of murder. Were those the other two people you mentioned? What were their names again? And how do you think I did it?"

He leaned across the table and glowered at Johnson.

"What do you guys think I am, some kind of a psycho?" he said.

Riley felt a slight jolt at those words.

He'd said them with a distinct note of contempt, as if he looked down his nose at so-called "psychos."

She wondered if a real serial killer would put it quite like that. Of course none would be likely to consider himself a psycho, but something about his tone sounded out of character for the kind of man they were looking for.

But could I be wrong?

She knew that her reservations were too vague to be useful. She just had to stay put and watch and listen.

And that was getting harder and harder to do by the moment.

Her phone buzzed. She looked at it and saw that it was from Jake Crivaro.

I can't talk to him right now, she thought, looking back at the suspect through the two-way mirror.

But then she thought, *I* need *to talk to him right now.*

She excused herself from the booth and stepped out into the hallway and took the call.

Chapter Twenty Two

Jake Crivaro jerked awake. Looking at the clock beside the bed, he saw that he had slept very late.

Good, he thought. His retirement had really begun.

It was a strange feeling not to have to bound out of bed early like he always did. It wasn't a bad feeling, though. Jake thought maybe he could get used to it. In fact, he felt very different this morning than he had since ... he actually couldn't remember how long ago ... many years, probably.

He got out of bed and shaved and brushed his teeth. Still wearing his bathrobe and pajamas, he went out into the kitchen and poured himself a cup of black coffee and a bowl of cereal with milk. Looking around his apartment where he'd lived during most of his career, he realized that even this place didn't feel the same. Although he was still living in the town of Quantico, he had no duties at the BAU. The world was surely still filled with murderous monsters, but they were no longer his concern. And he didn't mind that at all.

He realized that he'd actually started feeling the difference yesterday in the parking lot outside the BAU building. The minute he'd finished talking to Riley, telling her what he was doing, some new sensation had come over him. Thinking about it now, about everything he'd done next, he decided that must have been a sense of newfound freedom.

He'd driven to the nearest diner and ordered an enormous plate of pancakes with sausage. He'd come back to his apartment for a couple of hours, then gone to his favorite deli, where he'd eaten a fat Reuben sandwich with fries.

Then he'd caught an afternoon movie—one that he'd been wanting to see, but hadn't had the time. It hadn't impressed him. Today he couldn't even remember much of the plot. But he'd enjoyed going to see it all the same.

Then he'd taken a nice drive out into the country to enjoy the colors and smells of spring. On his way back home, he'd stopped at a bookstore and bought several novels, including some cozy mysteries, the kind he'd always liked because they had so little to do with reality.

After eating a TV dinner, he'd alternated between reading the books and watching inane reality shows on TV. He'd had a couple more bourbons than usual—not enough to get him drunk by any means, but enough to make him sleep much harder and deeper than he normally did. And he couldn't remember dreaming at all, which was rare for him. Nightmares had become so common that he was perfectly used to them. He could barely remember ever having any other kind of dreams.

And now Jake felt... well, he wasn't sure how he felt, but it was different, and it wasn't bad. A habitually painful tightness that he normally carried between his shoulders simply wasn't there.

Am I starting to relax? he wondered.

Wryly he wondered—would he even be able to tell if he *were* relaxed, after having been a stranger to relaxation for pretty much his whole adult life?

Did he have any point of reference to what normal life was like?

Most likely, normal people didn't try to cram everything they could think of into one day.

Then an unsettling question was starting to nag at his mind.

What am I going to today?

And of course, there was the question of what he was going to do tomorrow, and the day after tomorrow, and...

The thought of all those tomorrows suddenly made him feel a bit dizzy.

He was going to have to fill up all those days?

He'd never given much thought to his prospective retirement.

He knew that he was going to have to do something. He'd have to travel, take up some kind of hobby, get involved with other people, make new friends.

Jake growled under his breath at the very idea.

Making friends had never been his strong suit. Most of his relationships had been purely professional, and a lot that had started off friendly hadn't ended that way. He couldn't think of a single former partner or colleague he'd like to get to meet and reminisce with—or for that matter, any who would want to have anything to do with him.

And as for getting in touch with family—he hadn't spoken to his brother and sister in decades, and his parents were long gone. Sure, maybe he could call his ex-wife, Andrea, and see how she was doing…

Yeah, and ruin her day in the process.

The last time he'd heard from Andrea, she seemed to be perfectly happy in her second marriage. After her years of numbing hell as a homicide investigator's wife, Jake sympathized and wished her nothing but happiness.

Of course, he could try to get in touch with his grown son, Tyson. But really, would an effort at reconciliation be worth the pain and trouble to either of them?

Jake took a long sip of his coffee and stared at his half-eaten cereal.

What about Riley? he asked himself.

Yesterday he'd managed to convince himself that it was best to make a clean break—for her sake much more than his own. The truth was, he'd come to enjoy her company. She didn't seem to hate being around him, like so many other people did. But they'd both worked hard on their mentor-protégé relationship and it was hard to imagine transitioning to a normal friendship.

He'd had a call from her, he remembered. Late last night, when he'd been watching TV and starting into his second bourbon, his cell phone had buzzed. He hadn't bothered to pick it up, just listened to her message.

Now he reached across the kitchen table for his cell phone and listened to the message again.

"Hey, Agent Crivaro … I mean Jake. I'm still trying to get used to calling you that …"

Jake grinned. If he'd thought that making the rookie call him Agent Crivaro was going to keep her in line, he'd been wrong.

As he kept listening, he thought he heard a forced casualness in her voice as she asked how retirement was treating him—*"after twelve hours or so."*

Something's wrong, he realized.

After the message ended, he replayed her last few words.

"I'd just like to talk ... about things. Call me back whenever you get a chance."

She was trying hard not to sound too needy.

He felt a pang of guilt for not talking to her last night. He could call her now, of course. But wouldn't she already be hard at work at this hour of the morning? Surely this would be a bad time to interrupt her day ...

Jake growled aloud at the thought.

I'm making excuses.

But why? Why was he hesitating and wavering?

As he sat staring at the phone, he flashed back to a night last fall. Driving alone across the Appalachian Mountains into West Virginia, he'd gotten curious about Riley's father. She'd said that he lived like a hermit in an out-of-the-way cabin some miles off of that highway.

Without telling Riley, Jake had driven up to Oliver Sweeney's cabin. The crusty ex-Marine had almost shot him on sight, but once Sweeney had realized who Jake was, he'd been willing to talk to him.

And of course, they'd talked about Riley.

The visit had been a disturbing experience. Sweeney was an angry, bitter Vietnam veteran who'd turned his back on the world. He had obviously been hard on his family and everyone else who came near him. The encounter had helped Jake understand Riley better, had given him a window into her lurking self-doubts, but also her toughness and her drive.

He also remembered what Sweeney had told him before he had driven away from that cabin.

"You're a good man."

Those words had shaken Jake deeply at the time. Not only did he doubt that they were true, but he couldn't return the compliment. Captain Oliver Sweeney may have once been a good man himself—and possibly courageous in a way that Jake could truly admire. But those days were surely buried under years of bad behavior.

Nevertheless, the man had seemed to care about Riley in his own rough manner.

"Stick by my daughter," he'd said. *"She needs you. You can do her a lot of good. You're a lot better for her than I could ever be."*

Those words had echoed through Jake's mind ever since. Was there some truth in them?

He and Riley had once presented themselves as father and daughter when they went undercover on an investigation. Had there been a bit of reality in that disguise?

Jake drummed his fingers on the phone for a moment. Then he picked it up and put through a call to Riley. She sounded distracted and a bit breathless when she answered.

"Jake. What's up?"

"That's what I'm calling to ask you," Jake said. "I hope I didn't catch you at a bad time."

She hesitated before replying.

"I don't know, Jake," she said. "I don't know whether you did or not."

"Maybe I should call you back," Jake said.

"No," Riley blurted. "I think maybe I should talk to you right now. Things are bad here. We had a third murder last night—another electrocution."

Jake waited for whatever she had to say next.

"We've arrested a suspect," she said. "I was just watching my new partner interrogate him. I stepped out of the booth when you called. I'm alone in the hallway now."

"Then you should probably get back in there."

"No, I don't think so," Riley said. "Agent Johnson doesn't seem to need me—or at least he doesn't think he does."

Jake felt a tingle of concern.

Doesn't seem to need her?

He didn't like the sound of that.

"Besides…" Riley began.

She fell silent for a moment, then said, "Johnson is sure the guy is guilty."

"And what do you think?" Jake asked.

"I ... I'm not sure."

Crivaro stifled a sigh. It was a wishy-washy answer and he didn't like it.

"What does your gut tell you?" Jake said.

Another pause fell.

"I don't *think* he's guilty," Riley said. "Not of these murders, I mean. He's a horrible man, a terrible excuse for a human being. He might even kill somebody someday. But he didn't kill these three people. At least that's what my gut tells me. But I can't explain that to Johnson. I can't put it into words."

"That's because you've got to support your gut feelings with something more solid. Can you think of any good reasons to back up your instincts?"

He heard Riley groan aloud.

"I'm having trouble thinking at all right now," she said. "I'm so confused, Jake. This new partner, Agent Johnson ... well, I'm not used to doing things his way."

Jake liked what he was hearing less and less. Was this new partner of Riley's really the oaf he seemed to be, or was Riley just letting him walk over her?

A little of both, I expect.

"Have you tried explaining how you and I do things?" Jake said.

"Yeah."

"How did he take it?"

"Not well. I've told him all about you, and all that you taught me. He really doesn't get it. And he says stuff like ..."

Her voice faded again, but the situation was starting to become clear to Jake.

"Don't tell me," Jake said. "He says my ways—*our* ways, yours and mine—are out of date. He says I'm a dinosaur, a fossil."

Riley laughed a little.

"Uh, I think the exact word he used was *relic*," she said.

Jake chuckled.

"Yeah, I've heard that one too," he said. "I'll bet he also calls my generation 'Old BAU.'"

"Yeah, that's exactly what he said."

Jake said, "Riley, I wish I had a dime for every time somebody said something like that about me. I swear, I've been hearing it ever since I started working with the BAU. People have been calling me 'old guard' since before I even got a chance to be 'new guard.' They've been saying for years that the future belongs to information—as if you could solve any problem in the universe with ones and zeroes."

He could hear Riley let out a sigh of relieved agreement.

"What can I do to change his mind?" she asked.

"You can't," Jake said. "Don't even try. Just keep in mind—some things in this world are *old hat,* others are *new hat.* What we do is just plain *old hat.* Our techniques are useful ... for those of us who can use them. Not everybody can and a lot of people can't even understand them. You just have to keep faith in what you're doing. Have you got that?"

"Yeah."

"Good."

Jake stroked his chin and thought for a moment.

This would be a lot easier if I were right there helping her, he thought.

But of course, that wasn't an option.

"First things first," he said. "Have you gotten an intuitive sense of the killer?"

"I haven't had much chance," Riley said. "It's kind of hard to get into that kind of mental space when your senior partner has no idea what you're trying to do—or when he's going over the whole crime scene with a tape measure."

Jake smiled wryly.

"I hear you," he said. "But have you picked up anything about the killer at all?"

Riley paused for a moment.

Then she said slowly and thoughtfully, "I don't think ... he's an *angry* man. At least he's not habitually angry. True, he broke a wine glass at the scene of his second murder. But I think that was kind of a way of showing off. And I know this is going to sound a little silly, but ..."

"Go ahead," Jake said. "Silly is good."

"Well, I think he likes good wine. I think he likes nice things. He's got taste."

"So you think maybe he's kind of upper-class?" Jake asked.

"No, maybe more like the opposite. He might even be poor. But he's self-taught about a lot of things, and he's smart and probably well-read. He's even kind of... well, sophisticated in his way. And I believe he spends time with his victims just before he kills them, talks to them, perhaps even politely."

"So why *does* he kill them?" Jake asked.

"It's strictly personal," Riley said without hesitation. "He wants justice. He thinks these people have wronged him somehow. But it's not exactly vengeance. Like I said, I don't think he's even angry exactly. It's more that he's... purposeful. He's just trying to even the scale. And for a psychopathic killer, he's thinking about things pretty clearly."

Jake was pleased with what Riley was saying now.

She's really getting somewhere, he thought.

He asked her, "So tell me about the suspect you've got in custody."

Riley let out a grunt of disgust.

"He's just some thug, Jake. He's a wife-beater and a drunk and he's got no self-control. He's a hothead. He's also kind of stupid."

"He doesn't sound like the killer you just described," Jake said.

"No," Riley said, sounding much surer of herself than she had before. "He's a lineman, which means he's got some knowledge of electricity. But this guy didn't put together these complicated electrocution set-ups. He might wind up killing somebody in anger, but not this... I guess *intellectually* is the best word for it. We've got the wrong man, Jake. I'm sure of that."

She was quiet for a moment again.

Then she said, "Thanks for helping me think all that through."

Jake chuckled and said, "Hey, I didn't do any thinking at all. You had the whole thing pretty much figured out already, you just needed a chance to put it all together. You'd gotten distracted and flustered. I just asked the right questions."

"Well, thanks anyway."

"I wouldn't go thanking me just yet," Jake said. "You've still got a lot of work cut out for you."

"I know," Riley said. "We've got to find out how the three victims are connected."

"Don't look at that too narrowly," Jake said. "The killer might be the only connection. His vendetta against them might be the only thing they have in common."

"You're right," Riley said. "So we've got to find those he felt wronged by, whether they ever knew each other or not. But Johnson is stubborn, Jake. He's liable to stay sure we've got the killer in custody. Meanwhile, the real killer is moving faster, maybe getting ready to kill somebody else if he hasn't done it already."

Jake nodded and said, "I guess that means you're going to have to go it alone. That shouldn't be too hard. Hell, you've bucked *my* authority more than once."

He added emphatically, "But play it cool, OK? Try not to ruffle your partner's feathers. Just try to quietly carve out some space so you can work on your own. And whatever you do, don't get your ass fired—at least not before you solve this case. After that, you can piss off people as much as you like."

"OK," Riley said. "I miss you, Jake."

Jake almost said, *"I miss you too."*

But for some reason, he stopped himself.

He said, "Hey, by the time you wrap up this case, you won't miss me anymore. You'll have forgotten all about me."

"Fat chance of that," Riley said.

Jake chuckled and said, "Yeah, I guess you're right."

A silence fell between them. Neither of them seemed to know what to say. Jake wanted to tell her to call him whenever she needed his help. But somehow, that didn't seem like a good idea.

Finally he said, "Good luck."

"Thanks, Jake," Riley said.

They ended the call, and Jake sat staring at the phone. He wasn't surprised that Riley was at odds with her new partner. Jake had been through the same thing many times. He hadn't worked with many agents who could understand his unique methods. He knew that Riley would probably keep right on having the same problem during her career.

Unless, of course, she found the perfect partner.

Like she was for me, he thought.

He felt his throat catch at the thought of how rare it had been to have a partner he actually felt fond of.

He thought back to something he had told Oliver Sweeney about her.

"She's a diamond in the rough."

And he remembered what Sweeney had said in reply.

"Well, don't polish her up too pretty. And don't smooth out all that roughness. She's going to need it."

Jake figured the misanthropic old mountain man was right about that, at least.

She's doing OK, he told himself.

And he was sure she was going to solve this case.

She just doesn't know it yet.

Chapter Twenty Three

R iley stood in the hallway thinking about the conversation she'd just had with Jake Crivaro. Things seemed much clearer to her now. She needed to look at the victims one by one, try to find someone who would want each of them dead. She needed to start with some research.

She went into the front office and asked Ms. Raffin if there was a computer that she could use. The receptionist showed her to a free desk with a computer on it and told her its password.

As Riley sat down, the front door to the station opened. She was startled to see Sabrina Graves walk inside, accompanied by Officer Hayworth. The cop came over to where Riley was sitting.

"She's here to make a statement," Hayworth said.

"Good," Riley said. "Then I assume you'll get her to a doctor for a medical examination."

"Right," Hayworth said. "In addition to those new burns on her wrists, she's got lots of old scars and even signs of broken bones. And her kids are pretty scarred up too. Their bodies will be just about all the evidence we'll need. Thanks for your help."

"Don't mention it," Riley said.

Hayworth then led Sabrina away down the hall to a free room.

Riley felt a surge of satisfaction.

Although she was sure that Jared Graves wasn't guilty of the electrocution murders, he was plenty guilty of domestic abuse.

And now he's not going to get away with it, she thought.

Meanwhile, it was up to her to catch the serial killer they were looking for.

She logged onto the computer and got to work.

First she asked herself who might have hated Andy Gish enough to murder him. Riley hadn't heard or read anything that might suggest an answer for that question. Since she had immediate access to police records, it only made sense to find out anything she could about the local cop who had been the first murder victim.

Working on the police department computer, she soon found a folder that contained records for all the cops who had ever served here in the Prinneville police department. Inside that folder she found a file with Andy Gish's name on it. When she opened it, she saw that it was a straightforward list of all the arrests Gish had made during his years as a cop.

A good place to start, Riley thought.

After all, she was proceeding on the assumption that one of the offenders Gish had arrested had felt wronged enough to want to kill him. The list went back several decades, to when Gish had still been a rookie. Not that there were huge numbers of arrests for Riley to skim through. In a sleepy town like Prinneville, a beat cop's life was a quiet one.

Gish had a history of making arrests that seemed rather bland by Riley's standards—burglary, drug possession, graffiti, DUIs, disorderly public behavior, that sort of thing. Riley didn't see any murder cases listed here, although she saw occasional assaults, fistfights, and cases of domestic violence.

She figured she should focus on those.

She began to scan the arrests up on the screen, those of recent years.

But she quickly realized that what she was looking for wasn't likely to be there. All three of the victims had been in their sixties, and two of them had been retired. She asked herself—wasn't it possible that the arrest she was looking for happened quite a long time ago? That would help explain why no connections had been obvious to the local police.

She scrolled back a few years, then a decade, then further and further back, scanning the more violent crimes without knowing quite what she was looking for. The list was pretty bare-bones, little more than a summary of dates, locations, and offenders' names. But finally, an arrest of some thirty years before caught her attention.

It was the address that jumped out at her. Officer Gish had made the arrest at the very location that Riley had been to last night—the late Stacey Pugh's house.

Riley felt a tingle of excitement. A connection between two of the victims—Andy Gish and Stacey—was even more than she'd hoped to find, at least at this point in her research.

It must mean something, she thought.

Finding nothing more on that old case in the computer files, she got up and hurried over to Ms. Raffin's desk, where the receptionist was reading a magazine.

"I'm sorry to trouble you," Riley said, "but I need the complete file on an old arrest."

"What arrest are you looking for?" Ms. Raffin said, peering up from her magazine over her horn-rimmed glasses.

Riley told her about the arrest and the year it had happened.

Ms. Raffin squinted skeptically.

"That was a long time ago," she said. "Besides, don't you already have a suspect in custody?"

"There are always loose ends," Riley said, trying to sound surer of herself than she felt.

Ms. Raffin shrugged slightly and said, "Like I told you yesterday, nothing that far back has been digitized. It's all on paper over there."

She nodded toward the filing cabinet, then went back to reading a magazine, as though the conversation had ended.

Riley stifled a growl of annoyance.

Just yesterday, Ms. Raffin had gladly found the file Riley had been looking for. But that had been yesterday. Word must have gotten around the station that Riley was a bit of a nuisance. Perhaps Ms. Raffin had even been warned not to offer her any further help.

At least Riley knew where the files were kept. She walked over to the filing cabinet and opened it, and a pungent musty smell met her nostrils. She looked over the files and realized she had no idea how they were supposed to be organized—or if they were organized at all.

She was going to need Ms. Raffin's help, whether Ms. Raffin wanted to give it or not.

But Riley had an idea how to get her to help.

She fingered through the files for a moment, then took out a large bundle and set it carelessly on top of the filing cabinet. Then she reached back into the filing cabinet and pulled out another bundle and set it on the table next to the cabinet. She took out yet another bundle and set it on the floor.

Ms. Raffin looked up from her magazine with alarm.

"What are you doing?" she asked.

Riley replied cheerfully, "Don't worry, I'll put everything back the way I found it."

Ms. Raffin let out a grunt of disbelief. Obviously fearful of the mess Riley was making, she came over and began to finger through the files herself.

She said, "One of Andy Gish's arrests, you say? What was the date again?"

Riley told Ms. Raffin what she needed to know. The receptionist quickly found the file and handed to Riley. The file and its contents were old and yellowed.

Riley thanked Ms. Raffin, who nervously started re-filing the folders Riley had just removed. Riley took the folder back to the desk where she had been sitting and opened it up.

She began to read Officer Gish's own report of the arrest.

The offender is a juvenile, 12 years old ...

Riley paused and realized this was why no offender's name had appeared on the arrest list she had looked at a moment ago. The person wasn't an adult, and was never charged as one. She continued reading ...

His name is Lance Gruner, and he's a foster child in the care of Stacey Pugh. My partner and I responded to an emergency call from Mrs. Pugh. When we got to the house, we found Lance Gruner in the living room wielding a butcher knife. Everybody in the house had locked themselves in various rooms, except for Mrs. Pugh herself. We found her trying to talk the boy into putting the knife down.

As Riley read further, she learned that Lance Gruner had suffered from some kind of mental breakdown and had threatened the other kids in Stacey's care with the knife. He was large and strong for a kid his age, so his behavior had been truly terrifying and even life-threatening to the others in the house.

Riley paused for a moment. She remembered what Astrid Merrill had said about her neighbor, Stacey.

"I don't believe she ever said an unkind word to anyone, or about anyone. Everybody loved her. They loved what she was doing for children."

Riley also knew that Andy Gish seemed to have been well-liked and respected by everyone who had known him.

Riley found it easy to imagine the scene of the boy's arrest. When Andy Gish arrived with his partner, he'd found Stacey Pugh talking to the desperate boy with a knife, risking her own life to make sure that neither he nor anybody else came to any harm. Then Andy Gish joined Stacey Pugh in trying to calm down the troubled boy even while he must have been threatening them with violence.

Scanning Gish's report more carefully, she saw no indication that the policeman had used force to arrest the young offender. Gish and Stacey had probably persuaded him to go quietly to the police station.

They were good people, Riley thought.

Most importantly, she didn't believe that either of them had done the boy any deliberate harm. So, why, Riley wondered, would this boy have spent decades afterwards brooding about revenge against two people who had actually tried their best to help him?

Maybe I made a mistake, Riley thought.

Maybe I'm looking at the wrong suspect.

But as she scanned the rest of the report, she saw something else that Andy Gish had written that piqued her interest all over again.

The boy is a juvenile, and his behavior is obviously psychiatric and not criminal. Mrs. Pugh agrees strongly about this, so no charges will be filed. But he has no family to raise him, and Mrs. Pugh doesn't believe she has the expertise or resources to give him the care he needs. She suggests that he be certified into the Pittman Psychiatric Hospital ...

A mental institution, Riley thought.

It was a striking detail, although she still didn't think it told her why the boy might have harbored a lifelong murderous grudge against Andy Gish and Stacey Pugh.

But at least she had the name of a potential suspect to look into—someone who had some connection to both Gish and Pugh. Riley logged onto the Internet and looked for information concerning Lance Gruner. She found some sketchy details of his early years—how his parents were killed in a car accident when he'd been two, and how he'd been moved from one foster home to another until he'd finally wound up in the care of Stacey Hugh.

But the trail ended shortly after Lance had left the Pittman Psychiatric Hospital. Lance seemed to have lived for a time in the town of Jellicoe, near Salt Lake City. He'd left there a long time ago, and Riley could find no trace of anyone of that name living in this part of the country since then.

What became of him? she wondered.

Maybe, she thought, somebody at the hospital could tell her. At least they would have records of him having left the place. But when she searched for contact information for the hospital, she found that the place had closed down some twenty-five years before.

Another dead end, she thought with a sigh.

She wondered if she could get BAU researchers on the hunt for the man. Of course, Johnson might refuse to make the request since he was sure he'd already caught the perp. If she made the request herself, they wouldn't consider it a priority.

Voices from down the hallway interrupted her thoughts. Agent Johnson came into the front office with Sheriff Dawes and Chief Berry.

Chief Berry grumbled, "Too bad you had to stop when you did. You just about had him ready to confess."

Sheriff Dawes added, "I'm sure of it. It's too damned bad he's lawyering up like that."

"I expected him to ask for a lawyer sooner or later," Agent Johnson replied. We're closing in on him, and he's getting scared. Anyway, it's his right. If we'd pushed him any harder, his confession would be worthless. We just need to be patient and hunker down."

Berry chuckled cynically.

"Well, the public defender who's on his way here isn't exactly a legal genius," he said. "He's no good to anybody, and he won't get Graves off. Any jury will see Graves is as guilty as hell, and we'll get a conviction. I'm sure of it."

Johnson and Dawes both murmured in agreement.

Berry added with a sigh, "I just wish to hell Andy could be here to see justice done. The poor guy deserved that."

Then Johnson's eyes fell on Riley as she sat at the desk. He seemed surprised to see her there—almost as if he'd forgotten she'd even existed. At least he didn't seem angry that she had skipped out on hearing the rest of the interrogation. He clearly had other things on his mind.

He said to her, "I guess you heard that Graves's wife, Sabrina, showed up."

Riley tried not to smirk at his self-congratulatory tone.

As if he'd had anything to do with that happening, she thought.

Instead, she nodded silently.

"Tori is taking Sabrina's statement," Berry added. "My guess is it's going to be a doozy, and she's going to shoot down her husband's so-called alibis but good. She's finished covering for him, that's for sure. Serves the bastard right."

He said to Riley, "The three of us are going to get something to eat. We'll talk over lunch about how to proceed. Do you want to join us?"

"Not right now," Riley said. "I'm … uh, doing some research."

"What have you got?" Johnson asked.

Riley said cautiously, "Oh, it's just something … that might help with the case."

Johnson put his hands in his pockets.

"No kidding?" he said with an expression of mild surprise. "Well, that's good, I guess. Any evidence or information you can find against

Graves will be more than welcome. Can we bring you something to eat while we're out?"

Riley pointed to a nearby sandwich machine.

"No, I'll just buy something over there," she said.

"Suit yourself," Johnson said. "When we get back, we'll probably all head out to talk to Graves's neighbors and co-workers."

"OK," Riley said.

Still buzzing with confidence, Johnson and his two male colleagues headed on out the door.

Riley wondered—should she have told Johnson the truth about what she was doing right now? What would he have said if she'd told him she was all but sure they'd arrested the wrong man?

She remembered something Jake Crivaro had said over the phone.

"Try not to ruffle your partner's feathers."

Well, I didn't lie, she thought. *At least not exactly.*

It was true that she was doing research to help the case. And Johnson didn't seem overly curious as to the nature of that research. He'd just jumped to the conclusion that it had something to do with Jared Graves— and Riley guessed he didn't suppose whatever she was doing was very important. She simply hadn't bothered to contradict him.

And really, she was just as happy not to be having lunch with the guys—especially now that she was developing an idea of her own that she wanted to follow up on. She went to the lunch machine and got herself a sandwich and sat back down at her desk, planning her next move.

Riley soon realized exactly who she needed to talk to next.

Chapter Twenty Four

R iley wondered if she was making a terrible mistake. She remem-bered something that Jake Crivaro had said to her on the phone a little while ago.

"Whatever you do, don't get your ass fired—at least not before you solve this case."

It had sounded like good advice at the time.

But now Riley wasn't at all sure whether she could solve this case without getting fired. On her way to Beardsley in the beat-up, borrowed Ford hatch-back, she had time to think about everything she might have done wrong.

For one thing, she hadn't alerted Agent Johnson to the fact that she was leaving Prinneville on her own again. She'd considered giving him a call before she'd left the police station, but she'd quickly thought better of it—or maybe *worse* was a more apt word for it.

What would Johnson have said if she'd tried to explain that she was driving back to Beardsley to talk to Sheila Banfield again about her hus-band's murder? Riley didn't know, but she doubted very much that he'd approve, especially after the terrible blunder she'd made yesterday by arresting Ayers Hamby.

Besides, Johnson and his two colleagues were fully convinced that they had the killer in custody and were following up on that assumption. And for all she really knew, Johnson and the chief and the sheriff had the right man after all. It was a belief that Riley emphatically didn't share, but she felt sure Johnson wouldn't like it if she told him so. And right at this moment, stopping the killer before anybody else got murdered seemed like a more important priority than her budding career. If she got fired, she'd just have to find something else to do with her life.

And maybe that would be best, anyway.

Something else was worrying her. Before she'd left the station, she'd tried to call Sheila Banfield to let her know she was coming and wanted to talk to her some more. But the phone number was out of service.

Riley had then called the police in Beardsley to ask whether anything had happened to Sheila. The cop she'd talked to assured her that they'd paid the widow a visit a short time ago and had found her safe at home. Riley had tried to talk them into checking again, but they'd said the woman wanted to be left alone.

Riley couldn't help worrying about her safety. Was it possible that Sheila Banfield had already become the killer's next victim?

Riley drove on into Beardsley and into the upscale neighborhood where the woman lived. She parked in front of the Banfields' Spanish-style house and noticed that it looked larger than it had yesterday. The contrast to the houses where the other two victims had been killed was startling. This house was easily as big as those two homes put together. The lot where it stood would take up the space of an entire square residential block back in Prinneville.

The victims were so different, Riley thought again.

And yet she was following a hunch that she hoped would reveal some connection among them.

She walked up to the door and rang the bell. When no one answered, Riley rang again.

She heard a voice from the other side of the door.

"Leave me alone."

Riley cautiously called back, "Dr. Banfield, this is Special Agent Riley Sweeney, with the BAU. We met yesterday."

A silence fell.

"What do you want?" the woman called back.

"I ... I'm sorry to disturb you, but I need to talk to you again."

The door opened. Sheila Banfield stood there looking tired and distressed. She wasn't wearing makeup, and she was dressed more casually than she had been yesterday after having returned from a book tour.

"Come on in," she told Riley.

Riley followed her inside and accompanied her to the kitchen, where she sat down at the table.

"I was just about to make some tea," the woman said. "Would you like some?"

"I would, thanks," Riley said.

Sheila Banfield spoke as she started the teakettle on the stove.

"I didn't mean to be rude when you arrived. But reporters have been pestering me ever since... well, you know. I couldn't take the phone calls anymore, so I got my line disconnected. Still, the reporters kept coming around the house, and the police finally came this morning to make them leave. Of course, when you rang the doorbell, I thought..."

"I understand," Riley said.

This explained why she couldn't reach Sheila by phone, and also what the police had told her when she'd called them.

Sheila sat down at the table with Riley as they waited for the tea.

Dr. Banfield said, "I suppose I was just starting to kind of enjoy being famous. But right now it feels like a curse. When a bestselling author's husband gets—"

She inhaled sharply, unable to say the word "murdered."

Then she continued, "Well, it's news, of course. I should have expected all hell to break loose. But I really wasn't prepared for it."

"How are you coping otherwise?" Riley asked.

Sheila Banfield glanced around the spacious, sparkling kitchen.

"It's hard to say," she murmured, almost as if to herself. "It's such a strange feeling. Almost like being a house sitter for someone you don't know very well. Everything just... seems so unfamiliar."

Then she heaved a sigh and added, "Not to be curt, but..."

"You want to know why I came back," Riley said. "I'm afraid there's been another murder."

Sheila Banfield's mouth dropped open, and the pot started whistling at the same time, creating a weird effect that startled both of them.

The woman jumped up from her chair, turned off the burner, poured hot water into two cups that held teabags, and brought them back to the table.

"A third murder?" she asked, giving a cup to Riley and sitting back down.

"I'm afraid so," Riley said.

"Where?"

"In Prinneville."

The woman squinted silently at her tea, as if trying to convince herself she wasn't dreaming.

Then she looked Riley in the eyes and said, "The first victim was a policeman, wasn't he?"

Riley nodded.

"And the new victim?"

Riley said, "A widow who used to run a foster home. Her name was Stacey Pugh. Does the name ring a bell?"

The woman shook her head.

"No, I don't think so. Besides, Julian and I never really knew anybody over in Prinneville. And was the murder... done the same way as the others?"

"Exactly the same," Riley said.

"Do you have any suspects?" Sheila Banfield asked.

Riley was taken aback by the question. It reminded her that she was here under less than legitimate circumstances.

"We have a suspect in custody," Riley said. "His name is Jared Graves."

"That name doesn't ring a bell either," the widow said.

A flicker of a smile appeared at one corner of the woman's mouth.

She said, "I take it that you and your team have your doubts as to his guilt."

Riley felt herself blush.

She said haltingly, "Well... that's not exactly the situation."

"What is the situation?"

Riley swallowed hard, trying to think of what to say.

Then Sheila Banfield let out a faint chuckle.

"You're not exactly supposed to be here, are you, Agent Sweeney?" she said.

Riley nodded uneasily.

"Uh … how did you know?" she asked.

The woman shrugged slightly and said, "You're forgetting, I'm a psychiatrist. Or I was one until I got famous for other things. I know people. I pick up cues that other people would miss. Not unlike the work you do with the BAU, I imagine—profiling, isn't it called?"

Riley nodded again.

"Don't worry, I'm on your side," Sheila Banfield said. "Although I don't know the specific circumstances, I sense that you're a bright young woman with razor-sharp instincts. You might just be working with people who aren't on your wavelength, and don't understand your methods. Am I close?"

Riley smiled sheepishly and said, "Maybe too close, Dr. Banfield."

The woman smiled and said, "Of course. You're used to studying people, not having them study you. Well, since we've got so much in common, maybe you should call me Sheila. And I'll call you Riley. Notice that I'm not asking permission."

"That's fine," Riley said, suddenly feeling much more at ease than she had before.

She almost felt at home as she sat here with Sheila in her kitchen. It was as if they actually knew each other—and in a way, Riley figured, maybe they did, given their shared talent for reading people.

Riley could imagine what life might have been like for Sheila before her husband's murder. She pictured two intelligent, witty, affectionate people who never failed to enjoy each other's company, sitting right here and exchanging banter and ideas.

She thought about the book Sheila was famous for writing, *The Analog Touch*. Although Riley hadn't read it, she knew that Sheila was concerned with maintaining human values in the digital age—not unlike Riley herself, really. Sheila, too, was an instinct-driven woman trying to make her way in an increasingly data-driven time.

It seemed a shame that she and Sheila had to meet under such awful circumstances.

We might have been good friends, she thought.

But of course, this wasn't a social visit, as Sheila quickly reminded her.

"So why do you want to talk to me?" Sheila asked.

Riley hesitated, putting her thoughts together.

"I've done some research on my own," Riley said. "Stacey Pugh—the woman who was killed yesterday—once cared for a foster child named Lance Gruner. This was about thirty years ago, and Lance was twelve years old. They boy was mentally troubled, and he threatened Stacey and the other foster children with a knife. He was arrested by Andy Gish, the murdered policeman. But he wasn't charged with any crime."

Sheila was listening with keen interest.

"Of course not," she said. "He was a juvenile with a psychiatric problem. And you think this person—Lance Gruner—might be the murderer."

"Exactly," Riley said.

Sheila stirred her tea with her spoon.

She said, "And you're wondering, since my husband was a psychiatrist who sometimes worked with juvenile delinquents, if maybe he had something to do with the boy's case."

"It's a stretch, I know," Riley said.

"Not necessarily," Sheila said. "Julian was doing a lot of that kind of work during the time you're talking about. But what happened to the boy?"

"I don't have any idea," Riley said. "He seems to have disappeared over the years. I can't find any trace of him. But after he was arrested and taken out of Stacey Pugh's care, he was sent to mental institution ..."

Sheila's eyes widened.

"Don't tell me," she said. "It was the Pittman Psychiatric Hospital."

"Why—yes," Riley said. "I don't know what became of him after that."

Sheila grew a bit pale and leaned back and sighed.

"I'd hoped never to hear that place mentioned again," she said. "So did Julian."

CHAPTER TWENTY FIVE

As Sheila drummed her fingers on the table, Riley waited breathlessly to hear what she was about to say. For a few moments, the psychiatrist appeared to be searching her memories. Judging from her expression, those memories weren't pleasant. Finally, she spoke.

"Julian was a consultant at Pittman, many years ago," Sheila said. "At first he thought highly of their methods. He hoped they would be of special benefit to patients with antisocial and criminal tendencies. But after working closely with the staff at Pittman for a year or so, Julian became bitterly disillusioned. He severed all connections with the hospital."

Riley felt a sharp tingle of interest.

She said, "I found out that the hospital was closed down."

Sheila nodded.

"Yes, a couple of years after Julian broke ties with them," she said. "The Joint Commission took away its accreditation, closed it down for good reason. A lot of their techniques were experimental and haphazard—and even cruel and inhumane. For example..."

Sheila's words faded as something seemed to dawn on her.

Then she said quietly, "You told me that the new victim was killed in exactly the same way as my husband, right? And they were both killed in exactly the same way as the policeman? By electrocution?"

"That's right," Riley said.

"My God," Sheila muttered.

Then she fell silent again.

Riley's thoughts clicked away, trying to guess what Sheila might be thinking. Suddenly, new pieces of the puzzle seemed to be falling into place, and things started to make terrifying sense to her.

"Did they use electroshock treatments at Pittman?" Riley asked.

Sheila nodded and said, "ECT—electroconvulsive therapy—wasn't uncommon in those days, some thirty years ago. In fact, it's still in use today. It's considered especially useful for people suffering from depression or bipolar disorder—so-called manic depression."

"People like Lance Gruner," Riley said.

"Exactly," Sheila said. "And I can't help wondering whether he might be seeking revenge for some kind of harm that was done to him at Pittman."

"What kind of harm do you mean?" she asked Sheila.

Sheila fell silent for another moment.

Then she said, "ECT isn't as awful as its reputation would suggest. It doesn't turn you into some kind of zombie. When it's done correctly, it's really quite benign, and it can relieve severe psychiatric symptoms. It has side effects, of course—slight confusion and amnesia, usually. But those typically pass."

She shrugged and added, "It's still controversial, though. Antipsychiatry activists are deeply opposed to it. They insist that it causes long-term brain damage. But that's rather a fringe assumption, I think."

Riley asked, "Is it a voluntary procedure? On the part of the patient, I mean?"

Sheila nodded and said. "Oh, yes. And it's carried out by a trained team that usually includes a psychiatrist, an anesthesiologist, and a nurse. The patient is fully anesthetized and given a muscle relaxant. There's no trauma involved."

She breathed in deeply and added, "Or at least there's not supposed to be. At Pittman, the doctors developed their own methods and procedures—God knows why, exactly. They sometimes administered ECT without anesthesia, and even against the patient's wishes. They were especially cruel to those who had no families to look out for them. It must have been...horrible for those patients."

Sheila stared into her tea and continued, "During his time there, Julian saw some things that horrified him. He quit working there and reported his concerns to the Joint Commission. The commission didn't act right away, but eventually they received enough complaints to close the place down."

Riley squinted with interest.

"Do you think Lance Gruner might have been abused at Pittman?" she asked.

Sheila shuddered deeply.

"I don't know, but it's certainly possible," she said.

"Do you think your husband might have …?"

Sheila interrupted gently, "I can't believe Julian actually participated in any kind of cruel or abusive methods. But he might have had some connection to the young man, who might have blamed him for things that other people were doing."

She asked Sheila, "Where can I find records of what happened there?"

Sheila shrugged and said, "I don't know. It might be difficult."

"What about at the hospital itself?" Riley suggested.

"Oh, no, not there," Sheila said. "The place itself has long since been abandoned. It's not far away from Prinneville, over on the road to Mount Beville. But the building is a ruin."

With a rueful laugh, she added, "Some people say it's actually haunted. If I believed in such things, I wouldn't be surprised."

"Who was in charge of Pittman when it closed?" Riley asked.

Sheila tilted her head thoughtfully.

"I believe his name was Noel Burgess—Dr. Noel Burgess, although he was more an administrator than a practicing psychiatrist. I have no idea what happened to him, or whether he's still alive."

Sheila slouched a little in her chair.

"I'm not sure what else I can tell you," she said. "And the truth is, I'm feeling very tired. If you don't mind …"

Her words trailed off, but Riley took her meaning.

"I'll go," she said. "Thank you so much. You've been a wonderful help."

"I hope so," Sheila said with a sigh. "You know, I got famous because people thought I had answers to many questions about life in these strange times. I thought so too. I suppose I let it go to my head. But now … well, I don't feel like I know as much as I thought I did. In fact, I don't feel like I know anything at all."

"I'm terribly sorry for your loss," Riley said.

"Thank you," Sheila said.

Riley finished her tea and left the house and drove on out of Beardsley. Her mind was reeling now. Everything Sheila had told her confirmed and clarified the hunches that had brought her here. Now she was able to link all three of the victims to a single person—Lance Gruner. And maybe she was even on the verge of finding a motive for his killings.

He'd been in Stacey Pugh's foster care before he'd been sent to Pittman.

Officer Andy Gish had arrested him.

And as for Julian Banfield... Riley wasn't positive about his connection to Lance, but surely the psychiatrist's past association with Pittman Psychiatric Hospital was no coincidence.

She needed to find Lance Gruner.

Or whatever he's calling himself these days.

Or if he was even alive.

If Gruner was alive and didn't want to be found, she doubted that she could locate him on her own. She needed the help of a team—which meant she needed to convince Agent Johnson that she was really onto something. And she doubted that she was ready to do that. As far as she knew, Johnson was still absolutely convinced that he already had the real killer in custody.

She looked at her watch as she drove back toward Prinneville. She saw that she'd been away from the police station for longer than she'd realized. Apparently Agent Johnson hadn't noticed her absence—or possibly just didn't care. Otherwise he would have called her by now. Still, she figured she'd better get back there as soon as she could.

Just then she spotted a sign along the highway. It indicated that a side road was coming up in a mile—a road that led to Mount Beville.

Pittman Hospital is on that road, she reminded herself.

Not that there was really any point in her going there.

Or was there?

She felt an itch of curiosity.

Could she really pass so near the place without paying it a visit?

When she reached the turnoff, Riley veered off the highway and took the road toward Pittman Psychiatric Hospital.

CHAPTER TWENTY SIX

A s Riley drove along the road toward Mount Beville, her doubts were rising by the moment. Not only had she taken off on her own to interview Sheila Banfield, here she was on a secondary road traveling away from Prinneville again in search of a possibly nonexistent building.

This can't be a good idea, she told herself.

This was *literally* a detour from the case she was supposed to be working on. What she really ought to do was return to Prinneville and report to Agent Johnson honestly about why she'd gone AWOL this time.

She'd just have to leave it up to Johnson whether to fire her or find something for her to do that would meet with his approval.

She reminded herself yet again of Jake Crivaro's words.

"Whatever you do, don't get your ass fired."

Wasn't she risking that with every new choice she was making? What did she expect to find at an abandoned mental hospital, anyway?

Still, Riley kept driving along the road toward the mountains.

She had some idea that she might learn something about all the pain that had been inflicted there in the past. If her hunch was right, and Lance Gruner really was the killer, maybe she could get a sense of how he had suffered at Pittman Psychiatric Hospital. Maybe then she'd have a better sense of what was driving him. And maybe then she'd know how to find him and stopping him from killing again.

Or maybe ...

She sighed aloud. Maybe these were all just rationalizations. Maybe she was out here for no good reason at all. Maybe she was just being perverse and unprofessional. Worst of all, maybe she was just avoiding the truth about herself—which was that she wasn't any good at working on an investigative team, and therefore of no use to the BAU.

Riley was arguing with herself about what to do when a side road appeared to her right.

First she thought, *I could pull in there and turn around.*

Then, as she pulled off onto the side road she wondered, *Could this be where it is?*

A chain across the side road kept her from driving farther, so she stopped her car and got out to look around. A NO TRESPASSING sign hung on the chain, which was hooked at each end to a pair of concrete posts. The road beyond the chain was weedy and overgrown, and the pavement was cracked and pitted by years of neglect. But tire tracks in the layer of dirt covering the asphalt revealed that someone still drove this way, possibly quite frequently.

Riley couldn't see where the road led, but she spotted the turrets of an old building poking out above the treetops.

Surely that must be the abandoned mental hospital! With luck, maybe she'd find whoever drove this way—possibly a caretaker—and ask some questions.

She took down the chain that was across the road, got back in her car, and drove on, hoping her vehicle wouldn't stall out here in the middle of nowhere.

After a turn in the road, the large, Victorian-style brick building came fully into view. In the central section, tall, round turrets flanked a flight of stone steps that led up to a wide wooden door. On either side of the middle section of the building were two-story wings with smaller turrets on each end. Mountains rose up behind the building, adding a touch of majesty to the weird setting. Riley saw no other vehicle in sight.

The building was surrounded by a tall chain-link fence, but there was no padlock on the gate. Apparently, Riley supposed, nobody who was in charge of the place thought there was anything on the property worth stealing.

Or maybe even worth seeing.

But she was here now and she had to find out for herself.

Riley pulled the gate open and walked toward the building, feeling a bit daunted at the dilapidation of the place. She climbed crumbling stone steps to the front entrance and tried the handle of the door.

It wasn't locked either.

She pushed, and the door opened with a noisy creak.

Riley stepped inside.

There was enough sunlight spilling in through tall, dirty, broken windows for Riley to see that the building was truly the ruin Sheila had said it would be.

Everything in sight was covered with dust and cobwebs.

As Riley's footsteps echoed through the chilly and drafty front foyer, she found it easy to imagine why some people thought the old building was haunted.

And in a way, maybe it is, she thought.

Not that Riley expected to encounter any actual ghosts here. But she hoped the place was haunted by traces of memories and even by possible clues.

At one side of the spacious foyer a sign above a double door read ADMINISTRATION. She headed toward it, but then stopped. Before going any farther, Riley turned slowly around and called out aloud.

"Hello! Is anybody here?"

She was startled by the noise her own voice made through the cavernous building. But no one answered.

She called again, "This is Special Agent Riley Sweeney with the BAU. I need to talk with whoever is here."

The only reply was the echoing sound of her own voice.

She opened the door marked ADMINISTRATION and walked inside.

Riley found herself in a large office area with roll-top desks and swivel chairs.

Facing Riley, an office doorway stood wide open. She walked on inside and saw a plaque on a large desk:

DR. NOEL BURGESS
ADMINISTRATIVE DIRECTOR

That was the name that Sheila had mentioned, the man who had been manager of the hospital! Riley was momentarily thrilled to see several enormous wooden filing cabinets there in his office.

Records! she thought hopefully.

But when she pulled one drawer open, she found nothing inside except dust and cobwebs and a few scraps of paper. She checked all the drawers one by one, but they were all empty. She heaved a discouraged sigh. The hospital's records might still be *somewhere,* but they certainly weren't here.

She went back into the foyer and then into the main hall. On her right and on her left the long hallway stretched away through the wings of the building.

Riley still had no idea what she was looking for, and even less of an idea of where she might find it, and she wondered again whether she was on a pointless errand. But she felt determined to keep exploring.

Making an arbitrary choice, she turned to her right and continued down the hallway on that side. A series of wooden doors stood open, letting light in from the rooms on either side. Plaster was crumbling and falling from the arched ceiling overhead, and a musty odor filled the air. And as she glanced down, she saw that the thick layer of dust was scuffed here and there.

Footprints, she thought.

They were too smudged to make out very clearly.

Was someone else here right now, in hiding somewhere? It seemed more likely that a watchman or caretaker, now absent, occasionally made rounds through the building—although she had no idea what such a person might be guarding or protecting. Perhaps he was off-duty now, at home from his shift.

She saw nothing of interest as she walked along, glancing into rooms as she passed by. The first few appeared to be offices or conference rooms, with rickety, broken-down chairs and desks and tables. Next she entered a section where patients had apparently been quartered. Each room had two beds with metal springs but no mattresses, and the light came in through barred windows.

Then Riley found a room that made her gasp with shock.

A tangle of metal rigging hung over what appeared to be some sort of a large medical examination table in the center of the space. The top of the table was of padded leather, and tattered leather straps with steel buckles hung from its metal sides. Metal lampshades were all focused on the table. On both sides of the table, rows of raised seats had apparently been for students or spectators.

A knot of horror formed in Riley's chest.

She'd stumbled across a treatment room.

This is where it happened, she realized, as the imagined screams of helpless patients echoed through her mind.

CHAPTER TWENTY SEVEN

For the first time since she'd gotten here, Riley had the feeling that ghosts were all around her—ghosts of cruel therapists who, for reasons of their own, delivered powerful shocks without permission or anesthesia, and ghosts of the patients who had suffered fear and pain at those therapists' hands.

She looked around the room with horror. It was an evil place. Riley could feel that in her bones. Her every instinct told her that her vague theory about the connection between the killer and his victims was proving true.

Many of those victimized here must have been scarred. She felt sure that *one* of the victims of this clinical abuse had been scarred in some uniquely terrible way, turning him at long last into a killer bent on personal justice against his tormentors.

But Riley knew even this grisly discovery wasn't the hard proof she'd need to persuade Agent Johnson. It still seemed unlikely that she'd find that sort of evidence anywhere in this building, not after so many years of abandonment.

With a deep shudder, she left the treatment room and continued on down the hallway.

At the end of the hall, double doors opened into a large round room that occupied this entire level of one of the turrets she had seen from outside. Light was pouring in through all the surrounding windows, and it was obvious that someone was using the remains of this decaying structure as a private home.

Not the caretaker, she was sure. *And this is no ordinary squatter.*

The huge space was oddly but attractively decorated with various styles of furniture. Several rugs covered much of the clean tile floor. Oil lamps with decorative shades and candleholders with half-burnt candles were scattered on small tables. On one side of the space, an ornate screen sectioned off a bedroom area where a nice quilt covered a single bed. A large wooden wardrobe apparently served as a closet.

On the other side of the room, a dining table and chairs were placed near a glass-doored cabinet displaying china plates and nice glassware. Original paintings hung on the walls—landscapes and still-lifes of fruit and flower arrangements.

A plush sofa was placed in front of a fireplace and a pot on a swing arm hung over the fireplace grate. The person who lived here apparently used it for cooking.

On a table Riley found a battery-powered Walkman and a large collection of cassettes and CDs—an eclectic assortment that included classic rock, country jazz, and classical music that seemed to be carefully arranged by periods and composers.

Interesting tastes, she thought, *for a brutal killer.*

A bookshelf held an equally varied array of volumes—classic novels, nonfiction, art history, poetry, philosophy, and other types of literature. The books all looked worn and thoroughly read. Some had white Dewey Decimal labels on their spines. One section consisted of self-help books for learning about a range of subjects, from gourmet cooking to car repair to wine-tasting.

Finally Riley came across a small rack of wine bottles. Her eye fell on a bottle standing beside the rack. It had been opened and corked again, and it was now a little more than half full. The label had what appeared to be genuine handwritten signatures of two wine makers. Riley read the label aloud.

"1987 Opus One."

Riley felt a slow tingling all over her body. A connection with the man who lived here was beginning to kick in.

Don't overthink it, she reminded herself. *Let it happen.*

Following her impulses, she pulled out the cork, poured some wine into the glass, and sat down on the plush sofa with it.

She swished the wine around in the glass, admiring its deep color in the sunlight that poured in from one of the windows. She sniffed the wine and relished its rich smell—much richer and more pleasant than anything Riley was used to.

Then she tasted it, letting the liquid coat the inside of her mouth and circulate all around her tongue.

Though hardly a wine connoisseur, even Riley realized that this was an excellent vintage. She savored a whole range of fascinating tastes— dark fruits, she thought, and plums, and even a hint of chocolate.

And ...

Untrained though she was in winetasting, Riley sensed yet another startling and especially delicious flavor hovering amid the other flavors.

She slowly took another sip, and this time the unknown flavor had a name.

Justice!

Riley felt a jolt of understanding. She became light-headed and dizzy as the presence of the killer swept over and through her.

She was fully inside his mind, enjoying the wine in exactly the way he had.

"Sweet justice," she murmured aloud with a smile ...

Yes, that was exactly how it tasted—like justice.

The wine gave the man pleasure beyond any vintage he had ever tasted.

And that was because he had obtained the bottle in a special way.

As he sat here in his lair, he remembered sitting in front of Dr. Julian Banfield in the psychiatrist's wine cellar. The doctor had been bound hand and foot in preparation for his intended fate. The man tried to coax Banfield to remember him. But too many years had passed. The boy was now a man. The doctor didn't recognize him anymore.

It was a shame, of course.

But the man hadn't yielded to impatience—at least not yet.

Instead he'd opened bottle of Dr. Banfield's wine—not this bottle, but another with a fancier name that he recognized from his reading. He tasted the wine, which of course was excellent, but he couldn't enjoy it as he otherwise might, not while his business remained unfinished.

In a spasm of frustration, he'd thrown his glass at the wall.

But then he'd seen traces of awakening memory in Dr. Banfield's eyes.

Then Dr. Banfield's face lit up fully with recognition—and more important, with guilt.

And that was when he threw the electrical cord into the water at Dr. Banfield's feet ...

Riley shuddered violently and almost dropped the glass she was holding in her hand.

The spell suddenly over, she gasped and choked, unable to breathe for a moment. Then she gradually managed to calm herself. The experience she'd just had, though brief, was more intense than anything she'd ever known.

Of course the wine she had just tasted had been stolen from Dr. Banfield's cellar.

So far the killer had only drunk from this bottle twice—once in honor of Dr. Banfield's death, and then again to celebrate the murder of Stacey Pugh.

She jumped to her feet and whirled around, more than half-expecting the killer to walk in the door at that very instant and catch her in the act of helping herself to his purloined vintage.

But no one was there.

Still wobbly on her feet, Riley carried the glass back to where she'd found it and set it down by the open bottle. Then she walked around the room, trying to decide what to do next.

Maybe, she thought, all she had to do was wait for the killer to come back to his lair. Dangerous though he might be, she would be ready to greet him with her weapon in hand and promptly place him under arrest.

But of course it wouldn't be that easy.

For one thing, her borrowed Ford was parked outside, and he'd surely see it when he returned, warning him of her presence.

Maybe he's seen it already, Riley thought.

Then a darker possibility began to lurk in the corners of her mind.

She hurried over to the wardrobe and opened it. The variety of men's clothing inside—ranging from a workman's coveralls to a formal suit—provided a glimpse into the life of a chameleon-like man who could blend into just about any social situation, and who cobbled together a living by doing any kind of work he could find.

It revealed a man who had little money, but spent it cunningly on the finer things in life. And whatever he couldn't buy, he simply stole.

Like library books.

And like Dr. Banfield's wine.

On the floor of the wardrobe were six pairs of shoes, ranging from sneakers to well-polished black dress shoes. But something about the arrangement of footwear troubled her.

There was a telltale space between the sneakers and a pair of hiking boots. The empty space was wider than it would be for an ordinary pair of shoes. Riley guessed that the man was currently wearing whatever he kept right there.

She took out her penlight and peered closely at that spot. It revealed the slightest trace of a print. Peering at it, she thought she detected a familiar-looking tread mark. In fact, it could well be the same as the rubber boot print Agent Johnson had found at two of the crime scenes.

This could mean that the killer was out there somewhere, wearing the very utility boots he had worn when he'd committed three murders.

And he's going to kill again—right now, today.

Perhaps he's killed someone already.

Riley's heart was beating painfully. Waiting patiently for the murderer to return here to his lair was not an option. Wherever he was, somebody had to find him and stop him.

Right now.

But how was that even possible?

Could she possibly get Agent Johnson to mobilize his team on the basis of her raw intuition?

She didn't even know who the man's next intended victim might be.

Or do I?

Suddenly she flashed back to the nameplate on the desk back in the office.

DR. NOEL BURGESS
ADMINISTRATIVE DIRECTOR

Riley dashed out of the room, reaching for her cell phone. As she ran down the hallway, she punched in Agent Johnson's number.

I've got to make him understand, she thought frantically.

CHAPTER TWENTY EIGHT

The man who liked to call himself Sparky was driving toward the home of his next victim...

Victim? he asked himself, as he had at other times.

Can that be the right word?

It didn't seem right at all. *He'd* been the victim. The lives he was taking weren't from random victims. They were the lives of people who had done him irreparable harm. It was only just that they paid for the wrongs they had committed against him—and against others as well.

As he steered his car into the neighborhood, he reflected on the three people he had executed so far. He'd been pleased to keep personal animus out of those killings. He hadn't hated any of those people. They were simply human beings who had done terrible deeds.

Officer Gish, for example, had thought he was only doing his job by arresting Sparky. He'd meant no harm. He hadn't known the role he was playing in Sparky's terrible fate.

Neither had Mrs. Pugh, who'd felt genuinely endangered by Sparky when she'd called the police.

Not that their ignorance had been any excuse or justification. He knew it wasn't entirely rational for him to think so, but...

They should have known.

They should have known what would happen to me.

Their ignorance was exactly what they'd had to be punished for.

Of course, Dr. Banfield had been a different case.

He knew.

He knew what was happening to me even while it happened.

Worse, the psychiatrist had led Sparky to trust him.

Dr. Banfield had been Sparky's personal therapist during his early days at Pittman Psychiatric Hospital. Dr. Banfield had nothing to do with the actual shock treatments. Instead, he'd been kindly and nurturing and empathetic, and he'd made Sparky believe that someone understood him at all last.

That was why Sparky had told him about the shocks, about the pain.

Dr. Banfield hadn't known whether to believe Sparky at first. Sparky had understood why. He'd been a troubled boy back then, and he was prone to saying strange things that weren't true.

But Dr. Banfield had looked into Sparky's claims, and had found out to his horror that they were absolutely true.

Sparky remembered what he had said to him during their next session.

"What they're doing is unforgivable. I can't allow it to go on. I'll do everything I can to stop it. But first I've got to leave here ..."

Those words echoed through Sparky's mind again.

"I've got to leave here."

Dr. Banfield had left, all right.

That had been their last session together.

He'd left Sparky alone, in the care of cruel people who saw him as some sort of lab animal whose pain and suffering were insignificant in the grand scheme of things.

Perhaps, he thought, even Dr. Banfield's intentions had been good. Perhaps he had meant what he'd said, and he'd been doing everything he could to stop what was going on at Pittman. The place had eventually closed down.

But the doctor had taken too long.

By the time they released him, Sparky had been confused about what had actually happened during those nightmare years. He wasn't sure how long he'd endured such cruel torments or the specific day that he'd been released from Pittman. He had simply struggled to make his way in a world that he considered alien, even hostile.

He'd gotten better over the years, but he'd never made the mistake of trusting another human soul. He'd lived a quiet, ordinary life. Without much education, he'd taught himself whatever he needed for working at innocuous jobs in places far away from where he'd grown up and been held.

He had lived among people who barely noticed him, would never know him. He had spent his free time alone, learning about fine wines, art, music, but never sharing such things with any other human being.

It had been a solitary life, but it had felt safe to him. He'd even considered himself to be reasonably happy.

Until ...

He'd been living in Jellicoe, a town just south of Salt Lake City, working as a grocery store clerk, when his old toaster broke and he'd had to buy another one at a thrift store. The appliance looked almost new, and he thought he'd gotten a good bargain.

But when he'd plugged it into his kitchen wall socket, he'd received a shock that knocked him to the floor.

That shock had brought everything back.

It unleashed horrible memories of being held down, feeling the pain, screaming, begging them not to do it again. After that the memories and flashbacks kept coming on ruthlessly, and he didn't know what to do about it. It was as though ghosts of those who had tormented him were threatening him again.

Finally he'd decided that the only way to deal with his ghosts was to face them head-on. That was why he'd left Jellicoe and moved back into the place he had most feared. He'd been surprised to find the ruins of Pittman Psychiatric Hospital remarkably comfortable. A home without electricity suited him just fine.

Of course, he didn't believe in ghosts, not literally. But figuratively speaking, Pittman was full of ghosts, and he was surprised to find them to be warm and welcoming company. At long last, he didn't feel alone. It was as if he were surrounded by phantoms who had suffered the same as he had suffered, and understood him well.

He'd also found the inner calm to understand what he needed to do.

He had to pursue justice—not just for himself, but for the ghosts he lived among.

He'd started with the policeman who had arrested him. Afterward, Sparky had felt better than he could remember ever feeling. He took it as a sign that he was doing the right thing.

Of course he'd realized that his job wasn't finished. So he'd kept on.

But tonight he felt much more nervous than he had before. He knew he was entering a new phase of his task.

Deserving of death as they had been, Officer Gish, Dr. Banfield, and Mrs. Pugh had all been *human beings.* He'd recognized their humanity even while he'd snuffed out their lives. He'd acted without either mercy or malice, which had been right and proper.

But this *person* he was about to confront...

No, he corrected himself.

Not a person at all.

A monster.

None of the other people he'd killed had actually witnessed his so-called treatments.

But this monster had been right there when everything had happened.

This monster had even taken part in those ghastly doings.

He felt bile rising up in his throat at the memory of the monster's face watching during his terror and suffering.

He reminded himself sharply that he was seeking justice, not revenge. He had to keep his motives pure.

Of course the one he was looking for now deserved to die. He would feel just fine again after he carried out his responsibility to take care of that.

And then what?

Would this be the end of his responsibilities? Would he be able to rest?

No, I won't, Sparky realized.

Many others in this world had done great harm. They all needed to be found, to feel the punishing volts pass through their bodies.

As he approached the house Sparky realized that this would be his next execution, but it would not be his last.

CHAPTER TWENTY NINE

R iley was hurrying down the ruined hallway at a brisk trot when Agent Johnson took her phone call. He didn't sound happy to hear from her.

"What's going on, Agent Sweeney? And where the hell are you, anyway?"

Riley blurted breathlessly, "I think I know who he's going kill next."

"What are you talking about? *Who* are you talking about?"

"Our killer. I think I know who his next target is."

She heard an angry growl on the other end of the line, then Johnson's words poured out.

"We've *got* our killer, Agent Sweeney. In case you didn't notice, his name is Jared Graves. And we've got him safely locked up where he can't kill anybody. Now it's just a matter of proving him guilty. Which is what the rest of my team and I are trying to do right now. The others are scattered around town interviewing people. I'm at the power company where he works. I was talking to his boss before you interrupted me just now. And if you don't mind, I'd like to get back to the task at hand."

Riley hurried out the front door of the building and trotted toward her car.

This is going to be tough, she realized.

She said, "Agent Johnson, you've got to believe me. Jared Graves is not our killer."

"OK, I'll bite. Who do you think *is* our killer?"

Riley pulled the driver's door open and got into the borrowed car.

Panting and unnerved, she tried to explain things as rationally as she could.

"His name is—or used to be—Lance Gruner. He was in Stacey Pugh's foster care until he got too violent and she couldn't handle him anymore. Officer Gish arrested him at Stacey's house, but he wasn't charged with any crime. Instead he was committed to a mental hospital, where he was treated by Dr. Banfield. He got some kind of terrible electric shock treatments there, and now he's hunting down all the people he considers to be responsible."

A silence fell. Riley put the key in the ignition and was about to start the engine.

But where do I think I'm going to go? she asked herself.

She had no idea.

She said to Johnson, "Don't you see? Lance Gruner connects all the victims so far. He had motive to kill all of them. And I think he's on his way to kill his next victim—if he hasn't already. It's a man named—"

Johnson interrupted her, "Where are you right now?"

Riley stifled a sigh of despair. How could she begin explaining all that she'd done since she'd left the station, starting with her visit to Sheila Banfield? If she tried, wouldn't she only provoke Johnson into further doubts? But she had no choice but to be as honest as possible.

"I'm at the Pittman Psychiatric Hospital—or at least what's left of it. It was abandoned years ago, and it's now in ruins. I found the killer's lair here. He's been living in a room here as a squatter."

"Was he there when you got there?" Johnson asked.

"No," Riley said.

"Then how do you know it's *his* lair? People squat in old buildings like that all the time. Did you find his name written on anything?"

"No."

"So it could be any old bum. Do you have a single piece of actual hard evidence that what you're saying is true?"

"I found a bottle of wine in the room," Riley said. "It's expensive. I think he stole it from the Banfields' basement."

"How do you know?"

Riley didn't know what to say.

Johnson let out another growl.

"Agent Sweeney, I decided not to worry a little while ago when I realized you'd gone AWOL again. I'm starting to get kind of used to it. But the last time I saw you at the station, you said you were doing some research. 'Something to help with the case,' you said. I understood that to mean you were trying to help us prove that Jared Graves was guilty. Was that a mistaken assumption on my part?"

Riley swallowed hard.

The answer to his question was, of course, "yes."

But she couldn't bring herself to say it.

She said, "Agent Johnson, you've got to believe me. The killer is still out there somewhere. And I'm all but sure he's getting ready to kill somebody else right now."

She heard a scoff, and then he said, "And I'm all but sure you're wrong. In fact, I know it for a virtual certainty. But if you've got other ideas, go ahead and knock yourself out and try to prove them. I'm through trying to rein you in."

"But Agent Johnson—"

"I mean it, Agent Sweeney. You're on your own, and you can do as you damn well like. We can sort out our differences with Lehl when we get back to Quantico. Just don't harass anybody else. And whatever you do, don't *arrest* anybody."

Before Riley could say another word, Johnson ended the phone call.

Riley sat staring at her cell phone.

She started to punch in Johnson's number again.

But then she thought, *What's the use?*

Johnson had just made it clear that she was on her own. He wasn't interested in her ideas, and to keep trying to persuade him would only make things worse.

She took a few deep breaths to clear her head.

First things first, she thought.

If she was right, the killer had another victim in his sights right now—a man named Noel Burgess. She had to find the man before the killer could get to him.

If that's even possible.

But maybe it wasn't such a daunting task. It occurred to Riley that, unlike everything else about this case, it might even prove to be fairly simple. She dialed the number of Ms. Raffin, the receptionist at the police station.

When the woman answered, Riley told her who was calling.

Ms. Raffin said, "Have you talked with Agent Johnson? He called here a little while ago looking for you."

"Yes, we talked a few minutes ago," Riley said. "We just had a misunderstanding. Everything's ... all right now."

"How can I help you?" Ms. Raffin replied.

Riley heard reticence in the woman's voice. Riley remembered Ms. Raffin's reluctance a while ago when she asked her to help her track down the arrest records she was looking for. She hoped she hadn't already exhausted whatever might be left of Ms. Raffin's goodwill.

Riley forced a laugh and said, "Oh, it's a silly thing, really. I'm trying to find out whether there's a Noel Burgess—a *Dr.* Noel Burgess— living somewhere in the county. I'd take care of it myself if I were anywhere near a phone book, but I'm not. Could you have a look for me?"

After a brief pause, Riley was relieved to hear the sound of turning pages.

"I've got an address and phone number for him," Ms. Raffin said. "He lives right here in Prinneville."

Ms. Raffin gave Riley the address and phone number. As soon as she and the receptionist ended the call, Riley punched in Noel Burgess's phone number. Somewhat to her surprise, the man answered right away.

"This is Noel Burgess. How may I help you?"

Riley struggled to collect her thoughts.

What should she tell him? Perhaps she should be careful not to alarm him. But if she was right, he had ample reason to be alarmed.

She said, "Dr. Burgess, this is Special Agent Riley Sweeney with the BAU, and I have..."

She hesitated, then said the words aloud.

"I have reason to think your life is in danger."

Riley wasn't surprised that a baffled silence fell.

"Please explain," Burgess said, sounding mildly surprised but remarkably calm.

Riley tried to breath slowly as she talked.

"Are you at home?" she asked.

"Yes."

"First, I need to know—have you noticed anything unusual so far today? Have you had, say, an unexpected visitor, somebody you might not know right away?"

"No," Burgess said. "I've been quite alone all day. I haven't even gotten any phone calls."

Riley felt a surge of relief.

If Burgess really was the killer's next target, at least Riley had contacted him beforehand.

Riley said, "I'm going to drive to your house right now."

"Where are you calling from?" Burgess asked.

Riley hesitated. Was it really a good idea to tell him? She quickly decided that it was best to be truthful.

"I'm at the ruins of a mental hospital—the Pittman Psychiatric Hospital."

She heard a gasp of alarm.

"Oh, dear," Burgess said.

Riley wondered, *Does he have some idea of what this is all about?*

Seeming to recover his composure, Burgess said, "Well, if you start right now, I expect you can get here in twenty minutes."

Riley said, "Meanwhile, I want you to stay locked inside. Go right now and look out your windows and see if anyone might be lurking around your house. Above all else, do not let *anyone* inside. Not even anyone you know. Not even a next-door neighbor. In fact, if anyone should so much as knock, I want you to call nine-one-one to get the police there. Tell them your life is in danger."

"This sounds very dire," Burgess said. "But how can I be sure…?"

His words faded, but Riley knew what he was about to ask.

"How can I be sure you're who you say you are?"

And of course, she had no way to convince him over the phone.

To her relief, he said instead, "Never mind. I'll be right here. I'll do as you say."

Riley nervously thanked him and ended the call. For a moment she wondered—should she go ahead and call the police and tell them?

Tell them what?

For one thing, a new wave of self-doubt was starting to kick in. Could Riley be absolutely sure that her hunch wasn't wrong? And anyway, Dr. Burgess didn't seem to be in immediate danger. The important thing was for her to get to him as soon as she could.

She turned the ignition and the engine sputtered to life. She patted the dashboard and spoke to the ailing car.

"Hang in there. I need you keep running for a while longer."

As she drove back toward the main road, she remembered something that Agent Johnson had said to her over the phone.

"Just don't harass anybody else. And whatever you do, don't arrest anybody."

Riley couldn't help but scoff aloud at what struck her as a rather quaint command.

If she was right, making an arrest was going to be the least of the tasks she would soon have to face.

CHAPTER THIRTY

It was getting dark by the time Riley arrived in the upper-middle-class area of Prinneville where Noel Burgess lived. As she pulled into the spacious driveway of his handsome brick house at the end of a cul-de-sac, she was relieved to see that nothing seemed to be going on there. There certainly weren't any cop cars around, so apparently Dr. Burgess hadn't made an emergency call.

Not that Riley could be sure that all was well inside that house. She knew that the murderer was nothing if not cunning. He had made his way in and out of other homes without attracting attention. She shuddered at the possibility that he had already gotten to Dr. Burgess during the time it had taken Riley to drive here.

As she got out of the car and looked at the well-lit house, she saw a curtain lift and a face peek out through a window. Riley guessed that it was Dr. Burgess himself. She reminded herself of what she had told him over the phone.

"Do not let anyone *inside. Not even anyone you know."*

Under the circumstances, he would have good reason to be alarmed by the arrival of a woman he'd never seen before. Hoping to reassure him, she stood where she was and waved her badge in the air. Then she pulled out her cell phone and punched in his number.

The voice that answered sounded vaguely amused.

"I take it that you are FBI Agent Riley Sweeney."

"That's right," Riley said.

"Which means it's safe for me to let you in."

"Yes, it's safe. I'm the one who called to warn you."

"Very well, then," he said, ending the call.

The face disappeared from the window. A moment later Burgess opened the front door.

As Riley strode toward the house, he spoke up. "I'd like a better look at your badge, if that's all right, young lady."

A bit surprised by his skeptical tone, Riley produced her badge again. The short, thin, and dapper elderly man peered at it through reading glasses. Then he glanced over the tops of his glasses at Riley's vehicle in the driveway.

"An interesting mode of transportation for a BAU agent," he mused.

Riley stifled a sigh. Naturally, the decrepit car had puzzled him a bit.

"It's, uh, a loaner," she said. "And it's…"

"It's a long story, I'm sure," Burgess said with a kindly smile. "Well, I won't nag you about it. Judging from what you said on the phone, I'm sure we have more important things to discuss. Come on inside."

Riley said, "First, I think I'd better have a look around outside."

She got out her flashlight and walked around Burgess's entire house. Seeing no sign of anyone lurking outside, she went back to the front door, and Burgess let her inside.

He led her through the entry hallway into a carpeted living room with large windows and a fireplace. Riley thought the furniture looked comfortable and fairly expensive without being ostentatious. From what she could see, it was a nice house—well-kept, orderly, and tasteful. It was not as spacious and strangely vacant as the Banfields' house. Still, it did seem rather empty in a different way.

Riley didn't see the slightest clue that a family had ever lived here. There were no photos of children or grandchildren or family groups of any kind. In fact, no photos at all as far as she could see. The house also lacked any decorative touches that a woman might have brought to it. The current occupant was apparently a bachelor, and had probably been living here alone for a long time.

Might the killer be in the house already? Riley wondered.

Could he have slipped in without Dr. Burgess even noticing it?

She doubted it. And besides, she couldn't do a thorough top-to-bottom search on her own. She kept looking around warily.

Dr. Burgess leaned back in his chair and gazed at her with a kindly, rather sad expression on his face.

He said, "So tell me why you think my life is in danger."

Riley sat upright and replied, "I hope I'm wrong."

"Well, I hope so too. It's not impossible, I suppose. I do have enemies."

"Enemies?" Riley asked.

"I'm the director of a non-profit ethical organization—one of its founders, actually. It's the American Psychiatric Accountability League. We're sort of a watchdog over the mental health profession. We appraise and assess institutions and practitioners, give them grades and rankings."

Riley said, "I don't suppose everybody is always happy with your conclusions."

Burgess let out a slight chuckle. "No, but they tend to hold their peace about it. Furiously raving against a bad rating isn't the best way to prove that rating to be inaccurate. The best option is to try to improve one's methods. Anyway, I can't remember any medical professionals ever taking the trouble to try to kill me. It wouldn't be in their own best interests."

He folded his fingers together and leaned toward her.

He said, "But you mentioned that you were calling me from the Pittman Psychiatric Hospital. What took you to that godforsaken place? I don't imagine anyone has set foot in there for years."

Riley took a slow breath.

"Dr. Burgess, I understand that Pittman was closed down over the very sorts of abuses your organization fights against today."

A cloud of sadness crossed the man's face.

He said, "Yes—closed down while I was its administrator, I'm sorry to say. Do you think…what happened there…has something to do with any danger I might be in?"

"That's what worries me," Riley said. "Can you tell me exactly what went on at Pittman?"

Dr. Burgess let out a long, bitter sigh.

"It was the first administrative position in my career—and my last, if you don't count my work with the League. I had the training and credentials of a practicing psychiatrist, but the habits and inclinations of a bookkeeper. That suited the hospital's trustees, whose motives were entirely profit-driven."

He shook his head and continued, "I paid little attention to what my staff was doing with our patients. I took their expertise for granted and only considered the bottom line. So when my chief psychiatrist, Dr. George Beck, managed to drastically cut expenses in his department, I didn't ask questions."

He trembled, and for a moment, he looked as though he wanted to end the conversation and simply get up and walk away. But he seemed to force himself to continue.

"Dr. Beck was ... I still don't even know how to describe him. He was intelligent and dedicated ... and fixated on his own theories."

Only his closest subordinates at Pitman understood anything about what he was doing—and they didn't dare oppose him. It wasn't just about saving money on the medications. He was obsessed with pain and terror, and wanted to study their effects on live human subjects. He turned Pittman into his own experimental laboratory."

Riley nodded and said, "He performed electric shock treatments on unwilling subjects, with minimal anesthesia."

"Often it was with *no* anesthesia," Burgess said with a shudder. "And of course his techniques—brutal though they were—were cost effective. That was all I knew at the time, and all I wanted to know."

Riley flashed back to a memory of her last semester at Lanton University, and the first psychopathic killer she had encountered. Professor Brant Hayman, too, had been obsessed with pain and terror. He'd wanted to know what effects they would have on a community and he'd studied that question by murdering individual students and examining their classmates' reactions to those crimes.

Dr. Beck at Pittman had obviously been caught up in a similar madness.

But the killer I'm looking for has a different motive, she thought. *Nothing so impersonal as academic research.*

Justice was the word she'd connected with him when she was back at the old hospital.

Dr. Burgess continued, "Finally some professionals who worked at Pittman saw clearly what was going on and reported it. An investigation was conducted, and Beck wound up in prison. As for the rest of us..."

The psychiatrist got a faraway look in his eye.

"We did nothing wrong," he said. "We did everything wrong. Both of those assessments are perfectly accurate. I'm not sure which is the most damning. But none of us except Beck suffered any legal consequences. Partly that was because Beck kept such a small, tight circle of subordinates, who could plead that they were only doing as they were told, while I... well, I could deny having any knowledge of what he was doing. I received a fine and a reprimand for my negligence, and that was the extent of my punishment."

An odd feeling was starting to come over Riley. She wondered—was Dr. Burgess really the killer's next intended victim? She had plenty of reason to believe so. Burgess even fit the profile of the other victims—someone who had never meant any personal harm to Lance Gruner, but whose actions or inactions had wounded him very deeply.

But for some reason she couldn't put her finger on, she was starting to doubt Dr. Burgess was Gruner's target.

And yet...

After her visit to the hospital, she felt strongly that the killer was stalking his next victim right now. And if Dr. Burgess wasn't his prey, who was? Suddenly a possibility occurred to her.

"Whatever became of Dr. Beck?" she asked.

Burgess shrugged and replied, "He died in prison. And there have been times I've almost envied his fate. My wife left me out of sheer loathing for what I had allowed to happen, and we'd never had children. I've not been married since, and I've got few real friends. My life has been poisoned by guilt and self-blame. All I can say in my own defense is that..."

His voice faded, but Riley understand what he meant.

"At least you've tried," she said. "You've devoted your life to making sure the same terrible things don't happen somewhere else to other people."

Burgess nodded and said, "And I've never lied about what I did. Not to you, nor to anybody else. I've made an example of myself. My life has been an open book."

A silence fell between them. Riley felt sorry for this man whose conscience had tormented him for years, and would continue to torment him until he died. And yet part of her couldn't help feel that he deserved to suffer.

But she still found herself questioning whether she'd come to the wrong person and the wrong place.

She said cautiously, "Dr. Burgess, do you remember having a patient named Lance Gruner?"

Burgess shook his head.

"No, why?" he said.

Riley explained, "Three people have been murdered during the last week. I have reason to believe that Lance Gruner is the killer. I know that he suffered at Dr. Beck's hands, that he received those electric shock treatments. And I believe Gruner is killing people who he holds responsible for what happened to him—a cop who arrested him, a foster mother who allowed him to be committed to Pittman, and a psychiatrist who treated him."

"A psychiatrist?" Burgess asked.

"Dr. Julian Banfield," Riley said.

"Oh, yes—Dr. Banfield," Burgess said with a note of approval. "He was a consultant back then. He was also one of the whistleblowers who went to the Joint Commission and helped close Pittman down. He was a good man—a better man than I was in those days. I'm sorry to hear of his death."

Burgess squinted at Riley thoughtfully.

"And you think I might be the killer's next target?" he said.

"I—I don't know," Riley said. "I thought so, but I'm not sure anymore. Do you remember Lance Gruner? He was only twelve years old when he came to Pittman, but he was big for his age, and he suffered from bipolar disorder and had violent tendencies…"

Burgess shook his head again.

"No, I didn't know him. I wouldn't have known him. Like I said, my work at Pittman was almost purely administrative. I had virtually no interaction with the patients there, and more's the pity. I should have paid better attention to what was going on right under my nose. Mine was a terrible failure of human neglect."

Riley felt a tingle of realization coming on.

She quickly remembered how she'd felt a little while ago at Pittman, when she'd gotten such a swift, vivid look into the killer's mind. And now she felt that she knew one thing about him with virtual certainty.

Everything is personal for him. It's not just impartial justice. Whether he admits it or not, this is retribution for his own suffering.

He had looked each of his three victims in the face during those terrible days, and he had never forgotten them.

And they probably hadn't forgotten him either.

Perhaps they had even murmured his name during the last moments of their lives.

But that couldn't be true of Dr. Burgess.

Riley managed not to gasp aloud. She was sure that Lance was ready to kill again—if he hadn't done so already.

And I'm not there to stop it.

Chapter Thirty One

S parky crouched down in the driver's seat of his car. It was dark outside now, and he thought he wasn't likely to be spotted since he was
parked some distance away from the single streetlight. But he could
clearly see the little house across the street. The woman he sought—the
monster—wasn't at home yet.

Will she even get home tonight? he wondered.

He reminded himself to be patient. He knew from spying on her
before that she worked highly irregular hours, and sometimes spent
whole nights away—working, apparently. Even if she didn't show up
tonight, he'd have other opportunities. He had all the time in the world.

But the longer he waited, the more he had to struggle with his anger.

He kept having to remind himself that he had to keep his emotions
out of it. He had to act coolly, intellectually, ethically.

"Without mercy or malice," he murmured aloud.

It was becoming something of a motto—a good one, he thought.

When he heard a car approaching, he glanced around and saw that it
was hers.

He kept very still, watching as she parked at the curb in front of her
house and got out, then went to the trunk and took out a couple of bags
of groceries.

He could see her face clearly and he recognized her easily even now,
thirty years after he'd suffered at her hands.

The monster.

So much worse than the other three.

Of course she was older now and her face had changed in other ways.
She looked softer, more...

Broken, he thought.

He felt like slapping himself for letting the word slip into his mind.

Don't sympathize! he told himself.

Sympathy would be just as bad as anger. It, too, was a hot-blooded passion that would corrupt his cold justice just as fully as anger would.

Without mercy or malice!

That was how he had to act. He owed it not only to himself, but to the cause of justice and fair play.

For a moment Sparky was afraid the woman had seen him, but then she turned away and went on into the house with the groceries.

This would be the night. Her last night.

He just had to decide how to proceed.

If she'd arrived home earlier, while there was still a hint of daylight, he might have walked up to her door and knocked and used his carefully studied, calculated charm in order to talk his way into her house.

But not now, he thought. It was late, and she might know about the recent murders. A woman alone wouldn't just let a stranger in.

And of course, if she did recognize him…

He picked up his satchel of equipment and walked across the street. Her small cottage was conveniently isolated from neighboring homes by tall hedges, and for a few moments he just stood in her side yard and watched as she put her groceries away in the kitchen. Then he followed to another window to watch as she went into her little living room and turned on her TV with the sound way up.

He smiled. That suited his evolving plan well.

Now he just had to find the best way in.

He circled the house and saw that a bedroom window was partly open. He'd only have to remove the screen and push the window a little higher.

She'd never hear him over the blare of the TV.

Riley's brain clicked away furiously as she sat in Dr. Burgess's living room. She was sure that this man was not the killer's next target.

But who might be?

She asked, "Dr. Burgess, do you know who else would have been in the room when Lance received those electric shocks?"

Burgess's eyes widened.

"Oh, yes—I can think of one person. A registered nurse at Pittman, Inga Nussbaum. Normally ECT treatments are carried out by a team of at least three people—a therapist, an anesthesiologist, and nurse. But Dr. Beck didn't bother with an anesthesiologist. He was a strong man and he could subdue most patients by physical force without anyone's help. He insisted that he and his nurse could administer whatever he deemed necessary. Inga was his only assistant during those treatments."

"Didn't she ever report what he was doing?" Riley asked.

Burgess shook his head ruefully.

"Tell me, Agent Sweeney—have you ever heard of the so-called Milgram Shock Experiment?"

Riley immediately remembered studying about the Milgram experiment as a psychology student back at Lanton University.

"Why, yes," she said. "Volunteer experimental subjects were ordered to deliver electric shocks to another person. They weren't told why."

Burgess added, "They also weren't told that the buttons they were pushing to deliver their shocks were dummies, and that the people they were 'shocking' were only actors pretending to be in pain. The results of the experiment were deeply troubling. The subjects willingly delivered stronger and stronger, more and more painful 'shocks,' simply because someone in authority told them to."

Riley now fully understood what he was getting at.

"It was the same with Nurse Nussbaum, wasn't it?" she said.

"Indeed, it was," Burgess said. "Dr. Beck was a commanding and charismatic figure. The whole staff at Pittman was in awe of him, including Inga. She couldn't help doing what he told her to do. It was only after those terrible sessions finally ended that she began to come to terms with the harm she had helped to inflict on innocent people."

"Is she still alive?" Riley asked.

"Why, yes," Burgess said. "She lives right here in Prinneville. Her license was suspended for a time, but she eventually got it back. She works as private duty nurse, taking care of patients in their own homes. She told me she never wanted to work for any kind of institution again. We're actually close friends, and we talk to each other, often commiserating about all that happened at Pittman and—"

"I need to call her," Riley interrupted, taking out her cell phone. "Right this minute."

Wide-eyed with alarm, Burgess told Riley the nurse's telephone number. Riley punched in the number and soon heard a woman's voice speaking over what sounded like a TV show playing loudly in the background.

"Hello, this is Inga. Who may I ask is calling?"

"Inga, this is—"

Riley was interrupted by the woman's sharp cry, followed by scuffling sounds.

Then there was a click and the dial tone.

Riley frantically dialed again, only to hear an outgoing voicemail message.

Riley stared at the phone, which was shaking in her hand.

The killer is there with Inga, she realized.

Right now.

CHAPTER THIRTY TWO

T he phone was shaking in Riley's hand as rushed out of Dr. Burgess's house. Climbing into the car, she punched in the number for the Prinneville police station. When a familiar voice picked up the call, she was grateful that the receptionist apparently worked late into the evenings.

Riley spoke as calmly as she could, "Ms. Raffin, I believe another murder is in progress. Is Agent Johnson there?"

"No," Ms. Raffin said with alarm. "What should I do?"

"What about Sheriff Dawes? Or Chief Berry?"

"They're still out interviewing people about the subject we've got in custody. So are a most of the other officers. I'm just about alone here."

Riley stifled a sigh of discouragement. She remembered Johnson telling her over the phone that he'd sent personnel all over town to try to prove Jared Graves's guilt. And it was only a small-town police department, after all.

So who does that leave to help me?

She spoke urgently, "Ms. Raffin, I'm heading to the potential crime scene right now. I need backup—whoever can get there, as soon as possible. Can you help me with that?"

"I'll do what I can," the receptionist said.

Riley gave Ms. Raffin the address, then added, "I especially need for you to contact Agent Johnson. Make sure he gets there as soon as he can. Tell him the killer is about to strike at that address. I'll need his help."

"I understand," the receptionist replied briskly. "I'll find him."

Riley ended the call and sat there wondering whether Ms. Raffin would be able to get her any backup at all—and whether Agent Johnson would pay any attention to Riley's appeal.

All she knew was that she had to get to Inga Nussbaum's house right away. As she turned the key in the ignition, the engine sputtered.

Slapping the dashboard, Riley cried out, "Oh, please. Please don't fail me now. I need you to work just one more time."

She turned the key again, and this time the engine started.

She drove away from Dr. Burgess's house, desperately hoping she wouldn't be too late.

Sparky finished strapping Nurse Nussbaum to the chair in the basement, and made sure that her bare feet were properly positioned in a pan of water on the floor. He put on his rubber gloves, and just as he finished connecting a length of cable to the breaker box, he heard the woman let out a low, miserable groan.

He went back over to his prisoner, lifted up her chin and stared at her face. Her mouth was covered with duct tape, and her eyes were closed. She still hadn't regained consciousness from the dose of chloroform he had used to knock her out. She hadn't even heard him approach while she was watching TV, and he wanted her to know what was happening to her.

He said in a kindly voice, "Wake up, Nurse Nussbaum. We need to talk. We've got some unfinished business to attend to."

But the only response he got was another groan, a weaker one than before.

He worried that maybe this time he really had used too much chloroform. It wouldn't suit his purposes if she slipped into a coma—or worse, died right here and now without regaining consciousness. Though not as old as his other three victims, she seemed frail.

And this face ...

The truth was, she didn't look much like a monster anymore.

It was as if life had driven the monster out of her.

Perhaps she had become a kindly person over the years.

Should I just let her go? he asked himself.

Then he felt a wave of fury.

Don't be stupid! It's not my decision to make.

I'm an instrument of justice!

I have duties to perform!

This woman must be punished right now, because other responsibilities awaited him. He didn't yet know who they might be, but other people out there in the world had also committed terrible crimes. They had done great harm in other ways and deserved the same fate. He would find them, one by one. It was up to him, and him alone, to put the scales of justice right.

He couldn't waver this time.

Not when he was just getting started.

When Riley pulled up to the tiny cottage where Inga Nussbaum lived, she saw that the lights were on inside. Did that mean that the intended victim was still alive? At Stacey Pugh's home the power had been blown when she was electrocuted. This house appeared to be just as old, so maybe the lights were a good sign.

She got out of the car and looked around.

She saw no flashing lights and heard no sirens.

Am I going to get any backup? she wondered.

She didn't look forward to dealing with this situation solo.

If only Jake Crivaro were here, she thought.

But of course he wasn't.

Get used to it, she told herself as she ran up onto the front porch and banged on the door.

She called out, "This is Agent Riley Sweeney with the BAU. Let me in."

She could see no one through the door glass, though she could hear the TV blaring.

She'd heard that same sound just before her phone call had been interrupted.

She tried the door handle, but of course the door was locked. Riley stepped back, then raised one foot and threw her whole weight into kicking the door hard right beneath the latch. To her relief, it flew open. She would just have to ignore the pain in her knee.

She drew her weapon and charged into the house. An overturned and broken floor lamp showed there had been a struggle here, all right.

It'll be happening in the basement, she told herself.

Riley raced down a hallway and found a door standing open in the kitchen. She saw stairs that led downward.

She tore down those stairs, then skidded to a halt at the bottom.

The victim was here, and so was the killer.

Like the three victims before her, the woman was bound hand and foot with duct tape. She was taped to a wooden dining chair, and her bare feet were in a wide pan of water.

The woman wasn't moving, and her head was hanging on her chest.

Is she dead already? Riley wondered.

The tall, muscular, middle-aged man standing beside her was wearing rubber gloves and rubber-soled boots. He was holding a length of heavy cable in his hand.

The cable was cut off at one end, revealing bare metal wires.

The man stood staring at Riley, clearly surprised by her arrival.

Holding her gun on him, Riley said, "Are you Lance Gruner?"

The man nodded. "And who, may I ask, are you?"

Riley was gripping her Glock with both hands, so she couldn't produce her badge.

"I'm Special Agent Riley Sweeney with the BAU," she said.

"And you're here to stop me, I suppose," Lance said. "But you can't. You don't have any idea how important this is."

Riley replied, "OK, put the cord down—safely, slowly, several feet away from her—and then explain it to me."

The man shook his head.

"I don't think so," he said.

Riley said, "If you do her any harm, I'll shoot."

"I don't doubt it," Lance said. "But then it will be too late, won't it?"

He just stood there smiling at her. Riley realized they'd already reached a stalemate. Given the circumstances, she'd be justified in taking a shot at him right this very instant. But if she did, he'd probably drop the electric cable straight into the water, and the woman would die anyway.

Lance said, "You see, Agent Sweeney, I don't much care about my own life. I learned a long time ago that fate had no interest in treating me kindly. Lately I've learned that I have certain responsibilities, and I have carried out some of those very well. But perhaps this is meant to be my final task after all. If it's time for me to die, I'm content with that."

A note of resignation in his voice told Riley that he wasn't bluffing.

So what could she do to stop him?

As she hesitated, she heard a distant sound that might be approaching sirens.

Was her backup arriving?

Or was it just some car chase playing on the TV upstairs?

Before she could decide, the woman in the chair groaned loudly. Lance Gruner looked at the nurse with sudden interest, then reached down and pulled the duct tape off her mouth. She stared at him wide-eyed for a moment.

Then she said in a hoarse voice, "I know who you are."

He smiled a smile that seemed almost warm and kindly.

"Do you?" he said. "That's good. The others didn't—at least not at first. What do you have to say to me?"

Tears trickled down the woman's face, and she spoke through sobs.

"I know this is going to seem … strange, but … I'm glad we're here. I'm glad we're face to face again. I've been haunted by your face—and the faces of those other poor souls—for years and years. And I've always longed with all my heart to say something to you—or to any of the others …"

She stared into space for a moment, then looked Lance in the eye.

"I'm sorry," she said to him. "That's all I have to say. It doesn't change anything, it doesn't help, it doesn't make anything better, but … I'm terribly, terribly sorry. I'm sorry from the bottom of my heart, every hour of every day. And I'm tired of living with all this guilt. And if you want to take my life … well, it's up to you, I guess."

A silence fell between Lance and the nurse. Riley still thought she could hear sirens. She still didn't know if they were real or televised, and she didn't feel reassured by the possibility that they might be real. The Prinneville police were hardly skilled in SWAT techniques. If they came blundering in here, they would probably only seal the poor woman's fate.

Meanwhile, as Lance stared fixedly at Inga, Riley understood what sort of moment she was witnessing. She had sensed all along that the killer had shared a moment of communication with his victims—and now she understood what sort of moment it had been.

Recognition.

It meant everything in the world to Lance that his victims knew exactly who he was, and why he felt that he had to kill them. Otherwise, the executions would be meaningless to him. But she could tell by his expression that this moment of recognition was somehow different from the others.

Riley thought maybe she could take advantage of that difference.

"You heard her, Lance," she said quietly. "She's sorry. More than that, she's lived with her guilt all these years. And she's suffered. You don't need to punish her. She's punished herself more than you ever possibly could. Just let her go."

Lance turned from staring into the nurse's eyes and looked at Riley.

She could see that he was wavering. But he was still holding the cable directly above the pan of water. She saw no way to take him down without killing the nurse.

Moving slowly, she lowered her weapon and holstered it.

"You're not a monster, Lance," she said.

Lance's eyes widened at that word, *monster*, and his face grew pale.

I hit a nerve, Riley thought.

Riley knew that she had to make a bold move—perhaps the boldest single move she had ever made in her life.

If her luck failed her, it might also be the last.

And it had to be right now.

Holding Lance's gaze, she stepped closer to the woman in the chair, then took hold of her hand.

Lance still stood there with the electric cable in his hand.

She told him, "If you close the circuit now, I'll be part of it. I'll die too. But I never did you any harm. Is that what you want?"

A long silence fell. Riley couldn't tell what Lance was thinking.

Did I reach him? Riley wondered.

Riley wondered whether she needed to say something more to bring him around.

Then a strange, awed, almost ecstatic glow came over his face.

Riley felt a twinge of relief.

Yes, I reached him after all.

But she quickly sensed that his rapt expression meant something else entirely.

Finally he said, "You are very noble. And it is good that she doesn't have to die alone."

His hand moved, as if to drop the cable now.

But a loud smashing sound off to one side made him jerk around.

Riley had no time to think. She pushed hard on the back of the chair, tilting it back so that the woman's feet lifted out of the water.

She glimpsed the cable falling, striking the woman's leg.

She felt a powerful jolt of electricity, and everything went black.

Several beams of light were bobbing around in the midst of complete darkness. At first Riley thought she was dreaming. Then she heard a voice speaking, as if from out of nowhere.

"I found the breaker box over here. There's one switch off. Let's see if I can reset it."

Suddenly Riley was blinded by bright light, and she had to cover her eyes with her hand.

She heard Agent Johnson say, "Yeah, that fixed it all right. I guess the wiring wasn't completely fried this time."

As Riley's eyes adjusted, she moved her hand and looked around. She realized she was lying on the basement floor, surrounded by several men wielding flashlights. Agent Johnson smiled down at her as he crouched beside her.

"It's nice to have you back, Agent Sweeney. You got quite a shock— although I guess it could have been a lot worse. You were pretty much out cold for a few minutes, but you were breathing and you had a pulse and you kept groaning and mumbling under your breath. I figured we hadn't lost you for good."

Riley ached all over as she sat upright. She saw that Sheriff Dawes and Chief Berry were putting Lance Gruner in handcuffs. A couple of other cops—Tori Hayworth and Forrest Banks—had set down their flashlights and were cutting Inga Nussbaum loose from the fallen chair.

"Is she ...?" Riley asked.

Johnson said, "She's shook up, naturally, but she's going to be OK. It looks like she's got a nasty burn where the cable hit her. But like I just said, it could have been worse. She's still alive, thanks to you."

"But—what just happened?" Riley said, rubbing her forehead.

Johnson let out a grunt of self-disapproval.

"I screwed up, that's what happened. The team and I were out interviewing people around town, trying to get the goods on Jared Graves, to prove once and for all that he was our serial. Finally I went into a bar and talked to the bartender and the manager and several customers. They all agreed that Graves was right there drinking with them when Andy Gish was killed."

Riley asked, "But didn't Graves say ...?"

"Yeah, he said he was at home hung over. I guess he was shook up and just didn't remember what the hell he'd really been doing at the time. Anyway, if he hadn't killed Andy Gish, he almost certainly didn't kill Dr. Banfield or Stacey Pugh, either. That was when Ms. Raffin reached me from the station, to tell me you'd called and needed backup."

Johnson shrugged, looking more than a little embarrassed.

He said, "I got to thinking about that bottle of wine you said you'd found—the one in the room at the hospital that you thought was stolen. I gave Sheila Banfield a quick call, and she confirmed that an expensive bottle was missing from her cellar."

Johnson sighed and added, "Well, it suddenly hit me—your instincts had been right all along, and I'd been flat-out wrong. I got the troops together and we drove on over. When I got out of the car, I saw that a light was on in the basement. I knew what that could mean. So I came to look and kicked out the window and ... well, I guess you can figure out the rest."

"Thanks for saving my life," Riley said to Johnson.

"Hey, don't thank me," Johnson said. "If I hadn't acted like an idiot, maybe you'd never have been in that much danger."

He stared at the floor for a moment, then said, "It was close. Too close."

Then he looked at her and grinned. "I guess stats and numbers and data aren't all that matters. Do you think maybe I can grow some of those gut instincts of yours? Or do you have to be born with it?"

Riley was pretty sure that someone had to be born with it.

But she only smiled without saying so.

Chapter Thirty Three

It was the wee hours of the morning by the time Riley pulled up to the building where she and Ryan lived in DC. As she parked the car she saw that lights were on in their basement apartment.

Oh, God—Ryan stayed up waiting for me, she thought with a sigh.

Of course she'd called him before she'd gotten onto the plane to fly her back to Quantico. But she'd told him she'd be late and tired, and not to wait up for her.

And now it appeared that he'd been doing just that.

She felt a renewed aching all over as she got out of the car and walked toward the building—a reminder of just how much physical trauma she'd been through tonight. Her knee hurt from when she'd kicked open the door at Inga Nussbaum's house, and she still felt as though a trace of current was buzzing through her body from the terrible electric shock that had been Lance Gruner's last attack on both her and Inga.

She went into the building and down a few stairs, then opened the door to their tiny apartment. When she walked inside, no one was in the living room, although the lights were on. Then she saw that Ryan was fast asleep in the kitchen, in his pajamas with his head lying on the table, surrounded by note pads and law books and legal documents.

She walked over and gave him a gentle nudge. He groaned without quite waking up.

"Wake up, sleepyhead," she said in a soft voice.

"Huh?" Ryan murmured.

"It's way past your bedtime," Riley said with a gentle laugh. "Didn't I tell you not to wait up for me?"

Ryan picked his head up and looked at her through bleary eyes.

"I didn't," he said. "I had work to do." He looked around at the clutter on the table and added, "See?"

Riley sat down in the chair beside him. She knew that all-nighters weren't his style. Although he might have actually brought work home from his law office, he'd only stayed up this late on her account. But she wasn't going to argue with him about it.

Ryan's head seemed to be clearing a bit.

"You look like hell," he remarked.

Riley laughed.

"Wow, that's some way to welcome a girl home," she said.

"No, that's not the way I meant it," Ryan said. "I'm just..."

"I know, concerned," Riley said, touching his face affectionately. "I appreciate that. And yeah, it's been a pretty rough case."

Ryan got up from his chair and went to the kitchen cabinet to pour Riley some bourbon.

Just what I need right now, she thought.

And she found it sweet that he didn't even have to be asked.

"Aren't you having one?" she asked as he poured a single glass.

"Maybe I will," Ryan said. "If you don't mind peeling me off the floor to put me to bed."

Riley laughed again.

"We could both end up sleeping right here," she said.

Ryan sat back down with her and they both sipped their drinks.

"I heard on the news about some strange murders in Utah," Ryan said. "Was that...?"

"Yeah, that was my case," Riley said.

Riley felt a sudden wave of exhaustion. With it came all sorts of memories from the last couple of days. During the flight back here, she'd had plenty of time to think about the whole cycle of deliberate cruelty that had led to three murders. Those thoughts had unsettled her. More than that, they'd made her consider her own life and relationships.

She took a long, slow breath and added, "I'll tell you about it later. But Ryan, I'd just like for us to promise each other one thing."

"What's that?" Ryan asked.

"Let's always be kind to each other. More than that, let's be kind to everybody—at least as kind as we can possibly be. Let's not be mean or cruel. I've learned one thing from this case—and it's that the world needs a whole lot more kindness."

Ryan took her left hand and peered closely at her engagement ring.

"It's a deal," he said. "Meanwhile, I think we should..."

His voice faded, and Riley smiled lovingly at him.

"Make plans?" she asked, finishing his thought.

Ryan nodded, touching the ring with his finger.

"I think it's time we set a date," he said.

Riley felt flooded by a surge of warmth.

"I think so too," she said. "But maybe it's not a decision we should make right now, while we're both in a state of near-collapse."

"I agree completely," Ryan said with a nod. "That's why I made a dinner reservation for us at Hugo's Embers for tomorrow night. We can plan our lives then."

"Perfect," Riley said, feeling happier than she'd felt in a long time. "Now let's see if we can both make it from here to our bed."

❧ ❧ ❧

The next morning when Riley drove to Quantico, she felt almost uncannily refreshed. She still ached all over from her ordeal, and she'd only gotten about three hours of sleep, but for some reason she felt ready to take on the world.

As usual, she was using Ryan's Ford Mustang to commute to her job, and of course it was a pleasure to drive. Still, she remembered the sputtering Hatchback she'd borrowed in Utah with a certain amount of affection—especially how it seemed to have given up the ghost once and for all just when she returned it to the police station.

She remembered patting it on the wheel and speaking to it.

"Good job. You really pulled both of us through. Now you deserve some rest."

Riley wondered—was she going to get any rest herself, or would she be put back in the field right away? She find out soon enough when she reported to Special Agent in Charge Erik Lehl. But before she went to the BAU building, she had one stop to make. She was sure Lehl wouldn't mind if she didn't arrive there bright and early.

Instead of driving onto the base, she turned into the town of Quantico and parked in front of Jake Crivaro's apartment building. When she went inside and knocked on the door, Jake greeted her cheerfully.

When she stepped into his apartment, Riley was surprised to see a couple of large suitcases just inside the door.

"Uh, did I catch you on the way out?" she asked.

"I'm taking a trip," he replied.

"A vacation at last?"

Jake chuckled and said, "Kind of. Actually, I might be moving."

Riley's heart leapt up in her throat.

"Moving?" she said. "And you didn't tell me?"

"Hey, don't get upset," Jake said, gesturing for her to sit at his kitchen table, which she did. "I just found out about this yesterday. I heard that you wrapped up that case in Utah last night, and I didn't want to bother you right away. I was going to call. I promise."

Riley nodded glumly.

"I still don't know if it's going to be permanent," Jake continued. "I wouldn't leave without saying goodbye."

That word, "goodbye," hit Riley almost as hard as the electric shock she'd gotten yesterday.

She asked, "Where are you thinking about moving?"

"To Miami," Jake said.

Riley was surprised, but only for a second.

"Where your son lives," she said.

"That's right. Tyson called yesterday, said we'd been strangers way too long, and I definitely agreed. We're both ready to patch things up. He thinks I should come down there to stay. It makes sense, doesn't it? I mean, isn't Florida where old folks are supposed to wind up sooner or later? At least it's worth finding out if I like it there down where it never snows. Maybe I'll even be able live an ordinary life."

Riley couldn't help laughing.

"You, an ordinary life? Good luck with that!"

Jake laughed too. "Yeah, I might need it. But who knows? Life on the beach and wearing checkered pants and playing golf and shuffleboard might agree with me."

"It just might," Riley admitted.

"So tell me all about the case," Jake said, fetching them both mugs of coffee.

As they drank their coffee, Riley told him everything, including personal feelings that she didn't plan on putting into her official report. It felt weird to be letting it all spill out like this, but it also felt good. She realized how much she was going to miss talking freely about their work. She could never tell Ryan all the details and Agent Johnson wouldn't even understand most of what she was saying.

When she finished, Jake heaved a deep, heartfelt sigh.

"It was one of those cases, wasn't it?" he said.

Riley didn't need for him to explain what he meant. They'd discussed this sort of thing before. From time to time, Jake had told her, she was going to work on cases that made her question everything about human beings and their capacity for good and evil.

"Yeah, it was definitely one of those cases," she said. "Thanks for your help when I called yesterday."

"I'm always just a phone call away," Jake said.

"I know," Riley said. "I appreciate it. I've got to say, I had my doubts yesterday about whether I could pull this one off."

"I didn't have doubts," Jake said. "Not for a second. I'm proud as hell of you, Riley Sweeney. You're through with your apprenticeship. You're ready to take my place. So I can retire in peace. I'm as proud of you as if you were my own daughter. You've come into your own at last."

Riley hastily brushed away a tear.

Jake jabbed a finger at her and scolded, "Don't you dare cry. That's carrying the father-daughter thing too far."

Riley giggled and brought her emotions under control. "But something's worrying me, Jake. It's Agent Johnson."

Jake crossed his arms.

"So I gathered when we talked yesterday," he said. "Is he still mad at you?"

"No, he even admits he was wrong," Riley said. "He was actually kind of friendly during the plane trip home. But even so ..."

Her voice faded.

Jake shook his head and said, "He's wrong for you, Riley. He's a good agent but not a good match to be your partner."

"I know, but am I going to have any choice?"

Jake smiled knowingly.

"Don't worry about it. You won't get stuck with him. And he won't get stuck with you.

Riley squinted and asked, "How do you know?"

"I know a lot of things," Jake chuckled. "Hey, if I wind up moving to Florida, maybe you can come down to see me from time to time. I can take you on fishing trips."

Riley laughed again.

"Have you ever been fishing in your life, Jake?"

"Not once," Jake said.

"Then I'll come down and teach you," Riley said, raising her coffee cup.

"Now there's an idea," he replied.

They clicked their coffee cups together.

As soon as she walked into the BAU building, Riley received a page from Erik Lehl's receptionist. The chief wanted to see her right away. She headed straight for Lehl's office, where the receptionist ushered her on inside.

Riley's gangly, taciturn boss was sitting at his desk with his fingers steepled together.

"Have a seat, Agent Sweeney," he said.

Riley sat down, suddenly feeling nervous. Although she considered herself to be a pretty keen observer of people's moods, she always found it hard to read Erik Lehl. Since he was in charge of a group of particularly insightful agents, she figured that it was to his advantage to stay a bit inscrutable. For all she could tell about him at the moment, he was about to give her a sharp reprimand.

Considering her own insubordinate behavior on the recent case, she wouldn't find that shocking.

Lehl swiveled slightly in his chair and pointed to a folder on his desk.

"Agent Johnson filed his report this morning," he said. "I'm glad to hear that the two of you solved the case."

Riley stammered, "I—I'm glad too."

"I expect you to file your own report later today."

"I'll do that, sir."

Lehl opened up the folder and glanced over its contents.

He said, "Meanwhile, I must say—Johnson's report is rather unusual."

"Oh?" Riley said with a spasm of worry.

"He goes into a lot of detail about everything that happened, but ..."

Lehl perused the contents in silence for a moment.

Then he continued, "But he's very critical of his own work on the case. He admits to making some pretty serious mistakes. Would you agree that his judgment was ... well, flawed in some ways?"

Riley swallowed hard and said, "I'm—I'm sorry to say that I do, sir. I guess I would call it ... limited in scope."

Lehl's lips twisted into the slightest trace of a smile.

He added, "And also that your own actions were—well, unorthodox?"

Riley swallowed again.

"I'd have to agree about that as well, sir," she said.

Still skimming the report, Lehl said, "He also writes very highly of you. He says that your insights were absolutely key to closing the case, and he wishes he'd paid better heed to your ideas from the very start."

Riley simply didn't know what to say.

Lehl drummed his fingers on his desk and continued, "He says he thinks he has a lot to learn from you. I wonder—what's your opinion about that?"

Riley felt a surge of anxiety.

What on earth am I supposed to say? she wondered.

She quickly decided that she needed to be honest.

"Sir, I appreciate Agent Johnson's kind assessment of my work. But I don't think we're well-suited to be partners. Our styles are just too far apart. I don't think either one of us would be able to fully adapt to the other."

Lehl nodded and said, "Yes, that's exactly what Agent Crivaro told me."

Riley's mouth fell open.

"Agent Crivaro?" she asked.

Then she remembered what Jake had said about Agent Johnson back at his apartment.

"You won't get stuck with him. And he won't get stuck with you."

Now Riley understood why Jake had seemed so sure of himself.

Lehl said, "Agent Crivaro called me a little while ago. Of course, he knows you as well as anybody. And he says you need to work with someone... well, less cerebral might be the word. He doesn't think we'll be able to pair you with someone whose instincts are as sharp as yours. But he thinks someone more grounded, more down-to-earth might suit you well—and also might restrain some of your more wayward impulses."

Lehl smiled and added, "The phrase he used was 'meat and potatoes.' He said you ought to have a really good 'meat and potatoes' partner. But one with an open mind. And I think I've found just the agent. He recently transferred into the BAU from a field office, and he hasn't got a lot of experience under his belt. He's only been with the FBI for a year longer than you. But he's already doing excellent work."

Just then his receptionist's voice came over the intercom.

"He's here, sir."

Lehl responded, "Perfect timing. Send him right on in."

A youngish man came through the door. He looked solid and strong, but somehow less polished than most of the younger agents Riley knew. His hair was a tiny bit shaggy and his clothing was somewhat rumpled.

Lehl said, "I want both of you to meet your new partners. Agent Jeffreys, this is Riley Sweeney. Agent Sweeney, this is Bill Jeffreys."

Riley recognized the name.

Bill Jeffreys.

He already had an excellent reputation here at the BAU.

Agent Jeffreys said, "I understand you were Jake Crivaro's partner."

Riley nodded.

Agent Jeffreys let out an admiring chuckle.

"I hear he was one hell of an agent," he said. "Too bad about him retiring. But you learned from the best, and you must be pretty damned good. I hope I can keep up with you."

As they shook hands and smiled at each other, Riley took an immediate liking for him. From his grin and his handshake, she thought that he felt the same way about her.

I do like meat and potatoes, Riley thought wryly.

And she was sure that she and Agent Bill Jeffreys were going to work together just fine.

A New Series!
Now Available!

LEFT TO DIE
(An Adele Sharp Mystery—Book One)

"When you think that life cannot get better, Blake Pierce comes up with another masterpiece of thriller and mystery! This book is full of twists and the end brings a surprising revelation. I strongly recommend this book to the permanent library of any reader that enjoys a very well written thriller."

—Books and Movie Reviews, Roberto Mattos (re Almost Gone)

LEFT TO DIE is book #1 in a new FBI thriller series by USA Today bestselling author Blake Pierce, whose #1 bestseller Once Gone (Book #1) (a free download) has received over 1,000 five star reviews.

FBI special agent Adele Sharp is a German-and-French raised American with triple citizenship—and an invaluable asset in bringing criminals to justice as they cross American and European borders.

When a serial killer case spanning three U.S. states goes cold, Adele returns to San Francisco and to the man she hopes to marry. But after a shocking twist, a new lead surfaces and Adele is dispatched to Paris, to lead an international manhunt.

Adele returns to the Europe of her childhood, where familiar Parisian streets, old friends from the DGSI and her estranged father reignite her dormant obsession with solving her own mother's murder. All the while she must hunt down the diabolical killer, must enter the dark canals of his psychotic mind to know where he will strike next—and save the next victim before it's too late.

An action-packed mystery series of international intrigue and riveting suspense, LEFT TO DIE will have you turning pages late into the night.

Books #2 and #3 in the series – LEFT TO RUN and LEFT TO HIDE – are also available for preorder!

LEFT TO DIE
(An Adele Sharp Mystery—Book One)

Did you know that I've written multiple novels in the mystery genre? If you haven't read all my series, click the image below to download a series starter!

Made in the USA
Monee, IL
11 June 2022